Hadley's Hellions

Four friends united by power, privilege and the daring pursuit of passion!

From disreputable rogues at Oxford to masters of the political game, Giles Hadley, David Tanner Smith, Christopher Lattimar and Benedict Tawny live by their own set of *unconventional* rules.

But as the struggle for power heats up so, too, do the lives of these daring friends. They face unexpected challenges to their long-held beliefs and rigid self-control when they meet four gorgeous, independent women with defiant streaks of their own...

Read Giles Hadley's story in:

Forbidden Nights with the Viscount
Available now

And watch for more Hadley's Hellions stories coming soon!

Author Note

Change: it's necessary for life to progress, yet most of us resist or fear it. How do we know which essentials should remain the same and which we should let go of to make room for something better? The period of the Great Reform Act of 1832 has always fascinated me for that reason; men of honor and conscience held radically opposing views of what change should take place.

For Giles Hadley, estranged son of an earl, restricting the power of the aristocracy—including the father who rejected him and his mother—has very personal overtones. On the opposing side, Lady Margaret Roberts, daughter of a conservative marquess, grew up with a love of the land and a deep sense of responsibility toward the people who live on it.

Maggie and Giles agree on almost nothing—except a desire to give full rein to the passion that flares between them. Neither the widowed Maggie, who lost her true love and refuses to risk her heart again, nor the embittered Giles, product of a marriage gone horribly wrong, have any interest in more than a mutually agreeable interlude.

But passion—and love—don't follow rules or preferences. When a mysterious attacker puts Maggie in danger, prematurely ending their liaison, both the conservative lady and the liberal lord must decide whether they dare risk a radical change of view in order to claim the love of a lifetime.

I hope you'll enjoy their journey.

Julia Justiss

Forbidden Nights with the Viscount

HARLEQUIN® HISTORICAL

Recycling programs
for this product may
not exist in your area.

ISBN-13: 978-0-373-29876-1

Forbidden Nights with the Viscount

Copyright © 2016 by Janet Justiss

Printed in U.S.A.

www.Harlequin.com

Julia Justiss wrote her first ideas for Nancy Drew stories in her third-grade notebook, and has been writing ever since. After publishing poetry in college, she turned to novels. Her Regency historicals have won or placed in contests by the Romance Writers of America, *RT Book Reviews*, National Readers' Choice and Daphne du Maurier. She lives with her husband in Texas. For news and contests, visit juliajustiss.com.

Visit the Author Profile page
at Harlequin.com for more titles.

To the Beau Monde group of RWA,
without whose historical expertise and
graciousness in sharing it this book could not
have been written.

Prologue

London—late April, 1831

'So your half-brother is getting married.'

At his best friend's comment, Giles Hadley, ostensible Viscount Lyndlington and Member of Parliament for Danford, looked up from the reports he was studying in the small private room of the Quill and Gavel, a public house near the Houses of Parliament. 'George?' Giles asked, not sure he'd heard correctly.

David Tanner Smith, Member from the Borough of Hazelwick, gave Giles a patient smile. 'Yes, George. Have you another half-brother?'

Stifling his first sharp reply—that he didn't care who or whether his irritating half-brother married—he said instead, 'What makes you think George is getting leg-shackled?'

'It all but says so in the *Morning Post*. "Lady M., daughter of the Marquess of W.," David read, "has been seen frequently of late in the company of the Earl of T.'s younger son, the Honourable G.H. The lady has wealth and impeccable connections, the gentleman aspirations to high office, even if he is not to inherit. Might this be a match made in political heaven?"'

'Lady Margaret, daughter of the Marquess of Witlow—if I'm correctly filling in the newspaper's discreet blanks—certainly possesses the credentials to make an ideal wife for any man wanting to dominate Tory circles,' Giles admitted. 'No wonder George is interested.'

'Indeed. With the marquess's wife in delicate health, Lady Margaret has played hostess for her father for years, ever since she lost her husband—Lord Roberts. Died in a carriage accident, tragically soon after their marriage.'

'Five or six years ago, wasn't it?' Giles asked, scanning through memory.

'Yes. Besides that, her brother doesn't care for politics. Which means the man who marries Lady Margaret will not only gain a wife with extensive political expertise, but also inherit all the power and influence the marquess would otherwise have expended on behalf of his son.'

'A shame she supports the wrong party,' Giles said. 'Not that *I've* any interest in marriage, of course.'

'A greater shame, if reports I've heard about the lady's charm and wit are true, to waste even someone from the wrong party on George.'

Just then, the door slammed open and two men hurried in. With a wave of his hand towards the stacks of paper on the table, the first, Christopher Lattimar, MP for Derbyshire, cried, 'Forget the committee reports, Giles! The session's going to be dissolved!'

'Truly, Christopher?' David interposed. Looking up at the last arrival, Benedict Tawny, MP for Launton, he asked, 'Is it certain, Ben?'

'For once, Christopher isn't joking,' Ben replied, his handsome face lit with excitement. 'Grey's tired of the Tories making endless delays. He's going to take the issue to the people. Which means a new election!'

'That's great news!' Giles cried. 'Sweep the Tories

out, and the Reform Bill will be sure to pass! Equal representation for every district, a vote for every freeholder, an end to domination by the landed class—everything we've dreamed of since Oxford!'

'An end to rotten boroughs, for sure,' David said. 'I doubt we'll get the rest—yet. Though I'm not sure why, as a future earl, the rest is so important to you, Giles. To any of you, really. I'm the only one here not of the "landed class".'

'You're the son of a farmer—which makes you "landed" by occupation,' Christopher said with a grin.

'My late father's occupation, not mine,' David replied. 'I'd be lucky to tell a beet seed from a turnip.'

'Whether we get the reforms all at once or by stages, it's still a landmark day—which calls for a toast!' Ben said. Stepping to the door, he called out, 'Mr Ransen, a round of ale for the group, if you please.'

'Did you truly believe, when we sat around in that dingy little tavern in Oxford recasting the future, that we would ever see this day?' David asked, shaking his head with the wonder of it. 'Our views certainly weren't very popular then.'

'Neither were we, except with the inn's doxies. What a mismatched set!' Christopher laughed. 'Me, ostensibly the son of a baron, but really the offspring of one of Mother's lovers, as the snide were ever fond of remarking. Giles, ostensibly heir to an earldom, but estranged from his father, with the favoured half-brother dogging his heels, practically panting with eagerness to step into his shoes.'

'And making it clear to our classmates that, should he attain that earldom, he'd not forgive or forget anyone who befriended me,' Giles added, suppressing the bitterness that always simmered beneath the surface.

'Then there was me, illegitimate son of a lowly governess,' Ben chimed in. 'The snide never tired of recalling that fact, either.'

'But all still gentry born,' Davie said. 'Unlike this true commoner. It's selfish, I know, but I'm glad you three never quite fit in with your peers. I can't imagine how lonely Oxford would have been otherwise.'

'You wouldn't have been lonely,' Christopher replied. 'You're too clever. You always knew the answers, no matter the subject or the don. Who else could have coached us so well?'

Before his friend could reply, the innkeeper walked in with their ale. Claiming glasses, the four friends raised their mugs.

'To Giles, our impatient leader; to Davie, our philosophical guide; to our rabble-rouser, Ben; and to the final accomplishment of our dreams,' Christopher said. 'To the Hellions!'

'To the Hellions!' the others repeated, and clinked their mugs.

While the others drank, Davie turned to Giles. 'A new election means new strategy. Will you campaign?'

'I'll make a run through the district,' Giles said, 'but my seat's secure. I'll probably go canvass in some of the boroughs we're still contesting. Maybe we can pry more of them out of the hands of the local landowners.' He grinned. 'Maybe we can even steal some away from the father of the oh-so-accomplished Lady Margaret.'

Davie laughed. 'I hear his seats are pretty secure. But by all means, give it a try.'

Giles downed the last of his ale. 'I just might.'

Chapter One

A month later, from her seat in the open carriage in front of the hustings in the market town of Chellingham, Lady Margaret Roberts smiled out at the crowd. 'You will all turn out for the election tomorrow, won't you? I'd be most grateful if you'd vote for my cousin, Mr Armsburn! I assure you, he will do his very best to serve your interests in Parliament.'

'If he promises to send you back every time he needs a vote, it's his!' one of the men next to the carriage declared.

'Aye, and mine, too, for such a pretty smile,' the man beside him shouted.

'Thank you, gentleman,' she replied, blowing each of them a kiss. The crowd's roar of approval made her laugh and blow another.

Ah, how she loved this! The excitement of the milling crowds, the rising anticipation on election day as the votes were given, knowing that the winner would take his place in Parliament and help forge the destiny of the nation. The thought that she might in some small way have a part in the making of history was a thrill that never faded.

Since the bitter pain of losing her husband Robbie, resuming the role of her father's hostess and political assistant had been her chief pleasure in life, the only pursuit that distracted her from grief.

The love of her life might be gone, but there was still important work to do. Or at least, she told herself so in the loneliness of her solitary bed.

Pulling herself from her reverie, she looked up—and met a gaze so arresting she instinctively sucked in a breath. Deep-blue eyes—like lapis sparkling in moonlight, she thought disjointedly—held her mesmerised, the pull so strong she felt as if she were being drawn physically closer to him.

And then she realised they *were* closer. The owner of those magnificent eyes was making his way through the crowd towards her carriage. At the realisation, her heartbeat accelerated and a shock of anticipation sizzled along her nerves.

Those fascinating eyes, she noted as he slowly approached, were set in a strong, lean face with a purposeful nose, sharp chin and wide brow over which curled a luxuriant thatch of blue-black hair. The gentleman was tall enough that his broad shoulders, clad in a jacket of Melton green, remained visible as he forced his way through the crowd.

Just as he drew near enough for her to note the sensual fullness of his lips, he gave her a knowing smile, sending a shiver of sensation over her skin.

How could he make her feel so naked while she was still fully clothed?

And then he was before her, smiling still as he extended his hand.

'How could I not wish to shake the hand of so lovely a lady?' he asked, his deep voice vibrating in her ears like a caress. And though she normally drew back from physical contact when there were so many pressing close, she found herself offering her hand.

His grip was as strong and assured as she'd known it would be. Waves of sensation danced up her arm as he clasped her fingers, and for a moment, she could hardly breathe. If she were given to melodrama, she might have swooned.

Taking a deep breath, she shook her head, trying to recover her equilibrium. 'I hope you will be equally amicable about according your vote to Mr Armsburn?' she asked, pleased her voice held a calm she was far from feeling.

His smile faded. 'I hate to disoblige a lady, but I'm afraid I'm here to support Mr Reynolds.'

'The radical Mr Reynolds? Oh, dear!' she exclaimed, her disappointment greater than it should have been. 'I fear our politics will not be in agreement, then, Mr—'

Before the gentleman could answer, a tide of men washed out of the tavern across the street. 'Free beer, free men, free vote!' they chanted, pushing into the square. From the corner, a group of men wearing the green armbands of her cousin's supporters surged forward. 'Tories for justice!' they cried, shoving against the free-vote supporters. Several of the tussling men fell back against her horse, causing the gelding to rear up and fight the traces. Alarmed, she tugged on the reins, but the panicked animal fought the bit.

The gentleman jumped forward to seize the bridle, settling the nervous horse back on his feet. 'You should get away in case this turns ugly,' he advised. Making liberal use of his cane to clear a path, he led the horse and carriage through the throng and on to a side street.

'There's a quiet inn down Farmer's Lane,' he told her

when they'd turned the corner. 'I'll see you safely there, then locate your cousin.'

She opened her lips to assure him she'd be fine on her own, but in truth, the sudden rancour of the crowd, the shouts and sounds of scuffling still reaching them from the square, disturbed her more than she wished to admit. 'I would appreciate that,' she said instead.

Within a few moments, they reached the inn, the gentlemen sent the horse and carriage off with an ostler and offered her his arm into the establishment. 'A private parlour for Lady Margaret, and some cheese and ale,' he told the innkeeper who hurried to greet them.

'At once, sir, my lady!' the proprietor said, ushering them to a small room off the busy taproom.

Once she was inside, shielded from the view of the curious, the gentleman bowed. 'It is Lady Margaret, isn't it?'

'Yes. But I don't believe we have been introduced, have we? I'm sure I would have remembered you.' No woman under ninety with eyes in her head and any sense of appreciation for the male of the species could have met this man and forgotten him.

'We've not been formally presented—a lapse I am delighted to rectify. But the Borough of Chellingham has long been in the pocket of the Marquess of Witlow, so what other lovely lady could be canvassing for his candidate than his daughter, the celebrated Lady Margaret?'

'Oh, dear! That makes me sound rather...notorious.'

He shook his head. 'Admired and respected—even by your opponents. I don't believe the squabbles outside will escalate into actual violence, but with "free beer" and elections, one can't be sure. Promise me you'll remain here until your cousin can fetch you. Though I cannot help but feel a man lucky to have so lovely a canvasser working on his behalf should take better care of her.'

'How can I thank you for your kindness—and to a supporter of your opponent?' she asked. 'Won't you at least allow me to offer you a glass of ale? I hate to admit it, but I would feel easier if I had some company while I...calm my nerves.'

That might have been overstating the case—but for once, Maggie didn't mind imposing on the gentleman's obvious sense of chivalry, if it meant she could command his company for a bit longer.

And discover more about the most arresting man she'd met in a very long time.

He smiled then—setting those sapphire eyes sparkling, and once again sending shivers over her skin. 'I wouldn't want to leave you...unsettled.'

Oh, the rogue! She bit back a laugh, halfway tempted to rebuke him. Those knowing eyes said he knew exactly how he 'unsettled her' and didn't regret it a bit.

With that handsome figure, fascinating eyes and seductive smile, he'd probably unsettled quite a few ladies, her sense of self-preservation argued. It would be prudent to send him on his way before he tempted her to join their number.

After all, she'd had a lengthy page from that book, and wanted never to pen another.

But despite the voice of reason, she didn't want to let him go.

The landlord hurried in with her victuals on a tray, offering her a perfect excuse to delay. 'You will allow the innkeeper to bring you a tankard of his excellent home brewed? Mr Carlson, isn't it?' she asked, turning to the proprietor. 'My cousin, Mr Armsburn, told me you have the best ale in Chellingford. I know he's drunk many a pint when coming through to campaign.'

'That he has, Lady Margaret, and bought rounds for

the taproom, too,' Carlson replied. 'I'm happy to stand a mug to any of his supporters.' After giving them a quick bow, he hurried back out.

'Now, that is largesse you cannot refuse,' she told her rescuer.

'Even if I'm accepting it under false pretences?'

'We needn't upset Mr Carlson by telling him that. He's been a Tory voter for many years.'

'No wonder you charm the electorate—if you know even the names of the local innkeepers.'

She raised an eyebrow. 'Of course I know them. One cannot represent the best interests of the district unless one knows the people who live there, and their needs. But you have the advantage; you know who I am, but have not yet given me your name. All I know is that you're misguided enough to support a Radical.'

He laughed, as she'd meant he should, and made her an exaggerated bow. 'Giles Hadley, ma'am, at your service.'

The note of challenge in his tone puzzled her for the few seconds it took for the name to register. 'Giles Hadley!' she repeated with a gasp. 'The leader of the Hellions, the infamous Viscount Lyndlington—although you do not use the title, do you? Should I be expecting a whiff of fire and brimstone?'

He laughed again. 'Rumours of our exploits have been highly exaggerated! I doubt we were any more given to frequenting taverns and consorting with the, um, gentle ladies who worked there than most undergraduates. We just patronised a humbler class of establishment, and consulted, rather than patronised, the patrons.'

'So what was this about being hell-bound?'

He shrugged. 'One of the dons who was a clergyman heard that, if we ever had the power, we would eliminate churchmen's seats in the Lords. The sacrilege of wanting to upset the established order, along with our "dissolute" activities, led him to denounce us all as the Devil's minions. As for my title as a viscount, it's only a courtesy accorded to the son of an earl. I prefer to be known for what *I've* accomplished.'

'Which is quite a bit, I understand! I've heard so much about you!'

'If you heard it from my half-brother George, no wonder you've been imagining me with wings and a forked tail,' he said drily.

She shook her head. 'Most of what I know comes from my father and his associates—who see you as a rising star in the Whigs. My father, who does not praise lightly, has several times lamented that Lord Newville managed to snag you for the Reform cause before he could persuade you to join the Tories. I am honoured to make the acquaintance of a man so esteemed by my father!'

And she was—awed enough at meeting the man even his opponents spoke of as likely one day to become Prime Minister that for an instant, she forgot his physical allure.

But only for an instant. With her next breath, the shock of learning his identity was once again subsumed in awareness of the powerful attraction he generated.

What a combination! she thought dazedly. That intense masculine appeal embodied in a man pursuing a career she admired above all others. And despite what he'd said, there was something of the wicked about him.

Rather than preening a bit at her obvious admiration, though, as most men world, he seemed somewhat discomforted—an unexpected display of modesty that only enhanced his charm.

She barely suppressed a sigh, immobilised by eyes that seemed to look deep into her soul.

'Thank you for the compliments, though I'm sure I

do not deserve them,' he said after a moment, as if only then realising that they'd spent the last several minutes just gazing at each other. 'And forgive me for speaking slightingly of George. From the article I read recently in the *Morning Post*, it appears I should wish you happy?'

'Wish me happy?' she echoed. As his meaning grew clear, irritation flashed through her. 'Certainly not! As a member of my father's Tory caucus, I see Mr Hadley quite often, but there's no understanding between us. Newspapers!' She shook her head impatiently. 'The gossips have been pairing me off ever since I came out of mourning.'

'So you are not about to bestow your hand on my half-brother?' At her negative shake of the head, he smiled again—that brilliant smile that made her stomach do little flips and curled her toes in her half-boots. 'I have to admit, I am glad to hear it.'

No female he smiled at like that would ever look at his half-brother. Dazzled, she said without thinking, 'George Hadley isn't looking for a wife, but someone to reflect his glory, and I make a very poor mirror.'

Not until those honest but appallingly indiscreet words exited her lips did she realise how much Giles Hadley had unsettled her. She seldom voiced unflattering assessments of her acquaintances, and never to a stranger.

Flushing with mortification, she said, 'Pray, excuse me! That was most unkind, and I should never have said it.'

'Even if you know it to be true?'

'Whether or not it is true is irrelevant,' she shot back, flustered. 'I am not generally so critical. Or at least, I seldom utter such criticisms aloud,' she amended more truthfully.

'Then I am all the more honoured by your honesty.

And relieved, I must say. Women usually find George charming.'

'Truly?' She frowned, replaying in her mind's eye a typical exchange with the man. 'Perhaps with ladies he *wishes* to charm. When we converse, he always seems to be looking towards my father, as if he's much more interested in Papa's approval than in mine.' She made a wry grimace. 'Makes me feel rather like a prize pullet he's bartering to install in his hen house. And I should not have said that, either.'

Hadley laughed. 'If that's true, he's even more a fool than I thought—and *I* should not have said *that*! But there's bad blood between us, as I imagine you know.

'So I understand. I always find it sad when there is a dissension within a family.'

A bit more than dissension—there'd been a scandal of rather large proportions, she knew, although she'd heard none of the particulars. Hardly to her surprise, he did not attempt to enlighten her.

Before she could introduce some safer topic, her cousin's aide, John Proctor, rushed into the room. 'Lady Margaret, are you all right?' he cried. 'Armsburn and I have been looking everywhere for you! When I heard about the ruckus on the square, and then couldn't find you...' He exhaled a shuddering breath. 'I knew Michael would have my head for leaving you on your own, had you been harmed or even frightened! Please, forgive me!'

'Nothing to forgive,' she replied. Except his arrival, which would doubtless mean an end to her interlude with this fascinating gentleman. 'Mr Hadley took good care of me.'

The two men exchanged bows. 'Hadley, we are much in your debt for safeguarding Lady Margaret,' Proctor said.

'It was my pleasure,' Hadley replied. 'I'd advise you to take better care of your lovely canvasser in future, though. If I find her wandering unattended again, I might just keep her.'

His words, and the beguiling smile he directed at her as he said them, sent a little zing of pleasure through her. Empty gallantry, she told herself, trying to fight the effect.

Before she could try to determine how genuine the compliment might be, Proctor took her arm and all but tugged her out of her chair. 'Can I escort you back now, Lady Margaret? Your cousin is most anxious.'

'I wouldn't wish to worry Michael, of course.' With regret, she turned to her rescuer. 'I very much enjoyed our conversation, Mr Hadley. Despite holding opposing views, I hope we may continue it at some time in future.'

'You could not desire it more fervently than I! Good day, Lady Margaret,' Hadley said, and bowed over her hand.

As his fingers clasped hers, her heart fluttered and a flush of heat went through her. It took her a moment to remember to pull free from his grasp.

'Good day to you, Mr Hadley,' she said faintly, acutely conscious of his gaze on her as she walked out.

She *would* like to meet him again, she thought as her cousin's aide escorted her through the taproom. Though it would be better if she did not. She cringed inwardly as she recalled the unguarded words she'd let slip about his half-brother. A man mesmerising enough to cause her to suspend all of her breeding and most of her common sense was best avoided.

But oh, how he stirred her mind and excited her senses!

'I hope you weren't too friendly with Hadley,' Proctor said after he'd helped her into the carriage.

'Since when do I become "friendly" with men I hardly know, John?' she replied sharply.

Proctor held up a restraining hand. 'Please don't be offended, Lady Margaret! I know it's not my place to question your behaviour. But Michael—and your father—trust me to watch out for you. I'd have you steer clear of Hadley. He's a dangerous man.'

'Dangerous—how? Surely you don't believe all that nonsense about the Hellions! My father told me he admires him.'

'His own half-brother refuses to associate with him, and he's completely estranged from his father. His views are extreme, even for a Radical: he'd give the vote to every man in England, from the highest lord down to a common stew from the London slums. I've heard he even favours abolishing the House of Lords entirely!'

'Shocking, certainly,' she allowed, unsettled to have the radical nature of his positions confirmed—if what Proctor said was true. 'But Papa has always favoured an open exchange of views, even if the two parties cannot ultimately agree. I doubt I could be endangered just by talking with him.'

'Perhaps. But a man with such extreme political views might have equally radical social ideas—advocating Free Love and the abolishment of marriage, perhaps. I wouldn't trust a lady in his company, certainly not alone in a private room.'

Did Hadley believe in Free Love? No wonder he seemed wicked! The naughty idea sent a spark through her still-simmering senses. Oh, she could readily imagine making free with him!

She shook her head to rid her mind of the lusty—and pointless—thought. She had nothing more erotic in mind for her future than directing Papa's dinners—and perhaps throwing a kiss to a voter.

Turning back to Proctor, she said, 'At a busy inn, with the door to the taproom standing open? Hardly a convenient site to lure someone into impropriety. Although I wouldn't mind debating Free Love and the abolishment of marriage with him,' she added, watching Proctor's face.

At his look of horror, she laughed. 'Relax, John, I'm teasing! Though it serves you right, trying to lecture a woman of my age about her behaviour. How did the canvassing go? Does Michael think he'll hold against Reynolds?'

It took only that bit of encouragement to launch Proctor into a detailed explanation of how the campaign had fared in the rest of the town.

Normally, Maggie would have listened with rapt attention. Today, however, her mind kept drifting back to a certain gentleman with vivid blue eyes and a seductive smile that had made her feel more like a desirable woman than she had since…since the debacle with Sir Francis.

That memory ought to apply a fast brake to this runaway carriage of attraction. Recalling Hadley's flowery last words, she frowned.

Of course it had been gallantry. What else could it have been? They'd barely met, after all. And handsome as he was, he surely was accomplished in the fine art of flattery, and of persuading women who should know better that he found them more desirable than he did.

She sighed. It seemed she was a slow learner.

And yet… She had not imagined the spark that flared before them. She might have little experience, but she could still remember that enchanted time, when love for her childhood companion Robbie had transformed into something more, a layer of desire enveloping the friendship and tenderness. Ah, the mesmerising beauty of touch, the thrill of surrendering to passion, the ecstasy of possession.

How she ached for its loss!

No, she was not imagining the physical response she'd felt. But did Hadley truly find her desirable? Since an affair was too dangerous to contemplate, was there any point in pursuing this further?

Common sense warned to avoid a man who might prove such a temptation. But surely life was meant to be *experienced*, not hemmed in by caution. Such pleasures as it presented should be grasped greedily, before they were snatched away—losing Robbie had taught her that, too.

She was seven-and-twenty, a widow unwilling to risk her heart by marrying again, and she might not have many more opportunities to be tempted.

His seductive person aside, Hadley was a fascinating man, with views and values she would be interested to debate. From the not-so-flattering words his half-brother had dropped about him, she'd expected he might be something of a wild man, and he did have an untamed essence about him. An aura of purpose, too, with a trace of impatience, as if he were in a great hurry to do important things. And there was more than a trace of anger smouldering under the surface, particularly when he mentioned his half-brother.

Or was that just the passion that seemed to simmer in him? Recalling it sent a response swirling through her, and suddenly the carriage seemed too hot.

Yes, she would see more of him, she decided. He addressed the Commons frequently, her father said. Popular as he was, there was no question that he would be re-elected to the next Parliament. If she visited the Ladies'

Gallery after the sessions began again in June, she would surely hear him speak.

Before she heard more of his politics, though, she ought to learn more about the man. If he truly were dangerous, it would be best to know beforehand just how much of a risk he might pose.

But who to ask? Papa, who abhorred gossip, would be unlikely to tell her more than the bare minimum about Hadley's background.

Then she recalled just the person who would happily spill every detail she might want to know. As soon as she returned to London, she decided, she would pay a call on her great-aunt Lilly.

Lounging in his chair, Giles took his time finishing the home brew, which was as excellent as advertised. So he'd met the renowned Lady Margaret—and found her as witty and even more attractive than Davie had pronounced her.

He had to admit, he'd hoped to see her. When the four friends had drawn up that list of the boroughs to canvass, he'd chosen this one because it was known to be controlled by her father—and she was known to often canvass on behalf of his candidates. After the discussion of the possibility that she might marry George, and Davie's description of her, he'd been curious to meet the woman.

As he'd approached her carriage, he'd been impressed by her engaging smile and the ease with which she mingled with the crowd, by her obvious enjoyment of bantering with them and their enthusiastic response to her.

And then he'd caught her eye.

He shook his head, bemused. Some curious sort of energy had flashed between them, literally stopping him short. Despite the press of people, the babble of voices, the stamping of hoofs and rattle of passing carriages, he'd had the ridiculous feeling that nothing existed in the world but the two of them.

He didn't remember walking closer, but suddenly he was beside her, unable to keep himself from smiling, compelled to touch her—even if all that was permissible was for him to shake her hand.

He hardly recalled what he'd said to her during their interlude at the inn, and could only hope it hadn't been utter nonsense. He remembered only two salient points from their conversation: her father approved of him and she wasn't going to marry George.

The relief he felt about the latter was surely excessive.

He couldn't recall ever feeling such a powerful and immediate connection to a lady—and had no explanation to account for it. She wasn't a beauty in the traditional sense. Her hair was chestnut, not gold, her figure rather taller than average, her face longer than oval, with a generous mouth and pert nose decorated with freckles. But something in those vivid green eyes had sparked a physical attraction that went straight to his loins and drew him to her like a thirsty man to a cool, clear stream.

Though he was too bitterly conscious of his mother's fate ever to become a rake, he was hardly inexperienced, having enjoyed his share of discreet liaisons, always careful to take precautions to protect the lady. He wasn't some green lad just out of university, susceptible to being bowled over by an attractive woman.

In sum, he couldn't figure out what it was about Lady Margaret that had struck him so profoundly.

He did know he would seek her out again, if only to see if his unprecedented reaction would recur a second time. Or whether upon further acquaintance her attractions would seem no more remarkable than those of any other pretty, intelligent lady.

He paused a moment, frowning. Although Lady Margaret had emphatically disclaimed a relationship, if the newspapers had been puffing off a possible match between her and George, they must have been given some encouragement for the notion—very possibly from his half-brother. Marrying into an important political family would be just the sort of thing George would see as a prudent step towards the career as a government leader he coveted.

The prize pullet he's bartering to install in his hen house. Giles recalled her words with a chuckle. She certainly deserved better than that.

If associating with a woman George might have marked as his own caused problems with his half-brother, so be it. Pursuing this fascinating lady would depend on his—and her—inclinations alone.

Chapter Two

A week later, the butler ushered Lady Margaret into the front parlour of the Grosvenor Square town house of her great-aunt, the Dowager Countess of Sayleford. 'I've ordered a full pot of tea and a plate of biscuits to sustain us,' her great-aunt declared after receiving her kiss on the cheek. 'Make yourself comfortable, and tell me all about the campaign in Chellingham.'

As her great-aunt knew well, her preferred topic of conversation would normally be the elections. Though Maggie was fairly bursting with curiosity about Giles Hadley, she didn't want to open herself to the questions—to which she didn't have answers—Aunt Lilly would certainly fire at her if she delayed discussing politics to make enquiries about a gentleman.

So, though she had shockingly little interest in conveying the results in Chellingham, she dutifully gave a brief recitation of what had happened in the campaign.

'Glad to hear Armsburn held the seat,' her great-aunt said. 'My sources with an ear to Parliament tell me that one of the Grey's government's primary aims will be to eliminate boroughs like Chellingham that are controlled by the local landowner.'

'Yes, and I'm afraid it's virtually certain a bill to that effect will pass. I found the county full of inflammatory rhetoric! Even in normally placid Chellingham, there was alarming…disruption.'

'Disruption?' her great-aunt repeated, frowning. 'What do you mean? Surely you weren't endangered!'

'No, not really. Oh, there was a scuffle in the street next to my carriage between two rival parties, some of whom had imbibed more ale than was good for them,' she admitted. 'In any event, I was quickly rescued by a most charming gentleman.'

Her great-aunt's frown deepened. 'Where were Michael and Proctor? I would have expected them to rescue you, if rescuing were needful.'

'They were at another gathering place when the incident happened.'

'Your father will not be happy to hear that.'

'No, but there was no harm done, so you mustn't tell him.'

Her great-aunt eyed her for a long moment before finally nodding. 'Very well, it that's what you wish. So, who was this "charming gentleman" who protected you when your kin failed in their duty?'

'Another Member of Parliament—from the opposition, actually.' Trying to keep her tone as neutral as possible, she said, 'Mr Giles Hadley.'

Her great-aunt's eyes widened. 'Giles Hadley—you mean Viscount Lyndlington?'

At her nod of assent, her great-aunt continued, 'Oh, my! Charming, you say? To hear some of the rabid Tories tell it, he's the devil incarnate!'

'His half-brother often paints him in that light. But Papa admires him, and I give far more credit to his opinion. It did make me curious, though—the difference between Papa's view of him and his brother's, and I do wonder what happened to create such a breach in the family. I'm sure Papa knows, but I didn't think he would tell me much.' She grinned at her great-aunt. 'Whereas, I knew *you* would tell me everything!'

'What did you think of Hadley?' came the unexpected response.

Caught off guard, to her irritation, she found herself flushing. 'I suppose it's obvious I found him attractive.'

Her great-aunt raised her eyebrows, a mischievous twinkle in her eye. 'Since I cannot remember you ever enquiring about any other gentleman, I'd already assumed as much. Excellent! It *has* been six years since you lost Robbie. More than time enough for you to be moving on.'

'Don't be thinking that, Aunt Lilly!' she protested, raising a hand. 'I'm not angling for another husband!'

'Why not? You're still young, and attractive, and it's more than time enough for you to be over your disappointment about Sir Francis. And your grief.'

Once, she'd hoped Sir Francis might help her bury the grief—and look how disastrously *that* had ended. Both episodes being still too painful for her to discuss, she ignored the question, saying instead, 'I found Giles Hadley... fascinating, that's all. Those compelling blue eyes seem to look deep within you. There's a restless energy about him, a sense of anger lurking beneath the surface, to say nothing of what I understand are quite radical political views. He's certainly different from any other gentleman I've known! And yes, he does...attract me. But I'm not about to do anything foolish.'

Her great-aunt looked at her speculatively. 'You are a widow now. I don't advocate foolishness, but with discretion, you can do what you want—marriage, or not.'

'All I want right now is to know more about his cir-

cumstances. It's rather obvious that his half-brother hates
him. Not that I've discussed him with George, but when-
ever the opposition is brought up, he never loses the opportunity to get in a dig about his half-sibling. I suspect
much of his spleen stems from knowing the viscount
will inherit, even though George is the brother favoured
by their father. But why, Aunt Lilly? What happened to
fracture the family?'

'It's an old and quite interesting scandal.'

'About which, I am sure, you know all the details.'

'Naturally.' Her great-aunt smiled. 'What other benefit
is there in having lived so long in the midst of society?'

'So—what happened?'

'It began many years ago, just after the current earl
inherited. He and his best friend courted the same
woman—Giles Hadley's mother. She loved the friend,
not the young earl, but the friend was a younger son with
no title or income, and Randall Hadley, already Lord Telbridge, would have both. The friend intended to go to
India and make his fortune, but the girl's family, which
was in dire financial straits, wouldn't let her wait on the
possibility that he might one day return a nabob. Understandable, really; he might just as well die of a fever, or
be killed in one of the native wars. They pressured her
into agreeing to marry Telbridge, which she did ten days
after the friend left for India.'

'Poor lady,' Maggie said, thinking of how awful it
would have been if family duty had forced her to marry
someone other than Robbie. 'And then?'

'All was well until several years after the wedding,
when Telbridge somehow learned that his wife and the
friend had stayed alone together at a hunting cottage the
night before he left for India. Pressed by the earl, his wife
would not deny that they had been lovers—and that she

could not therefore assure the earl with perfect certitude that the son she bore him nine months after the wedding was in fact his. Wild with jealousy and anger, he sent them both away. Deaf to any pleas of reason, he divorced her and cut off all support—funds, lodging, even schooling for the boy. He remarried soon after the divorce bill was passed by the Lords, and has since devoted all his wealth and affection to the son of his second wife. As far as I know, Telbridge has not set eyes on the viscount in years. But all the rancour in the world will not alter the fact that since Giles Hadley was born after Telbridge married his mother, and was acknowledged for several years as the earl's son, under law, he will inherit, for all that Telbridge now shuns him.'

Maggie shook her head. 'Poor boy! No wonder he refuses to use his courtesy title. But from what you say, he grew up with no resources at all. I would expect him to be a simpleton or a savage, but he seems quite cultured. Did his mother's family step in to help?'

The dowager smiled thinly. 'Though admittedly, the scandal of the divorce placed them in an awkward position, I've always held that blood should care for blood. The girl's parents, however—doubtless with a glance over their shoulder at the financial boon the earl had provided them upon the marriage—disowned her. The boy might have grown up a savage, but for the intervention some years later by his aunt who, once she married, persuaded her husband to sponsor the boy and raise him as befitted his station.'

'Lord Newville?' she asked. 'Papa told me he had taken Mr Hadley under his wing.'

'Quite. The Newvilles took care of mother and son, financed Hadley's schooling, and sponsored his candidacy into Parliament. After what he suffered at his father's hands, it's not surprising he turned into a Radical, committed to limiting the power of the aristocracy.'

'What happened to the lady?'

'By all accounts, she was content, living in rural isolation with her son. I expect she hoped that one day the man she loved would return for her. But as it turned out, her family was right about that, if little else. He died in India several years after her divorce, and she did not long outlive him.'

'Now that his eldest son has made such a name for himself, and knowing he will one day inherit, isn't it time for Telbridge to make peace with his heir?'

The dowager shook her head. 'Randall Hadley was always a proud, unyielding man. I think it was more the satisfaction of winning the woman away from his friend, rather than affection for the lady, that led the earl to wed her in the first place, and he couldn't tolerate the idea that his wife had been touched by another. It's only thanks to the good sense of Hadley's aunt that the successor to the earldom won't be a complete Hottentot.'

'So there isn't much chance of father and son reconciling?'

'I wouldn't wager on it,' the dowager said. 'The earl is too stubborn; his second son, from what I hear, is so jealous and resentful of the heir he takes every opportunity to speak ill of him to his father. As for the viscount, he will inherit whether they reconcile or not. I would expect he has little desire to approach a man who left him and his mother destitute. Certainly, Telbridge has done nothing in the years since to prompt his son—if the viscount *is* his son—to seek a reconciliation.'

'Perhaps,' Maggie said with a sigh. 'But it is still sad.'

'Family squabbles are as old as time. Read your Bible,' the dowager advised.

'That doesn't make them less regrettable.'

'Indeed. However, if you do intend to…pursue an acquaintance with Giles Hadley, I would do so cautiously.'

'Why do you say that? Surely you don't think he's "dangerous", as John Proctor warned! Even if he should subscribe to Godwin's theories on abolishing marriage, I cannot see him forcibly seducing a woman.' She laughed ruefully. 'He wouldn't need to.'

'I've heard nothing of that—rather the opposite, actually. His *amours* have been few, and the ladies involved were treated with great courtesy. No, it's just that I'd not like to see a lovers' triangle descend to the second generation.'

'Lovers' triangle?' Her puzzlement gave way to irritation as she made the connection. 'That *Morning Post* article again! Surely you don't give any credence to newspaper gossip. I have no interest in wedding George Hadley, no matter how much he sidles up to Papa!'

'Though the writers do expend an inordinate amount of ink speculating about their betters, there is always some thread of truth in the reports. Perhaps George Hadley thinks he's "sidled up" to your father successfully enough that he's in a fair way to winning your hand. It would be an excellent match for him.'

'Well, it wouldn't be an excellent one for me,' Maggie retorted with some heat. 'I don't like the man, and I'm not so committed to the Tories that I would marry someone for their political advantage. Nor would Papa try to persuade me, no matter how much George Hadley tries to turn him up sweet.'

'Yes, but that's not the problem,' the countess continued patiently. 'Don't you see? There is no love lost between the brothers. Isn't it possible that, having read the newspaper reports as the rest of us have, Giles Hadley might seek you out, just to put a spoke in the wheel of his half-brother's plans? Now, I'm not saying Hadley turned up in Armsburn's borough with that in mind. Most likely he was in Chellingham for political reasons of his own, met you by chance, and admires you sincerely—why ever should he not? Given the history between the two, though, I would be cautious.'

For a moment, the thought that Giles Hadley might have approached her with the intent of beguiling her so he could crow to his brother about his conquest made her feel sick. That scenario was too reminiscent of the debacle with Sir Francis.

But an instant later, a deep conviction rose up to refute that scenario. Regardless of his reasons for coming to Chellingham, the attraction between them had been genuine—she was sure of that. Whether or not he would pursue the connection because of his brother's interest in her, or in spite of it, she didn't know, but the spark lit between them had not been the product of her imagination.

What she chose to do about it, now that she knew his full background, was still up to her. She was no more interested in becoming the bone of contention snapped over by two pugnacious half-brothers than she was in becoming George Hadley's prize pullet.

And she definitely didn't intend to risk falling in love.

'I will be cautious,' she promised the dowager as she finished her tea and set the cup back on the tray. 'That's why I came to talk to you, Aunt Lilly. You always give such excellent advice.'

'Advice is about all one has to give at my age,' her great-aunt said tartly. 'I'll let you go with one last bit: don't let anyone worry you into marrying again, unless you truly wish it. I had several offers after Creighton died, but none could hold a candle to him, and I wouldn't settle for a lesser man.'

'That's how I feel about my Robbie,' Maggie said, her eyes sheening.

'Not that I didn't amuse myself from time to time,' her great-aunt added.

'Aunt Lilly!' Margaret laughed. 'You'll make me blush.'

'As if I could, with all you must overhear, spending so much time around gentlemen! But I worry about you, child. You were inconsolable after losing your husband, and then when it seemed you'd found happiness again, the affair with Sir Francis ended so badly. I would so like to see you passionate about life again.'

'I enjoy my work with Papa.'

'I'd have you not just "enjoy" life, but be truly thrilled by it—illumined from within! You know what I mean— I can see it in your eyes. If Giles Hadley offers you the possibility of tasting such joy again, don't let the dull voice of prudence prevent you from furthering the acquaintance. After all, you cannot find what you won't risk looking for. Just keep in mind the possible complications.

'And I intend to end this homily with a recommendation about marriage, and you may as well not protest,' her great-aunt continued, holding up a hand to forestall any objection. 'Much as I would oppose you being pushed into marriage, neither would I like you to miss out on the blessing of children. A thought to consider, while you're still young enough to have them.'

Maggie worked hard not to flinch. That was a fact of which she was too bitterly aware.

Masking her discomfort from her perceptive great-aunt by rising, she said, 'I must get back. I've not been home yet, and Papa has a large party coming for dinner tomorrow night for which I haven't even begun to prepare. He'll want a complete account of the Chellingham elections, too. Thank you for tea—and your counsel, Aunt Lilly.'

'You are always welcome to both.'

As Maggie bent to kiss the dowager's cheek, her great-aunt reached out to pat hers. 'I pray for your happiness, child.'

Maggie felt the burn of tears and blinked them away. 'Thank you, Aunt Lilly. If something exciting should happen, you'll be the first to know.'

Her great-aunt chuckled. 'With my contacts, I certainly will—whether you tell me yourself or not!'

During the drive from her great-aunt's town house back to her father's in Cavendish Square, Maggie replayed their interview over and over. After hearing Giles Hadley's story, she was more fascinated by the man than ever. How had he reconciled the rural isolation of his early years with rejoining the world of the *ton* when his aunt had come to rescue him? Did he remember anything of the days he'd lived at his father's grand estate in Hampshire?

Despite his education and upbringing, if he knew nothing of that estate or its people, how could he become a good landlord to his tenants and a proper steward of the land entrusted to him, once he inherited? Or would he remain in London, furthering his career in Parliament, content to let some estate agent or secretary manage his acres and tend its people? What a tragedy for them that would be!

She would love to ask him about his plans, but their acquaintance was nowhere close enough for her to broach such personal matters.

Then there was the problem of the possible rivalry between him and his brother over George's supposed pretensions to her hand. Though she was certain there was a genuine attraction between herself and Giles Hadley, she'd already proven rather miserable at discerning whether a man's attentions stemmed from her charms, or the charms of her lineage, wealth and connections. Would Mr Hadley indulge her curiosity and encourage her interest because he found her as intriguing as she found him? Or if she followed through on her desires, might she be leading herself into another painful disappointment?

Yet, as even Aunt Lilly had implied, youth wouldn't last for ever. In the years since Robbie's death, she'd met many gentlemen, without feeling anything like the strong and immediate attraction she'd felt for Giles Hadley. If she let caution dissuade her from at least discovering where it might lead, she might never have another chance.

After all, she was wiser now, more suspicious of attention and flattery than she'd been before the episode with Sir Francis. As long as she kept her head, the worst that could happen by furthering the relationship would be the disappointment of discovering Giles Hadley was not as fascinating—or as fascinated by her—as she'd thought. She felt certain Giles Hadley would never endanger her, or compel her to go where she didn't wish to follow.

There'd be no question of 'compelling', though. Just thinking of the mesmerising blue gaze and the heated feeling in the pit of her stomach when he smiled at her set her pulses throbbing. But surely she was prudent enough to resist the most dangerous of all temptations, and restrict herself to friendship.

She really did wish to know him better…as a friend and companion, she told herself.

As a lover, if you could imagine a safe way to manage it, the voice of honesty answered back.

But only as long as she could invest herself just so far, without any possibility of committing her heart.

The short drive to the Witlow town house ended before she came to a definite decision. So much for thinking herself level-headed! Exasperated with such dithering, she decided as she descended from the carriage that she would attend some debates after the new Parliament convened. If an opportunity presented itself to speak further with Mr Hadley—or he sought her out—she would take it as a sign to proceed.

Because in the end, in that sphere beyond words or logic, the pull she felt to him was irresistible.

Chapter Three

Two evenings later, Giles arrived back in London and headed for the room at the Quill and Gavel, eager to compare notes with his friends about the election results. He found them all present as he walked in, Davie offering him a mug of ale, Ben Tawney urging him to a seat.

'What happened in Chellingham?' Christopher asked. 'Did Reynolds manage to snatch the seat from Witlow's man?'

'I'm afraid not,' he confessed, to the groans of his listeners. 'Michael Armsburn did so well in the verbal tally, we didn't bother asking for a formal vote. Riding around with Reynolds, one could tell it was hopeless. Even the unemployed former soldiers one would expect to rally to the Reform cause told us they intended to vote for Witlow's man. Said his lordship had watched out for their families while they were off fighting in the wars. How did all of you fare?'

'A win in Sussex!' Ben announced. 'We'll own the county now.'

'Wins in Merton and Warrenton as well,' Christopher added. 'The Whigs should return an overwhelming majority.'

'That calls for another round, don't you think?' David asked. After walking to the door to beckon the innkeeper to bring more ale, he said, 'Ben and Christopher, why don't you make a tally of the projected gains, district by district? I expect we'll be recalled to committee as soon as Parliament reconvenes.'

Once the two friends settled at the table, Davie raised his mug to Giles. 'So,' he said in a quiet voice pitched for their ears alone, 'what did you think of Lady Margaret?'

Surprised, Giles felt his face flush. 'How did you know I'd met Lady Margaret?'

Davie shrugged. 'You'd said you'd try to help the Radicals win one of Witlow's seats—yet you chose to canvass for one that we knew at the outset was very unlikely to be turned. A seat that just happens to be held by a cousin of Lady Margaret's, for whom she has often campaigned. And that, after hearing your brother might have matrimonial designs upon the lady. So, what did you think of her?'

'Sure the Home Office shouldn't employ your talents to keep track of dissidents?' Giles asked, disgruntled that his motives had been so transparent. 'Very well, I was quite impressed. She's a natural campaigner—the crowds love her. She seems passionate about politics and the welfare of the people in her father's boroughs.'

'A shame she's passionate for the wrong party,' David said, his perceptive friend watching him entirely too closely for Giles's comfort. 'Did you talk with her?'

'Yes. Her person is as appealing as her politics are not. I have to admit, I was quite…strongly attracted. By the way, she denied any interest in marrying George.'

'Did she? I don't know that her lack of interest would weigh much with your half-brother, compared to the advantages of the match. One can only hope her father has a care for her preferences, rather than for giving a leg up to a rising member of his party. Do you intend to pursue the connection?'

'Yes, I do.' *At least long enough to see if the extraordinary attraction he'd felt lasted beyond that first meeting.*

'And what of George?'

Giles shrugged. 'Having never in my life consulted George's preferences before doing something, I'm not likely to start now.'

Davie nodded. 'Very well. Just make sure the lady doesn't get caught in the crossfire, if there is any.'

Giles grinned. 'One thing you can count on: I will always protect a lady.'

Before they could join their friends at the table, a liveried messenger appeared at the doorway. 'A note for Mr Hadley.'

After Giles raised his hand, the man gave him the missive and walked out. Scanning it quickly, Giles frowned. 'It's from Lord Grey. He wants me to join a dinner meeting he's about to begin with some of his committee chiefs.'

Ben whistled, and David raised his eyebrows. 'Congratulations on having the party leader call for you!' Christopher said. 'Maybe there's a cabinet post in your future?'

'I doubt that. I'll have to go, though, unfortunately, it's at Brooks's Club—which is probably why Grey didn't invite all of us. He knows I never grace the halls of Brooks's unless I'm summoned.'

'Maybe you should go there more often,' Davie advised. 'Many of the senior party leaders are members; let them get to know you better.'

'I'd rather meet here, with all of you.' Giles smiled.

'Planning strategy and dreaming dreams of change, as we have since that grimy little inn at Oxford.'

'Being a Hellion was all well and good,' David allowed. 'But challenging the prevailing view has served its purpose. Now that the goals we dreamed about are going to be realised, shouldn't we turn our efforts into getting a hand in determining how they are implemented?'

'Very true,' Christopher said. 'Why not take advantage of whatever benefits membership at Brooks's can offer?'

'You could even pass them along to us,' David added with a grin. 'It's the only way *I'll* ever gain access to them, after all. Their politics might be liberal, but never in this lifetime are high-born Whigs going to allow the orphaned son of farmer into their club, regardless of how highly placed his sponsor might be.'

'Or the illegitimate son of a governess,' Ben added.

'A gently born governess, whose father is now a viscount and acknowledges him,' Giles reminded Ben. 'If you asked, your father would likely sponsor you at Brooks's.'

'So the members could mutter under their breath about my mother as I walk by, like the boys did at Oxford? I think not.'

'As for me,' Christopher said with a grin, 'being in the unusual position of being considered my legal father's son even though I'm not, I *could* be put up for membership. Except that dear legal Papa is a Tory who frequents White's.'

'I doubt they would have voted me in, had Lord Newville not been insistent,' Giles said. 'I can only imagine how much arm-twisting was involved.'

'Your nomination did place the members in an awkward position,' David said. 'Many of them are friends of your father, and there's the sticky matter of George. If anything happens to you, George gets the title; like our Oxford classmates, few there would want to befriend you and offend him, in case some day he attains real power.'

'We'll just have to see that he doesn't,' Giles retorted.

'Faith and the devil, that reminds me!' Christopher exclaimed. 'Wychwood told me that George lost his seat!'

'In Hampshire, my father's county?' Giles asked, astounded.

'Yes. Despite how strongly the voice vote went in favour of the Reform candidate, Wychwood said George insisted on a formal counted vote. And lost it decisively.'

The other three whistled as the significance of that registered. 'Pity his poor servants—and any other unfortunate who crosses his path in the next few days,' Christopher said. 'He'll be as quick to lash out as a temperamental stallion with an abscessed hoof.'

'He'll surely look for some way to transfer the blame to you,' David warned.

'And whine to his father about it,' Christopher added.

'I'd avoid him,' Ben advised.

'I always do,' Giles replied. 'But now, I'd better get to that meeting. With any luck, I'll be back to drink another mug before midnight.'

'Take good notes, so you can give us a full report,' Christopher said as Giles shrugged on his coat and headed for the door.

As he walked out, Davie followed him, then stayed him with a hand on his arm. 'This might not be the best of times to provoke a quarrel over a lady,' he said quietly.

'I don't intend to quarrel,' Giles replied. 'If he tries to start one, I'll ignore it, as I always do.' *No matter how much I'd like to plant a facer in the middle of that smug face,* he added silently.

'Just…watch your step. I've always thought George

like a coiled snake, ready to strike if cornered. Don't give him any more reason.'

'I shall be the soul of diplomacy.'

'Giles, the most hot-headed member of our group?' David retorted. 'Just remember that resolution, if you encounter George when I'm not there to restrain you. It would be…undignified for a rising Member of Parliament to mill down a former Member in public.'

'Besides which, George would be sure to haul me up on assault charges. Temper or no, I promise to be on my best behaviour.'

And he would be, Giles promised himself as he walked out to hail a hackney.

Several hours later, dinner and consultation with Lord Grey and two of his ministers complete and a sheaf of notes in hand, Giles had just left the small private dining room when an unwelcome voice assailed his ears.

Hearing his name called again, he turned towards the card room, girding himself for the always unwelcome encounter with his half-brother.

'It is you, then,' George said, and walked towards him.

At least he'd won that small satisfaction, Giles thought as he waited for his half-brother to approach: George had finally learned that Giles would not come running to him when his half-brother beckoned, like the lackey George wanted him to be.

As the man proceeded closer with his measured, self-important tread, Giles noted he was splendidly dressed, as usual, in a dark coat featuring the newly popular cinched-in waist, an elaborately tied cravat of fine linen with a large diamond winking out from the knot, and long trousers. A walking advertisement for his tailor, and for being a man who spared no expense on his person.

George stopped beside him, looking him in the eyes for a moment without speaking. His half-brother was of a height, but had the fairer hair and hazel eyes of their father and a pleasant face that, when it wore a congenial look Giles seldom saw, was accounted handsome, or so numerous society ladies seemed to think.

Apparently Lady Margaret wasn't of their number. That recollection pleased him more than it should.

When Giles refused to rise to the bait of asking his brother to tell him what he wanted, at length George broke the silence. 'Didn't believe at first you'd actually entered a gentleman's club, instead of hobnobbing with the lowborn sorts you usually associate with. Devil's teeth, to think how much blunt Lord Newville must have dropped, bribing the members to get you accepted here! But in this instance, I suppose I should thank him for sparing me having to track you down in that dive you frequent.'

Drawing in a deep breath through his gritted teeth to stem the rising anger, Giles made no immediate response. He'd long ago figured out the best way to deal with his half-brother's demeaning remarks was to ignore them, no matter how infuriating—thereby depriving George of the satisfaction of provoking him.

'Do you having anything of substance to say, or did you just want to tender the usual insults?' he said in a tone as bored as he could manage. 'If the latter, I'll bid you goodnight.' With a nod of dismissal, he turned to go.

'Wait! I do have something else to say.' George stayed him.

Much as Giles would love to snub him and walk out, if his half-brother truly wanted to speak with him, leaving now would only delay the confrontation. Tenacious as a bulldog, George would simply run him down somewhere else.

Wondering what his brother could possibly wish to discuss with him—unless he'd already figured out a way to blame Giles for his electoral defeat—he raised an eyebrow. 'Perhaps you might wish to do so somewhere more private than Brooks's entry hall?' With a gesture, he indicated a small anteroom.

After George followed him in, Giles said, 'I've still got work to do tonight, so I'd appreciate your keeping this short.' With what he considered true nobility, he refrained from adding that it involved important business for the new Parliament—the one in which George would not be serving. After closing the door, he said, 'Shall we dispense with the charade of exchanging pleasantries? Just say what you must.'

'I will be brief. I'm warning you to leave Lady Margaret Roberts alone. She's a gentlewoman from a distinguished family, her father a nobleman highly regarded by his peers. Neither need be embarrassed by it becoming known that she associated with *you*. And at a common inn, no less.'

Baffled, Giles stared at George—until his mind made the connection. 'You mean, in Chellingham?'

'As far as I know, that's the only time she's displayed such a lapse of judgement. Although I understand there was some disturbance that necessitated her removal, and that at the time she let you make off with her, she was not aware of who you were.'

'It being more acceptable for the lady to leave with a stranger than to leave with me?' Giles inserted.

'Well, of course she shouldn't be leaving with a stranger! Armsburn and Proctor were highly negligent in leaving her alone to begin with. Although it would have been better still if she'd not put herself forward, campaigning for her cousin.'

Although admittedly Giles was not conversant with who belonged to which circle of friendship among the Tory membership, he was not aware that Lady Margaret's cousin and his half-brother were close. And if they were not…

'How did you know what happened to Lady Margaret in Chellingham?' When his half-brother stuttered for an answer, Giles voiced the unbelievable, but only logical, conclusion. 'You weren't having someone *spy* on her, were you, George?'

'Someone should keep tabs on her, since it's obvious neither her cousin nor his aide were doing such a good job of it,' his half-brother replied defensively.

There could be but one reason for George to go to the trouble of having the lady watched: he *must* be set on marrying her. Even so, the behaviour was unsettling, and definitely raised his hackles on Lady Margaret's behalf.

'Is Lord Witlow aware of your…protective oversight?' He knew Lady Margaret couldn't be—and was reasonably sure what that lady's response would be if she found out.

'Lord Witlow would be gratified that I concern myself with the welfare of his dearest daughter,' George replied loftily.

So her father wasn't aware of the scrutiny either. Which made the behaviour even more disturbing. 'He might also not appreciate having someone wholly unrelated keeping his daughter under observation.'

George gave an impatient wave. 'My motives are of the purest. Besides, I cherish hopes that we will not long remain "unrelated".'

So George did intend to press his suit. 'You've spoken with his lordship on this matter?'

'He's doubtless aware of my regard,' George evaded.

'And the lady?'

'I haven't as yet formally declared myself,' George admitted. 'But on a matter as important as family alliances, she will follow her father's guidance, and he will certainly approve. Now that I have revealed my honourable intentions, I expect even someone like you to respect them, and not sully the lady with associations that could only be to her detriment.'

Keeping a tight hold on the simmering anger he didn't seem able to completely suppress, Giles said evenly, 'I would do the lady the honour of allowing *her* to choose with whom she wishes to associate.'

George stared at him a moment. 'Meaning, you *do* intend to pester her with your attentions?'

'I have never "pestered" a woman,' Giles retorted. 'If a lady indicates she is uninterested in my company, I am not so boorish as to inflict it upon her.' That shot flying entirely over his brother's head, he added, 'As I said, it is the lady's choice.'

'Excellent!' George said, a self-satisfied look replacing the hostility of his expression. 'I may be easy, then. Her father would never allow an association so detrimental to her good name and the regard in which she is universally held. That being all I wished to ascertain, I will bid you goodnight.'

Avoiding, as he always did, using either Giles's last name or honorary title, George nodded and walked back towards the card room.

Leaving Giles staring after him incredulously.

He should be happy, he told himself as he gathered up his papers again, that his half-brother's incredible arrogance spared him the necessity of wrangling with George over his intention to seek out Lady Margaret. Apparently, his half-brother thought the lady a puppet who moved at her father's command. And he was certain the marquess would command her to stay away from Giles, and marry George.

Fortunately, Giles already knew the first assumption was unlikely—Lady Margaret had told him plainly that her father respected him.

As for the latter, Lady Margaret seemed sincerely attached to her father, and probably would not willingly displease him. However, Giles doubted the independent lady he'd seen joking with voters on the hustings would let her father compel her into a marriage she did not want.

That conclusion cheered him almost as much as avoiding an ugly confrontation with his half-brother.

Nothing George had told him altered his intention to seek out the lady, at least until George or—he frowned at the thought—his watching minions discovered Giles had seen her again. By then, he should have confirmed whether or not his attraction to her—and hers to him—was strong enough for him to justify navigating the tricky course around his half-brother's presumptions.

He had no clear idea what sort of relationship he envisioned. Not marriage, certainly—his tenuous position and his past were too chequered to inflict that association on any woman. But the lady was a widow, and perfectly able to indulge in a discreet dalliance, if their respective desires led that way...

Tantalised by the thought, Giles set off for the hackney stand, eager to report back to his friends at the Quill and Gavel. As he climbed into the vehicle, it suddenly occurred to him that he had another pressing reason to seek out Lady Margaret, whether or not the powerful connection between them recurred.

Giles felt the lady ought to know that his half-brother was keeping her under surveillance.

At Lady Margaret's probable reaction to that news, he had to smile.

Chapter Four

Shortly after the opening of Parliament two weeks later, Lady Margaret climbed the stairs to the Ladies' Gallery in the upper storey of St Stephen's Chapel. The odd arrangement in that chamber—a round bench surrounding a wooden lantern at the centre of the room, whose eight small openings allowed a limited view down into the House of Commons below—would make watching the debates difficult, though she would be able to hear all the speeches.

And she'd *heard* that Giles Hadley was to give an address on behalf of the Reform Bill today.

She claimed a place, thinking with longing of the unobstructed view that, seated right on a bench beside the members, she enjoyed when she attended the Lords to listen to her father. The best she could hope for in this room, if she were lucky and the gentleman stood in the right place, was to catch a glimpse of Mr Hadley's head. Remembering that gentleman's magnificent eyes and commanding figure, seeing no more than the top of his head was going to be a great loss.

Would his voice alone affect her? Her stomach fluttered and a shiver prickled her nerves, just as it had each time she'd thought of the man since their meeting several weeks ago. And she'd thought of him often.

Doubtless far too often, for a man she'd met only once, who did not appear at any of the *ton*'s balls or parties—where she'd looked for him in vain—and who did not frequent the same political gatherings she attended.

But oh, how even the *thought* of him still stirred her!

She would certainly try to meet him today. After spending the last several weeks finding herself continually distracted by recalling their encounter, sorting through possible explanations for the magic of it, and wondering whether it might happen again, she was tired of acting like a silly schoolgirl suffering her first infatuation. She wanted her calm, reasonable self back. For even if he did seem as compelling upon second meeting as he had upon the first, at her age, she should be wise enough not to lose her head over him.

Besides, seeing him again in the prosaic light of a Parliamentary anteroom, it was far more likely that he would cease being the stuff of dreams and turn into just another normal, attractive man.

Soon the session was called to order and a succession of speakers rose to address the group, met by silence or shouted comments from the opposing bench, depending on how controversial the subject being addressed. After several hours, stiff from sitting on the hard bench, Maggie was about to concede defeat and make her way out when the voice that had whispered through her dreams tickled her ears.

Shock vibrating through her, she craned her head towards the nearest opening, hoping for a glimpse of him.

The light dancing on the wavy, blue-black curls sent another little shock through her. Nerves tingling and breathing quickened, she bent down, positioning herself to catch even the smallest glimpse as he paced below her.

His voice held her rapt—oh, what a voice! Her father was right—Giles Hadley was a born orator, his full, rich tones resonating through the chamber. As he continued to press his points, even the disdainful comments of the opposition grew fewer, and finally died away altogether.

When the rising volume and increasingly urgent tone indicated the approaching climax of the speech, Maggie found herself leaning even further forward, anxious to take in every word.

'For too long,' he exhorted, 'we have allowed the excesses of Revolutionary France to stifle the very discussion of altering the way our representatives are chosen. But this is England, not France. Are we a nation of cowards?'

After pausing to accommodate the chorus of 'no's he continued, 'Then let nothing prevent us in this session from doing what all rational men know should be done: eliminate these pocket boroughs that give undue influence to a few voters or the wealthy neighbour who can sway them, and restore to our government a more balanced system of representation, a fair system, a just system, one that works in the harmony our noble forebears intended!'

As his voice died away, he came to a stop right below her, his head bowed as he acknowledged the cheers and clapping from the Whigs, the mutter of dissent from the Tories. Then, as if some invisible force had telegraphed her presence, he looked up through the opening, and their eyes met.

The energy that pulsed between them in that instant raised the tiny hairs at the back of her neck. Then an arm appeared in her narrow view, pulling him away, and he was lost to her sight.

Straightening, Maggie found herself trembling. Thrilled by the power of his oratory, she remained seated, too shaken to move.

Papa had said everyone expected great things of him, and she now understood why. How could Lord Grey resist adding so compelling a Reformer to his staff? Even the Tories had fallen silent under the power of his rhetoric.

When he spoke with such passionate conviction, she suspected that he'd be able to persuade her to almost anything.

An alarming thought, and one that ought to make her rethink her intention to meet him again.

She was debating the wisdom of going downstairs and seeking him out, when suddenly the air around her seemed charged with energy. Startled, she looked up—into the blue, blue eyes of Giles Hadley.

Her mouth went dry and her stomach did a little flip.

'Lady Margaret!' he said, bowing. 'What an unexpected pleasure to see you again.'

She rose to make him a curtsy. 'And to see you, Mr Hadley. That was a very fine speech.'

He waved a hand. 'The plain truth, merely.'

'Perhaps, but the plain truth elegantly arranged and convincingly presented. It's no wonder the full chamber attended to hear you speak.'

He smiled, his eyes roaming her face with an ardency that made her pulse kick up a notch. 'I'd rather flatter myself that *you* came to hear me speak.'

'Then you may certainly do so. I did indeed come with the hope of hearing you, and was richly rewarded.'

His eyes brightened further, sending another flutter of sensation through her. 'Considering the many excellent speakers you've doubtless heard in both chambers, it's very kind of you to say so. Surely I ought to offer you some tea in gratitude? Normally, we could take it in the committee room, but with the session just begun, everything is rather disordered. Might I persuade you to accompany me to Gunter's?'

'I would like that very much.'

He offered his arm. After a slight hesitation, she gave him her hand, savouring the shock of connection that rippled up her arm.

She did have the answer to one of the questions that had bedevilled her since their last meeting, she thought as he walked her down the stairs. The effect he had on her was definitely not a product of election excitement or the danger of that skirmish in Chellingham. Leaving caution behind in this chamber of debate, she intended to enjoy every second of it.

'So,' he said after they'd settled into a hackney on the way to Gunter's. 'Did my speech convince you that the time is right for reform?'

'Your arguments are very persuasive,' she admitted.

'I hope your father and the Tories in the Lords agree. With so many Whigs returning to the Commons, passage of the bill in the lower house is certain. Though many in the Lords resist change, even the most hidebound cannot defend the ridiculousness of a pocket borough with a handful of voters having two representatives, when the great cities of the north have none.'

'True. But Members are not elected to represent only their particular district, but the interests of the nation as a whole,' she pointed out.

'Another excuse to oppose change that the Tories have trotted out for years!' he said with a laugh. 'Let's be

rational. When a borough contains only a handful of
voters who must cast their vote in public, they usually
elect the candidate favoured by the greatest landholder
in the area.'

'Who, since he does own the property, should look out
for its best interests and those of the people who work
it and make it profitable,' she countered. 'Which is why
giving every man a vote, as I've heard you approve, could
be dangerous. A man who owns nothing may have no
interest at all in the *common* good. With nothing to lose,
he can be swayed by whatever popular wind is blowing.'

'Just because a man owns property doesn't mean he
tends it well, or cares for those who work it. Oh, I know,
the best of them, like your father, do. But wealth and
power can beguile a man into believing he can do whatever he wishes, regardless of the well-being of anyone
else.'

As his father had? Maggie wondered. 'Perhaps,' she
allowed. 'But what about boroughs where the voters sold
their support to the highest bidder? Virtue isn't a product of birth. Noble or commoner, a man's character will
determine his actions.'

'With that, I certainly agree.' He shook his head ad-
miringly. 'You're a persuasive speaker yourself, Lady
Margaret. A shame that women do not stand for Parliament. Though since you favour the Tories, I expect I
should be grateful they do not!'

At that point, the hackney arrived at Gunter's, and for
the next few moments, conversation ceased while Hadley helped her from the carriage and they were seated
within the establishment. As Hadley ordered the tea
she requested in lieu of the famed ices, Maggie simply
watched him.

She'd been intensely aware of him, seated beside her

in the hackney during the transit. But she'd been almost equally stirred by his conversation.

Most gentlemen felt ladies were either uninterested in, or incapable of understanding, the intricacies of politics. Only her father had ever done her the courtesy of discussing them with her. Even her cousin Michael Armsburn, and the several other candidates for whom she had canvassed, valued her just as a pretty face to charm the voters.

None of the men she'd supported had ever invited her to discuss their policy or its philosophical roots. Giles Hadley excited her mind as much as he stirred her senses.

Or almost as much, she amended. He mesmerised her when he talked, not just the thrilling words, but watching those mobile lips, wondering how they'd feel, pressed against hers. She exulted in the tantalising magic of sitting beside him, the energy and passion he exuded arousing a flood of sensation in her, the heat and scent of him and the wondrous words he uttered a sea she could drown in.

Oh, to be with a man who burned with ardent purpose, who inspired one with a desire to be with him, not just in bed, but out of it as well!

Tea arrived shortly thereafter. Maggie forced herself to cease covertly studying the excellence of Giles Hadley's physique, the breadth of his shoulders and the tapered elegance of his fingers, and concentrate on filling his cup.

After they had each sipped the steaming brew, Hadley set down his cup with an apologetic look. 'I'm afraid I must confess to not being completely truthful about my reasons for inviting you here.'

Her great-aunt's warning returned in a rush, dousing her heated euphoria with the ice water of wariness. 'Not truthful? In what way?'

'Much as I am enjoying our excursion to Gunter's, we could have taken tea in the committee room. Except there is a matter I feel I must discuss with you that demanded a greater degree of privacy than would have been afforded in a Parliamentary chamber.'

Foreboding souring her gut, she said, 'Then by all means, let us discuss it.'

'I spoke with my brother not long ago. As you know, we…are not close, and he generally does not seek me out unless he wishes to dispute with me about something. The matter he wished to dispute about this time…was you.'

So she *was* to be a bone of contention? Not if she could help it! But perhaps she should hear him out before rushing to conclusions. 'What was the nature of that dispute?'

Hadley shrugged. 'You've read the journal reports— and so has George. Apparently my half-brother thinks you favour him—or he believes your father approves of him, and would favour his suit. He warned me to stay away from you.'

Some of the anger, hurt and despair of the episode with Sir Francis rose up, nearly choking her. 'And so you sought my company to spite him?' she spit out at last. 'Do you think to beguile me, and then boast to him about it?'

He straightened, frowning. 'Not at all! How could you imagine such a thing? Besides, if I were trying to charm you and boast of my conquest, would I have told you about our disagreement?'

'Do you think you *could* charm me?'

His irritated expression smoothed, a roguish smile replaced it, and he smiled at her, that smile that made her knees weak. 'Do *you* think I could?'

'If you did, and we were compromised, we might be forced to wed. Then you'd be stuck with me for life—

a fate which ought to give you pause,' she said tartly, mollified.

His smile faded. 'I would never do you the harm of marrying you.'

Before she could figure out that odd comment, he continued, his expression serious, 'But that's not what I meant to talk about. Did you speak with my half-brother about our meeting in Chellingham?'

It was her turn to be puzzled. 'No, I've not seen him since I returned to London. Why do you ask?'

'As far as you know, George is not a friend of your cousin Mr Armsburn?'

'They are acquainted, certainly, but not close.'

'The only place we've met, before today, was Chellingham. My brother specifically mentioned how detrimental to your reputation it would be if others discovered you'd been alone with me at the inn there. If you did not relate our encounter to George, and your cousin or his aide, Mr Proctor, didn't inform him, how could he have known about it?'

Maggie paused a moment, thinking. She'd spoken with Aunt Lilly, but that lady would never divulge, even to her friends, confidential information about her niece, particularly if it involved a gentleman and would therefore make her the subject of gossip and conjecture. She was quite certain she'd not mentioned their meeting to anyone else.

'I don't know,' she confessed.

'Then it seems my suspicions were justified. Outlandish as it sounds, in order for my half-brother to have known that you'd accompanied me to that inn in Chellingham, he must have been keeping you under surveillance.'

She shook her head a little, not sure she could have

heard him correctly. 'Are you trying to tell me that your brother has someone...*spying* on me?'

'You weren't aware of it?'

'Absolutely not!'

He nodded, looking grim again. 'Your father wouldn't have asked him to do such a thing, would he?'

'Why would he? I had my cousin and Proctor to watch over me. If Papa *had* thought I needed additional protection, he would have chosen someone I know better than your brother to provide it. And I am sure he would not have done so without informing me and explaining the need for it. No, I don't think Papa authorised this. Shall I ask him?'

'Perhaps you should. I wouldn't want to accuse my half-brother unjustly.'

The enormity of what he'd just told her registered. 'Why in the world would your half-brother want to have me watched?'

'He told me he intends to ask for your hand. Perhaps, with the turmoil over the Reform Bill and rumours flying of possible electoral violence, he wanted to make sure the woman he wants to marry didn't come to any harm.'

'Or he wished to make sure the woman he plans to marry did not behave in a manner of which he doesn't approve!' she retorted, more and more indignant as the implications registered. 'The effrontery! How dare he have someone tail me as if I were a...a petty thief he was trying to prove guilty of larceny!'

Giles's lips twitched. 'I didn't think you'd find the idea very appealing. May I assume from this that you are now even less likely to consider an offer from my half-brother?'

'If he has indeed so grievously imposed on my privacy, you may assume the chances of my accepting an offer from him to be non-existent!'

He smiled at that. 'Then I am almost glad of his arrogance. But…there is one thing more I feel I must say, before we drop the unpleasant matter of my brother.' He paused, his smile fading. 'I do hope you won't feel I'm telling you this just because the two of us do not get along.'

'I think I can count on your honesty.' She hesitated, unsure how much she could or should say, given how brief their acquaintance was. 'Even though I understand that you have not been…kindly treated, either by your father or your half-brother.'

He grimaced. 'We are estranged, that is certain.'

She respected his reticence, and admired his restraint in not pouring out the complaints her comment invited—complaints, according to what Aunt Lilly had told her, he would be well justified in making. 'So, what else did you wish to tell me?'

'Would your father compel you to wed a man of his choice, even if you had no particular desire to do so?'

'I cannot imagine he would. Besides, should he try to, I am of age, and have property and assets of my own over which he has no control. There would be no way he could force me to marry against my wishes.'

Giles nodded. 'So I thought. However, George has been…much indulged by his father.' Maggie noted he did not say 'our' father. 'He is quite used to getting whatever he wants. And it seems he wants to marry you. He believes your father would favour his suit, and that you would follow your father's guidance in the matter of the choice of a husband.'

She gave a short laugh. 'No wonder he seems so little

interested in charming me, and so much more interested in beguiling Papa.'

'George can be quite…unpleasant, when he is prevented from obtaining what he desires. If he does in fact make you an offer, and you refuse him, just…be careful.'

She'd been about to take another sip of her tea, but at that, she looked up to stare at him. 'You don't mean he would try to…force me! Or harm me, for refusing him!'

'No, no, probably not that. He would be more likely to start some malicious gossip in an attempt to blacken your name. So if you do refuse him, you might wish to be on your best behaviour.' He winked at her. 'No trysts at secluded inns in small market towns.'

She laughed. 'I will keep that in mind, Mr Hadley.'

'Very well. Now, much as I hate to bring this tryst at a very public place in the huge metropolis to an end, I fear I am due at a meeting in half an hour. Can I escort you home first?'

'No, I have some errands to complete.' Even more reluctant than he to have their time together come to an end, she added on impulse, 'Father is hosting a dinner tomorrow night for some friends, not a policy meeting, but a wide-ranging discussion of political ideas. The guests will be quite varied in background and opinion. Would you like to attend?'

'Are you sure your father would want me?'

'Papa enjoys a free exchange of opinions. I know he would be interested in hearing more of yours. And let me assure you in advance, your half-brother will not be invited.'

'Will you be acting as hostess?'

'For the dinner. I shall probably leave the gentlemen to their discussions afterward.'

'Then I should be delighted…' He paused, frowning. 'I

should be delighted, but I was not exaggerating George's malevolence. I didn't note anyone tailing us to Gunter's, so he may not discover that you accompanied me here, but my presence at your father's dinner will surely excite enough comment to reach his ears. Probably, the knowledge will merely increase his enmity towards me, which is a matter of no import—the fact that I breathe daily increases his enmity. He might, however, seek you out for an explanation. I would not have you harassed.'

His concern that she *not* be drawn into a squabble between brothers dissipated the last of the caution generated by Aunt Lilly's warning. 'I refuse to allow your half-brother to dictate whom I may or may not invite to my home. If he tries to take me to task for it, I assure you, I am quite capable of putting him in his place.'

'That I would like to see!' Hadley declared, then paused, still looking troubled. 'You are sure? The last thing I want is to introduce any unpleasantness into your life.' His frown dissipating, he gave her an intimate smile, his voice lowering to a seductive murmur. 'I would rather introduce you to pleasure.'

She looked up at him, her gaze caught and held by the power of his. Feeling a little breathless, she had to force herself to look away.

That comment made his amorous intent plain enough, she thought, thrown back into uncertainty by the realisation. She could put any potential affair to a stop right now…if she wanted. But did she want to?

Just because she was certain he would be amenable to dalliance, didn't mean she had to make a decision about it right now. Besides, there could be pleasure in less: conversing, flirting—even a simple kiss.

'My father and I would be honoured if you would

come to dinner tomorrow night,' she found herself replying.

His smile broadened and his eyes lit, as if she'd just given him a treasured gift. 'Then I will certainly be there.'

'Until tomorrow night,' she said, a little giddy. What was she getting herself into?

He escorted her out and summoned a hackney. 'You are sure you'll be all right? You don't even have a maid or a footman to carry parcels.'

'I never bring my maid if I'm visiting Parliament— she'd be bored to death, poor thing, and it would unnecessarily delay her work. Since I'm ordering supplies for dinner, they will be delivered later anyway, so no need of a footman to carry parcels.'

'What, no gowns or slippers or feminine fripperies?'

She laughed. 'At the risk of having you find me totally unwomanly, I confess I don't spend much time on gowns and slippers and fripperies.'

'I could never find you anything but delightful.'

At that, she looked back up at him, into eyes that once again seemed to see deep within her. Enchanted, mesmerised, she didn't *want* to look away. Every nerve quivering with awareness, had they not been standing on a public street, she might have gone into Hadley's arms.

A pedlar with his handcart pushed past them, breaking the spell, and Maggie stepped away. 'You'd better summon a hackney yourself, else you'll be late to your meeting.'

'Thank you again for accompanying me for tea.'

'And to you, for tea…and your warning.'

He turned as if to go, then paused, looking back at her over his shoulder. 'Do you really think I could beguile you?'

'All too easily,' she answered, before realising it would have been more prudent to turn that question aside.

He reached over to take her hand. Little eddies of delight swirled through her as he raised it and brushed his mouth against the thin kidskin sheathing her fingers. 'Then I'm very encouraged. Send me the invitation. I'll definitely come…exchange views with your father.'

With a bow, he handed her up into the carriage, waved his cane in farewell, and walked away.

Hand tingling, even more enchanted than she'd been after their interlude in Chellingham, Maggie watched him until the departing carriage set off, robbing her of the sight.

Chapter Five

That evening, Maggie waited up for her father, who had attended a dinner with some of his political cronies at Brooks's. Although she was certain the marquess would not object to including Giles Hadley in their gathering—the purpose of the entertainment being, as she'd told that gentleman, to explore a wide range of ideas—she also knew he would be surprised by her invitation, and curious.

Best to meet that curiosity head-on. Unfortunately, she wasn't sure she could do a very good job of explaining it to her father when she didn't fully understand it herself. She just knew she wanted to see more of Giles Hadley, and since he didn't attend society functions and was unlikely to turn up at Tory gatherings, luring him to her father's home was probably the only way she was going to manage it.

She really didn't want to tell her father that.

But since the invitation had been tendered, the gentleman had accepted, and she had no intention of revoking it—the need to see him again being greater than her reluctance to discuss the reasons for it with her sire—she'd have to tell Papa—something.

She was dozing over her book in the library when at last she heard her father's distinctive step in the hallway.

'Papa, could I have a word with you?' she called out as he passed the library door.

At the sound of her voice, he stopped short and peered into the room. 'Is that you, Puss? What are you doing still up?'

'There's something I wanted to inform you about. Nothing of importance, but I know you will be tied up in committee meetings all morning, and was afraid I might miss you. It will only take a moment.'

Her father came over to place a kiss on her forehead. 'I always have time for you, sweeting. Shall I pour you some wine?'

'No, this really won't take very long.'

'I think I will rest these old bones while we talk,' he said with a smile as he seated himself. 'So, what's amiss?'

'Nothing! It's just that I invited someone else to join us for dinner tomorrow night, and wanted to let you know beforehand.'

'I thought we'd included everyone we thought could contribute to the conversation. Who did we forget?'

'Well, it's not someone we normally include, but he does have quite interesting views. You've even told me you admire him, though you disagree on almost every particular. It's Mr Hadley—Mr *Giles* Hadley.'

He looked perplexed for a moment before the name registered. 'Viscount Lyndlington, you mean! Unusual that he insists on spurning the title, but I suppose, given the situation between him and Telbridge, understandable. Of course he's welcome, Puss—but how did you come to invite him? I wasn't aware that you were acquainted.'

'Oh, yes! I met him in Chellingham—you remember, I was canvassing for Michael, and he was there to rally support for Mr Reynolds. We spoke briefly, and I found him quite interesting. Then today, we spoke again when he came up to the Ladies' Gallery after he'd given a speech at the Commons.'

'An eloquent plea for passage of the Reform Bill, I understand.'

'Yes, he's quite an excellent speaker. If it is inevitable that the bill will pass the Commons, and he is certain it will, then it might be useful to have a thorough discussion before it comes before you in the Lords.'

'You must have found him persuasive.'

'I did. Not that I agree with all his views, of course. It's true, though, that there was quite a lot of reform talk even in Chellingham, and that borough is as conservative as conservative comes.'

'I will look forward to debating his views.'

'Very good, Papa. That's all, so I'll bid you goodnight.'

When she came over to give him a kiss, he caught her hand, staying her. 'Had I forgotten you telling me you'd met Mr Hadley in Chellingham?'

Maggie felt her face redden, and hoped in the dim candlelight, it wouldn't be apparent. 'I don't believe I mentioned it, specifically. Since at the time, I wasn't sure whether or not I would ever see him again, I didn't think it important.'

'Nor can I remember you visiting the Ladies' Gallery any time recently to hear the speeches.'

'I'd been remiss in not visiting sooner.'

'This young man must have made quite an impression on you.'

So much for thinking she'd got through their little chat without having to explain her interest in Giles Hadley. 'Yes, Papa, he did,' she admitted.

'I thought your favour might lie with a different Mr Hadley.'

'George?' She shuddered, and for a moment, debated telling her father it was almost certain *that* Mr Hadley had been spying on her. But asking Papa whether he'd authorised such a thing, especially when she was nearly certain he had not, might force her to disclose she'd seen a bit more of Giles Hadley than she'd thus far admitted. Deciding to say nothing, she continued, 'He may be a good Tory, but I cannot like him, Papa. He's too…calculating. And completely self-absorbed.'

Her father nodded. 'With the wealth and affection Telbridge lavished on the boy, small wonder he thinks of little beyond his own interests. It's probably just as well he lost his seat. In my estimation, his ambitions rather exceed his abilities.'

'That was my impression,' Maggie said drily. 'Unless the measure of a man is the inventiveness of his tailor.'

'Should I be asking Giles Hadley what his intentions are?'

'Good heavens no, Papa!' she protested, embarrassed by the very idea. 'Promise me you will do nothing of the sort. Yes, I find Mr Giles Hadley…attractive. An excellent and persuasive orator with unique ideas I would like to hear more about. But that's all!'

Her father retained her hand, rubbing the fingers. 'Would it be so bad a thing if you were interested in… more? I know losing Robbie broke your heart, and whatever happened with Sir Francis hurt you deeply. But it hurts *my* heart that you are wearing out your youth playing hostess for an old man, instead of enjoying a husband and setting up your nursery.'

Tears stung her eyes at the mention of those old wounds. 'I like being your hostess!' she protested. 'If

you're tired of having me preside over your table, I can
always retreat back to my house in Upper Brook Street,
or visit Mama at Huntsford.'

'You know I love having you here! Though your mama
would, of course, appreciate a visit.' He sighed. 'Sometimes I do feel…selfish, however, for not doing more to
urge you to go on with your life.'

'I have gone on with my life.'

'Have you, Puss? Or are you just treading water, holding your place against the current, refusing to allow yourself to be swept into something new?'

'Papa, how poetic!' *And unfortunately, how true.* But
how could she allow herself to be swept away when she
no longer trusted any man to tell her the truth? And even
if she could, when she no longer believed a mere marriage
of convenience would wash away the lingering ache of
loneliness and loss?

The possibility of opening herself to more—to anything that might cause the sort of devastation she'd experienced after Robbie's death—was unthinkable.

*A flirtation with Giles Hadley might make you forget
it for a while*, a little voice in her head whispered.

Ignoring it, she said, 'For now, enlivening conversation at dinner by adding an articulate, dissenting voice
is as "swept away" as I care to be. Will that suffice?'

'It's a start,' he said, patting her cheek. 'But don't keep
holding your place in that stream for too long. I still have
aspirations of bouncing your children on my knee before
I'm too decrepit to lift them.'

Her children. She swallowed hard. 'I'll try not to disappoint you. But please, let's not be tasking Mr Hadley
to help me provide you with them just yet.'

He laughed. 'Very well, Puss. We'll have him to dine
a few times first. An excellent young man, by the way.

Many an individual who suffered the setbacks he endured in his youth would have railed at his fate and become a bitter or frivolous wastrel, marking time until he inherited. Giles Hadley confronted his situation with courage, and with quiet determination and considerable effort, earned himself a place in the governing of this nation. I admire him for that.'

'So do I, Papa. And now I will bid you goodnight.'

After exchanging a kiss, they both walked upstairs to their bedchambers. But after blowing out her candle and settling back on her pillow, Maggie found she was no longer sleepy.

What had she really intended to accomplish with her impulsive invitation? To see if Giles Hadley could fit into her world—or she into his?

Did she want *him* to 'sweep her away'? She *wanted* him. That was certain. Every feminine part of her came to aching, needy life when he was near. The strength of that physical attraction made her only too acutely aware of how much she missed 'enjoying a husband'.

But it was a great leap from that to a more serious relationship, one she was nowhere close to being ready to take. Although, she suddenly realised, unlike every other man of her acquaintance, she probably didn't need to fear that *this* Mr Hadley would feed her sweet lies to win her favour—or her hand.

She had no idea what his current income was, but when he inherited the earldom, he would be a very rich man, with no need of her wealth. Though his half-brother George might prize her for her political ties, her Tory associations would be of no assistance whatsoever to the Reformist Giles; indeed, they would be a detriment.

Wedding her would offer him no real advantage, her only usable attributes—her lineage and breeding—being possessed by numerous other single females. Perhaps she could, cautiously, trust Mr Hadley when he told her how he felt about her.

And then she had to laugh. Had he not just told her quite plainly he had no interest in marriage? In fact, he'd made that odd comment about not 'harming' her by marrying her. As if she were a Tory candidate who would suffer for allying herself with a Reformer.

She considered the remark for a few minutes before dismissing it, unable to puzzle out the enigma. With neither of them interested in anything serious, perhaps she *could* let down her guard, feel free to be herself and simply enjoy his stimulating conversation and electrifying presence.

As for the physical attraction… He had all but invited her to a discreet affair, amicably conducted, no strings attached.

The very thought of it sent a spiral of warmth and longing through her. Even Aunt Lilly had admitted to 'amusing herself' after she'd been widowed. Oh, if only there were a truly safe way to do so!

But it was way too early in their acquaintance to worry about that. Before one directed a horse towards the highest fence, one must first saddle and bridle him, and get to know his paces. So for now, as she'd told her father, she would stick to the simple enjoyment of listening to his views…and the exquisite, tantalising pleasure of having him near.

In the late afternoon of the following day, Giles poured a glass of wine for Davie in the sitting room of their suite at Albany. 'You don't intend to accompany Ben and Christopher to dine with the committee members?' Davie asked.

Not wishing to reveal any more information than he had to, Giles simply shook his head as he handed Davie his glass.

'I promised Lady Greaves I'd come to Moulton Street tonight. It's their son Dickon's birthday. You'd certainly be welcome, if you'd like to join me.'

'I don't want to intrude on a family dinner.'

'You wouldn't be intruding. Sir Edward and Lady Greaves would love to see you.' Davie raised an eyebrow at him. 'You can't avoid polite society for ever, you know. Eventually, you will be an earl.'

Giles took a sip of wine, delaying the need to respond. How could he explain to Davie his continuing ambivalence about his eventual inheritance? As Davie knew all too well, he'd been angry and resentful as a young man, once he'd grown old enough to fully understand what his father had done to him and his mother. From the time his aunt pulled him from poverty and sent him to school, he'd been driven to prove he could become successful without any assistance from the earl. He'd thought, as time went on and he built his reputation, his achievements towards that goal would make it easier for him to reconcile himself to the future that must be his.

So far, it had not, nor had he been able to make himself act on any of Davie's increasingly frequent reminders that he ought to begin easing himself into his father's world.

'The current earl is, I understand, quite vigorous,' he said at last. 'Who knows, we may have abolished the aristocracy before he cocks up his toes. And since by then, you will most likely be Prime Minister, you will outrank me.'

'The farmer's whelp lording it over the lord?' David chuckled. 'Unlikely. Seriously, you really should become at least a little involved in the Season. Sir Edward and

Lord Englemere would be delighted to have you come to any of their entertainments, and once the *ton* discovered you would actually accept invitations, you'd have a flood of them.'

'What, subject myself to evenings of boring balls or tedious musicales with some dreadful soprano screeching away, or some equally dreadful young miss trying to display her limited prowess at the keyboard? If I want to waste time, I can take a nap.'

'What are you doing this evening? Not staying here napping, I hope.'

Tread cautiously, Giles told himself. 'Actually, I have a prior commitment. With, I should point out, a well-respected member of society. I'm invited to dine at the Marquess of Witlow's.'

Davie's hand froze with his glass halfway to his lips. 'At the Marquess of Witlow's?' he echoed, his eyes widening in surprise. 'With Lady Margaret as your hostess?'

'I expect so, since I understand she usually plays hostess for her father.'

'Did Lord Grey ask you to talk with Witlow? Try to negotiate to find some common ground before the bill comes to the floor that might persuade the Lords to pass it?'

'No, he didn't.'

'Then how—?'

Giles had hoped Davie, the most discreet of his friends, wouldn't press him, but it appeared that wish was not going to be fulfilled. 'I happened upon Lady Margaret after my speech at the Commons yesterday,' he reluctantly explained.

He had no intention of adding that he'd hoped she might come, had castigated himself as an idiot for thinking he sensed her presence while he was speaking, and then had been thrilled to glance up into the Ladies' Gallery and discover she was in fact in attendance. He'd found himself trotting up the stairs to the Gallery before he realised what he was doing.

And, ah, the strength of the desire that pulsed through him as she raised those lovely green eyes to meet his gaze… He'd felt an overwhelming compulsion to persuade her to remain with him—and the need to warn her about George had not, at first, even crossed his mind.

'I spoke with her afterwards…' At Davie's lifted eyebrow, he admitted, 'Very well, we took tea together. Before I sent her on her way, she invited me to dinner. Since I haven't heard from her today, I assume the marquess didn't tell her to rescind the invitation.'

Davie let out a low whistle. 'The lady must have cast quite a spell for you to voluntarily venture into the enemy's lair.'

Giles grinned. 'I don't expect they'll have me for dessert. And, yes, I find Lady Margaret intriguing; we had quite an interesting chat about politics during tea. But don't go picking out names for my firstborn.'

'None of us is ready for that!' Davie said with a laugh. 'But I admit, I am surprised. Though perhaps I shouldn't be. You've been alone for some time now, and you've never been interested in Beauties with more hair than wit.'

'Lady Margaret is certainly not that.' Now that he'd been forced to open up about the lady, Giles found it was…a relief, to be able to talk about the object of his inexplicable attraction with a perceptive friend. Davie would give advice if he thought it fitting, and unlike Ben and Christopher, do so without roasting Giles mercilessly about the connection.

'I was attracted to her from the outset, even more so

after talking with her after the session. She delivered a rather eloquent philosophical defence of conservatism, but at the same time, was willing to admit there are valid reasons for reform, as well as significant public support for it. I suppose I expected that, as a Tory, she'd be dogmatic and dismissive in her views, and was surprised to find her so open-minded. And so well spoken about politics.'

'She has been her father's hostess for years. One would have expected her to pick up some information about the process.'

'Perhaps, but you've observed many of the political hostesses. They create a congenial atmosphere to encourage dinner conversation, support their husband or relative's position ardently and campaign with enthusiasm. But most have neither interest in nor understanding of the intricacies of policy. I can't recall any who could articulate a position with as much eloquence as Lady Margaret. It was...energising to debate what I love with so knowledgeable and passionate a lady.'

'And she's so much more pleasing to the eye than most of your Reformist orators,' David agreed with a laugh. 'But—what of George? If you dine with the marquess, he's sure to hear of it. One can well imagine his reaction—especially now that he's lost his seat. Even though you said when you met him at Brooks's the other night, he didn't seem disturbed about it.'

Possibly because he was more disturbed about Lady Margaret—a concern Giles *hadn't* divulged to Davie. 'Perhaps he thinks the earl can countermand the election, as he has fixed every other setback George has experienced. In any event, I broached the problem to Lady Margaret. She was quite adamant that she wasn't going to allow George to dictate whom she entertained.'

'All very well, but she doesn't know him as you do. Can you feel easy, setting her up for his possible enmity?'

Giles shifted uncomfortably. He'd had second thoughts about attending for that very reason, despite his strong desire to further his relationship with the lady. 'I considered bowing out,' he admitted. 'But dammit, I don't want to allow George to once again try to dictate my life! In any event, he's more likely to direct his ire at me, rather than at the lady, and I'm used to dealing with it. If he should be unpleasant to Lady Margaret...he'll answer to me. Nor do I think the marquess would take very well to having his daughter harassed, and he has more power even than the earl. I'm confident I can proceed without causing difficulties for her.'

'If you are satisfied, that's good enough for me. Enjoy your dinner, then! I'll be most interested to hear what topics are discussed.'

'I intend to enjoy it—and hope to escape that Tory den with most of my hide intact.'

'I shall be back later to commiserate, if you need to return and lick your wounds.'

'I shall hold you to it.'

While Davie put down his glass and went off to change for dinner, Giles remained in the sitting room, sipping his wine. He was relieved to find his faith in his friend justified; after ascertaining the basic facts about Giles's relationship with Lady Margaret, Davie had neither pried for more nor quizzed him about it.

So, what did he hope to accomplish tonight?

There was the political aspect, of course. Lord Grey might not have sent him to the dinner, but the invitation did provide a sterling opportunity to sound out one of the leaders of the Lords about his position on the upcoming reform legislation. If he could discover from Lord Witlow what areas of compromise there might be, the bill could be tailored to accommodate that before it left committee. Anything which improved the chances for getting the bill approved as quickly as possible in this session would be a great advantage.

He would need to be on his guard, though. He didn't know who the other guests might be, but it was reasonable to expect some would be hidebound conservatives. He'd better prepare himself to be attacked.

Still, if he'd managed to survive the verbal and physical assaults mounted against him at Eton, before Christopher and then Ben had arrived to befriend him, he wasn't too worried about the venom of politicians. Especially as he came as an invited dinner guest. He doubted his host would allow anyone present to hurl at him the sort of vicious epithets about his mother that had resulted in so many bloody-knuckled exchanges during his schoolboy years.

The larger looming question was, of course, the lady: what did he intend to do about Lady Margaret?

As impressed with her—and attracted to her—as he was, he was not at all interested in marriage. As Davie noted, he and the other Hellions were still junior enough not to need a wife's connections to advance their political careers. And for reasons he'd never bothered to fully analyse, the very idea of marriage aroused some deep, nameless aversion.

Perhaps it was the disastrous aftermath of his parents' union, or the lingering guilt he couldn't shake at having inadvertently been the cause of that failure. Given his political aims and affiliations, as he'd informed her today, a union with him could do Lady Margaret no good whatsoever. And if anything happened to him before the current earl's demise, his unfortunate wife would inherit only the enmity of a half-brother more than ready to step into his shoes.

Fortunately, one of the few benefits of being estranged from the earl was it allowed him to avoid the society in which Telbridge and his half-brother moved. If there were any scheming, marriage-minded females who took the long view, figuring that enticing into marriage a man of modest means now would pay off later when said husband inherited a wealthy earldom, they could hardly weave any webs to trap him when he never appeared at any of their social events.

He intended to enjoy his ambivalent position in his single, solitary state for a good deal longer. Although, he did chuckle to imagine the consternation it might create in Reform circles were he to turn up with a wife who had as strong a Tory pedigree as Lady Margaret.

He *was* powerfully attracted to the lady, and was reasonably certain she returned the compliment. A widow with her own property who was not dependent upon some relative for her support—and therefore not under their control—was exactly the sort of female he'd looked to in the past for the few affairs in which he'd indulged.

And Davie was right—it had been a long time since his last liaison, which had ended amicably when the lady in question decided she wanted to pursue remarriage. He'd kept busy with work since, and when the need for intimacy could no longer be denied, had a friendly arrangement with a discreet lady of the trade, who accommodated his desires with expertise and enthusiasm.

Might Lady Margaret be amenable to an affair?

Desire dried his mouth and tightened his body.

How he'd love to bury his fingers in her thicket of auburn hair, pulling the pins free until the heavy mass billowed down around her shoulders! Watch those green eyes darken with passion as he slowly disrobed her, fanning her desire higher and higher as he kissed and caressed the flesh as he bared it. He could imagine the feel of her breasts, heavy in his hands, the nipples tightening under his tongue. Then to proceed lower, over the silk of her belly, into the valley between her thighs, to the hidden centre of her desires…

He was throbbingly erect, just contemplating it. But he'd better douse those amorous thoughts before dinner. He'd hardly be able to hold his own against the enquiries that were likely to be fired at him by the Conservative diners with the velocity of volleys from a British square, if he spent the meal in a glassy-eyed haze of lust.

Besides, though he had no doubt Lady Margaret was attracted to him as well, being attracted and inviting him to an affair were rather large steps apart. For the time being—or until she sent him unmistakable verbal or non-verbal cues indicating such a leap interested her—he had better just focus on enjoying the lady's conversation.

Taking a deep breath, he told himself to banish dreams of trysting and concentrate on politics.

To his surprise, it required an unusually strong application of will to do so, as his normally all-consuming passion suddenly seemed not so all-consuming.

But even with lust banished to simmer beneath the surface, his whole body still tingled with anticipation at meeting Lady Margaret again soon.

Chapter Six

Several hours later, Giles entered Lord Witlow's town house in Russell Square. So this was where Lady Margaret had been raised, he thought, noting the Adamesque decor in muted tones, augmented here and there with Greek statuary and Oriental vases. Tasteful, classic and understated, like the lady.

He took the stairs with alacrity, telling himself the excitement coursing through him stemmed partly from anticipation of the spirited political debate he expected at dinner—and not just because of his strong desire to see his hostess again.

He found the anteroom occupied by a dozen or so guests, gathered in clusters, and already so absorbed in their discussions that they scarcely looked up as the butler intoned his name. He did not at first see Lady Margaret, though the simmering undercurrent of energy heightening his senses indicated that she must be present.

And then he spied her, walking over with her father to greet him, beautifully dressed in a gown of deep green that set off her eyes. Though he lamented the demise of the fashion for very low-cut dinner gowns, Giles noted, running an appreciative gaze over her figure, that the new lower-waisted style emphasised her slender form and accentuated the swell of that far-too-well-concealed bosom. As he raised his eyes to her face, she extended her hand.

He bowed over it, feeling a tremor vibrate through her fingers as he raised them to his lips. He had to fight to keep himself from letting his lips linger over the soft kidskin, while his nostrils filled with scent of violets. Concentrate on politics, he warned the senses that urged him to cut her from the group and whisk her away somewhere they might be private.

'Father, I'm sure you remember Viscount Lyndlington— or Mr Hadley, as he prefers to be addressed. I was so impressed by his speech to the Commons, I took the liberty of adding him to our gathering.'

'I heard from several sources about the eloquence of that address,' the marquess said. 'Let's see if you can be equally eloquent in persuading some of my colleagues to your views tonight.'

'I hope in turn to become better acquainted with your objections to it,' Giles replied. 'Knowledge and openness to altering opinions will be the only way compromise can happen.'

'I shall look forward to the exchange,' the marquess replied. 'I believe you know most of the gentlemen?' He waved a hand towards the rest of the room.

Giles forced himself to take his eyes from Lady Margaret, who was shyly smiling at him, and gaze around him. He'd been expecting a gathering of Tory lords, but the group was in fact much more varied. Beside several of the marquess's associates from the Lords stood his good friend Lord Bathhurst and the irascible Baron Coopley, one of the most rigid Tories. But also present were the railroad man and inventor George Stephenson, several Tory MPs, and one of the Committee of Four whom Lord Grey had charged with drafting the Reform Bill, Sir James Graham.

This grouping should indeed provide for some interesting discussion, he thought, hopeful that prospect would make it easier to concentrate on politics—and ignore the allure of Lady Margaret, to whom his gaze kept returning, like a child's toy pulled by a string.

Another guest was announced, and host and hostess moved on to welcome him. Giles watched Lady Margaret's graceful sway of a walk as long as he thought he could get away with it without the raptness of his attention becoming notable, then made his way to the group which included Sir James.

'Hadley!' the Whig leader said in surprise as Giles joined them. 'I didn't know you were acquainted with the marquess. I'll look forward to having a friend in my corner during the debate tonight. Though you'll hear the variety of views Lord Witlow enjoys, I fear we shall still be outnumbered.'

Avoiding any comment about his connection to the marquess, Giles said, 'How does Lord Grey think the lines will be drawn, once the bill comes out of committee?'

As he expected, it required only that question to launch Sir James and the two MPs standing with him into a spirited debate about how the legislation would progress, a discussion Giles would normally have followed avidly. Tonight, he listened with half an ear, surreptitiously trying to keep Lady Margaret in sight.

She was a good hostess, greeting each newcomer, sometimes allowing her father to direct the conversation, sometimes, with gentlemen who were obviously old family friends, giving the newcomer a hug or a kiss on the cheek.

Giles never thought he'd be jealous of venerable gentlemen from the older generation. At least, he told the impatient little voice within that clamoured to be near her, she wasn't gifting her kisses to any man who looked virile enough to be his rival as a lover.

Startled to realise his interest in Lady Margaret had somehow progressed from admiration to evaluating other men as competition, he followed Sir James's group in as the butler called them to table.

To his disappointment, he wasn't seated near his hostess—the elderly Marquess of Berkley and Lord Coopley had that honour, as was proper for the two highest-ranking guests. He *was* surprised that he'd been seated adjacent to his host, a place that would normally have been reserved for a gentleman of higher status. Unless, he realised with a rueful grimace, one took into account his position as a courtesy viscount.

At first, conversation was general, with comments on the food and wine and an exchange of pleasantries and social news among the gentleman. Having nothing of interest to contribute, Giles listened politely, his glance straying to Lady Margaret at the other end of the table.

She was smiling at Lord Coopley—and what a lovely smile it was, he thought, those generous lips upturned and her eyes brightening. He liked what she'd done with her hair tonight, thick coils of auburn fire pinned atop her head, with little tendrils curling down to kiss her brow and earlobes—as he would love to. That luscious mouth, too.

'…do you not think so, Hadley?'

Startled by the sound of his name, he jerked his head back to find the marquess regarding him, a slight smile on his face. Realising he'd not only been rudely inattentive to the host who'd done him the honour of seating him beside him, he'd also been caught staring at the man's daughter, he gave himself a sharp mental rebuke, feeling his face heat.

If he were a parent worth the name, Lady Margaret's father must already be curious about the link between them. The last thing he needed was to give the marquess a distaste of him by exhibiting the sort of ill-bred behaviour his half-brother always accused him of—or worse still, have Witlow suspect the strength of his amorous interest in Lady Margaret.

That subject concerned the two of them alone.

'I'm sorry, my lord, I didn't quite hear. Could you repeat the question?'

'Certainly.' A little twitch to his lips, as if he didn't believe Giles's excuse for an instant, but didn't mean to call him on it, Witlow complied. This time, Giles listened closely, telling himself sternly for the remainder of the dinner to concentrate on his *host*.

Once the diners ventured into political matters, the conversation became stimulating enough to hold Giles's attention, despite the ever-beckoning temptation of Lady Margaret seated at the other end of the table. Giles deferred to Sir James, letting the senior Member shoulder the burden of defending the Reform cause, adding a comment only when called upon. Not that he was afraid of speaking out, but it would be presumptuous for a junior member to put himself forward when Grey's aide was present, an experienced man better known to this group than he.

Some time later, he heard Lord Coopley call his name. 'So, Hadley,' the baronet said in his gravelly voice, 'your half-brother tells me you carry a torch for the Friends of the People?'

'In a way,' Giles replied. 'Since Lord Grey himself formed the group, all of us who call ourselves Reformers are happy to carry on his ideals. Who could disagree with the notion that talent and virtue should be the chief requirements for a Member of Parliament?'

Apparently able to disagree, Lord Coopley sniffed. 'Every male eighteen and older to have a vote? Parliaments to be elected annually? One member of Parliament for each twenty thousand citizens? Bah! How could the nation's business be done, with Parliament forming and breaking up every season, and any Tom, Dick and Harry who could stagger to the polls after drinking a quart of election gin able to cast a vote? In private, no less, so one would never know where he stood! I suppose you sympathise with the Spencean Philanthropists, too, who would confiscate all our land and parcel it out, a few acres to every man, woman and child in the land?'

'Did my half-brother tell you that, as well?' Giles asked, irritated. Trust George to make him sound like the most rabid radical imaginable.

'He did. You're not going to call the Earl of Telbridge's son a liar, are you?'

Much as he would like to, he knew it wouldn't be prudent. 'Certainly not. Though it's true we agree on very little,' he replied, trying to walk a cautious line between dismissing the charge as nonsense and agreeing he supported a position he didn't.

Coopley uttered a bark of a laugh. 'Distributing land to everyone! I'd like to see what a tailor or a baker or a bricklayer would do with ten acres of prime farmland!'

'Or a Parliamentarian or lawyer?' Giles replied with a smile. 'I think we are all better off staying within our spheres of expertise. I'm sure Mr Stephenson would not like to have me conducting experiments on steam power, lest I blow him sky-high.'

As he'd hoped, the gentlemen laughed, easing the tension.

'Lord Coopley, could I beg your assistance?' Lady Margaret interposed, touching that gentleman's arm. 'Was it the Warrington Exetors who returned a Tory candidate for the last Parliament, or the Covington Exetors? Your memory for names is keen as a huntsman's knife, and you know everyone who is anybody.'

'Covington, my dear, Covington,' Coopley said, patting her hand. 'The family have been Tories since Peel's administration.' Either forgetting Giles or losing interest in baiting him, the older man launched into a detailed description of each administration in which an Exetor had served.

Giles risked catching Lady Margaret's eye to give her a quick nod of thanks, to which she replied with a slight smile and a lift of her brows before turning back to her dinner partner.

A short time later, the footmen cleared the table, and Lady Margaret stood up. 'Gentlemen, I'll leave you to begin your more...*lively* debates. Thank you all for coming, and I'll bid you goodnight. Papa, I'll be reading in the library; come see me later, if the vigorous discourse you're sure to enjoy after my departure doesn't totally exhaust you.'

Giles watched her walk out with appreciative eyes. Initially disappointed that she did not even glance in his direction before she left the room, he brightened when he recalled her parting comment about repairing to the library.

Had that been aimed solely at her father...or could he flatter himself that she'd meant it partly for him, too?

At the idea of having her to himself for a few moments, excitement flared, and he immediately began scheming how he might politely get away without exciting comment.

Sir James was watching her, too. 'She certainly rescued you deftly!' the baronet murmured to Giles after she disappeared from view. 'What a consummate hostess! I wish I had the like!'

'Lady Graham is a very gracious hostess,' Giles replied.

'My Fanny does her best, but she doesn't truly enjoy it,' Sir James replied. 'You need only look at Lady Margaret to see she thrives on discussion and debate. An excellent campaigner, too, which my Fanny most decidedly is not! The travelling, the dust, the crowds all exhaust her. There was talk a while back that Sir Francis Mowbrey might lure Lady Margaret away from her father to work her magic on his behalf, but in the end, it came to nothing.'

'Sir Francis Mowbrey, the Tory MP from Suffolk?' Giles asked, hoping he sounded like a politely interested guest—rather than like a man completely obsessed by the lady.

'Yes, he wooed her some years ago, not long after she came out of mourning. Sir Francis was making a name for himself in Tory circles and had all the right qualifications: old landed family, educated at Eton and Cambridge, related to many of the peers in the Lords, not to mention the ladies found him charming. They were engaged, but just before they were to wed, Lady Margaret cried off. Sir Francis was quite public about his displeasure over the break; understandable, I suppose—it was a better match for him than for the lady, as he would gain access to her considerable fortune, as well as her Tory contacts and political expertise.'

Surprised, Giles said, 'I wouldn't have expected Lady Margaret to be a jilt. Or capriciously change her mind at the last minute.'

'Well, let's just say Sir Francis was better at wooing than he was at fidelity. He liked the ladies as much as they liked him, and though he was discreet about it, apparently continued his little *amours* even after the engagement. The *on dit* was that Lady Margaret got wind of it, and decided she didn't want to become a wife who had to look the other way. Fair enough, I suppose.'

The man sounded like an arrogant jackass, Giles thought, though he made himself utter something appropriately banal. Better not to express his disgust, and risk alerting the baronet to the intensity of his interest in the lady.

But if Sir Francis had been foolish enough to lose the esteem of a woman of Lady Margaret's stature by trysting with other females, he didn't deserve her.

And if he'd led her on with declarations of love that turned out to be hollow, that might explain, Giles suddenly realised, why an eminently eligible female like Lady Margaret had chosen not to remarry.

Their attention was recalled by the marquess, who invited each guest to give his opinion on what would be the most important matter to be brought before Parliament in the current session. Mentally filing away what he'd just learned from Sir James, Giles returned his attention to matters political, biding his time until he could take his departure.

Finally, after an hour of intense debate came the lull that enabled him to make his escape. Pleading an early day working on committee reports, he expressed his appreciation to his host and took his leave. After enquiring of a footman where he might find the library, so he could bid his hostess goodnight, Giles walked in the direction indicated and towards the encounter he'd been anticipating all night.

The door to the library stood ajar. Intending to announce himself, he paused on the threshold, taking in the scene within.

Lady Margaret sat on a sofa near the fire, a full brace of candles on the table beside her, a slight smile on her face as she gazed down at the book she held. Light from the blazing hearth played in a teasing dance on her auburn hair, setting the burnished locks aglow and illumining her pale face with a blush of amber.

The sight of her, looking so solitary and yet so serene, struck his chest like a blow. In a rush of memory, he recalled how, after being put to bed, he'd sneak back to the small parlour in the little cottage he'd occupied with his mother, wanting another story or a goodnight kiss. He'd slip in to find her alone and reading, and think how beautiful she was. Long before he'd learned that they were poor, that they'd been cast off by his father, that she was living in exiled disgrace, he'd felt such a deep sense of peace and safety when she welcomed him with a hug before carrying him off to bed again.

Lady Margaret cast so similar an aura, for a moment he had the ridiculous feeling that he was coming home.

Before he could shake it off, as if that special energy that sizzled between them had alerted her to his presence, she looked up. 'Mr Hadley!' she exclaimed. 'Is the group breaking up so soon?'

'No, the rest of the gentlemen are still avidly engaged. I believe they'll be there until the brandy gives out.'

She laughed softly, a musical sound that made him want to smile. 'Since the supply is virtually inexhaustible, they should be there until dawn. But you need to leave?'

'Well…' He gave her a rueful grin. 'To be honest, I must admit I made my excuses early…hoping to have a private word with you.'

Her smile widened. 'And I was hoping you might slip away. Won't you come in?'

A body blow from a skilled pugilist couldn't have kept him from advancing towards her. 'With pleasure.'

Chapter Seven

Looking up to find Mr Hadley standing on threshold, so discretion-meltingly handsome with his broad-shouldered form outlined by the darkness beyond and his face illumined by candlelight, she at first thought she'd longed for him so fiercely, she was only imagining his presence. Then he smiled, confirming he was no illusion, and her foolish heart leapt in gladness.

'I'm so pleased you took my hint that I'd be in the library,' she said, trying to slow her pulse as she waved him to a seat on the sofa beside her.

'I'm so pleased you gave me the hint.'

Now that she'd got what she'd hoped for, she felt unaccountably shy. 'Did you enjoy the discussions?' she asked, feeling even more foolish for falling back on the prosaic, when she really wanted to ask him all about himself— his youth, his schooling, how he'd developed an interest in politics, what he wanted to achieve…whether he would reconcile with his father. Oh, she wanted to know *everything* about him!

He laughed. 'The exchange did indeed become more "lively" after your departure! With Sir James to buttress my position, I flatter myself that I gave as good as I got, and managed to rattle a few firmly held opinions. Enough that I thought it prudent to depart and leave them to enjoy their brandy in peace.'

'I thought you held your own admirably during dinner—and with great diplomacy. Especially with Lord Coopley.' She sighed. 'I'm afraid he can be quite dogmatic, but he's been Papa's mentor since he entered the Lords. He'd be so hurt if he learned Papa had hosted one of his "discussion evenings" and we had not invited him.'

'I did rather feel like a Christian in the arena after the tigers were released. Thank you again for the rescue, by the way. Browbeating aside, I found it useful to hear all the arguments the Tories may summon; it will help my committee prepare the best responses to counter them. Because the Lords *must* pass the bill this session.'

'Must?' she echoed, puzzled. 'Why "must" this time, when they've already failed several times before?'

'Surely you observed the mood of the country when you went out to Chellingham! There's even more agitation in the counties, especially in the northern industrial districts around Manchester, Liverpool and Leeds. Memories of the St Peter's Field Massacre are still vivid. By failing to vote for reasonable change, the Lords could foment the very rioting and civil discord they think to avoid.'

Alarmed, she was going to ask him to elaborate when he held up a hand. 'But enough politics for one evening! First, let me compliment you on a delicious dinner. After the bachelor fare I usually settle for, it was quite sumptuous! You really are, as Sir James asserted, the perfect hostess, providing for the needs of your guests, making sure everyone is included in the conversation, inserting a soothing comment here and there if the discussion gets heated—without the overheated gentleman ever noticing he'd been deflected. Quite masterful!'

'Thank you,' she said, flushing with pleasure at his praise. 'I do enjoy it, especially "discussion evenings" such as this one, where there are a range of views exchanged. Alas, despite the best pamphleteering efforts of Anna Wheeler and William Thompson, I fear women will not get the vote soon. This gives me some way to contribute.'

'Your lady mother does not enjoy playing hostess?'

'Mama's health is…delicate. She lost two babes in London in the early days when Papa first sat in the Lords; the experience left her with a permanent distaste for the city and, I'm afraid, for politics. Much as she and Papa dislike being apart, she now remains year-round in the country, while Papa resides here when Parliament is in session.'

'But your brother does not? As active in politics as your father is, I would have thought he would urge his son to stand for one of the seats in his county—or in one of the boroughs he controls.'

'I'm afraid Julian has no interest at all in politics—much to Papa's disappointment.' She laughed ruefully. 'I was the child who inherited that passion. After Mama took us into the country, it was always me, not Julian, who pestered Papa to tell us all about what had happened during the session after he came home to Huntsford. When I spent my Season with my great-aunt Lilly, I persuaded Papa to let me play hostess for a few of his political dinners—and loved it! And so, after…after I was w-widowed,' she said, not able even after all this time to speak of losing Robbie without a tremor in her voice, 'I took it up again.'

'Your brother stays in the country, as well? I don't recall ever hearing of him in town.'

'Yes, he watches out for Mama, to whom he is devoted, and manages the estate. After all, he will inherit it, and such a vast enterprise requires careful supervision. Papa began to train him for it when he was quite young, and Julian loves working the land.'

'While you prefer the city?'

'Oh, no, I love being at Huntsford! My husband's estate is in the same county, and had things…not worked out otherwise, I would have been content to live out my life there. Afterward, I…needed to get away. Fortunately, Papa was willing to take me on again as his hostess.' She gestured around her. 'So here I am, back in the bosom of my family, though I do return almost daily to my own house in Upper Brook Street. Father, Mama, Julian were everything to me when…when I lost my husband. I really don't know how I would have survived without them. Excuse me, I know I probably shouldn't say anything, but that is what I find so tragic about your situation—that you are estranged from your own father, and from the land and people it will one day be your responsibility to manage and look after.'

He seemed to recoil, and worried she'd trespassed on to forbidden ground, she said, 'It's none of my business, I know. I hope I haven't offended you.'

He'd clenched his jaw, but after a moment, he relaxed it. 'You're quite brave. Most of my acquaintance don't dare mention the earl.'

She gave him a rueful smile. 'Foolhardy, rather than brave. It just…makes my heart ache to hear about a family estranged from one another. After losing two siblings and…and my best friend and dearest love, those few I have left are so precious to me. One never knows how much time one will have with them. Another reason I enjoy playing hostess to Papa.'

He nodded. 'That's true enough. With the thoughtlessness of youth, I never imagined I would lose my mother so early.'

'She must have been wonderfully brave. To endure being isolated, with even her own family abandoning her.'

He laughed shortly. 'A child accepts what he knows as "normal". It never occurred to me while I was growing up in that little cottage on the wilds of the Hampshire downs that we were isolated or alone. Of course, like most boys, I wished I had brothers to play with, but Mama made the humble place we occupied a haven, full of joy and comfort. By the time I'd been away long enough to understand what had happened, why we lived as we did, it was too late. Too late to tell her how much I appreciated the love and care she gave, and the tremendous strength and courage she displayed in creating a happy home for her child, despite her own sorrow.' He shook his head. 'When my aunt came to take me away to school, I pleaded not to have to leave. I was certain I would be content to spend my whole life there, in that little cottage.'

Emboldened by having him answer her other questions, knowing she was pushing the bounds of the permissible, but unable to stop herself she said, 'So you don't think you would ever be able to forgive your father—the earl?'

His face shuttered. Alarmed, she feared he'd either say nothing at all, or give her the set-down she deserved for asking so personal a question. But after a moment, he said, 'Mama could have lied, you know. Denied that she and Richard had been lovers. My aunt told me that the earl had assured her he'd always known she loved Richard, and only wanted the truth. And then he punished her for giving it to him, in the most humiliating fashion possible. Disgraced. Divorced. Repudiated by her own family. How can I forgive him that?'

The anguish in his tone broke her heart, and she wanted to reach out to him—the isolated child whose adored mother had been mistreated and scorned.

'I don't know,' she said honestly. 'But I do know that anger eats away at the soul, creating a wound that festers. One cannot heal until one lets it go.' Advice she would do well to heed herself, she thought ruefully.

'Would that I could follow such wise counsel,' he said. 'Perhaps some day, I will.'

'It was presumptuous of me to offer it,' she admitted.

'Caring,' he corrected. 'You do offer it out of… compassion, don't you?'

Oh, it wasn't wise for her heart to ache for his pain—but it did. 'Yes,' she whispered.

With a sigh, he picked up her hand and placed a kiss on it. At his touch, their discussions of politics, her family, his past—all the words in her brain disintegrated, leaving her conscious only of sensation, as the simmering connection between them flamed up, powerful and resurgent. She caught her breath, her fingers trembling in his, fighting the urge to lean closer and caress his cheek.

Then he was bending towards her, his grip on her hand tightening as he drew her against him. She closed her eyes and angled her face up, offering her lips, filled with urgency for his kiss.

He brushed her mouth gently, as if seeking permission. She gave it with a moan and a hand to the back of his neck, pulling him closer. Groaning, he dropped her hand to wrap his arms around her, pressing her against his chest while he deepened the kiss.

At his urging, she opened her mouth to him. He sought her tongue and tangled his with it, sending ripples of pleasure radiating throughout her body. She rubbed her aching breasts against his chest, wanting to be closer, impatient with the layers of cloth that kept them from feeling flesh upon flesh.

Time, place, everything fell away. She was consumed by him, devouring him, afire with ravening need that raged stronger with every stroke of his tongue.

Lost in mindless abandon, she wasn't sure how much further she would have gone, had he not suddenly broken the kiss, pushed her away, and jumped up to stumble to the hearth.

'Voices!' he rasped, his tone breathless and uneven. 'Coming this way.'

She heard them then, the shock of cold air against her heated cheeks as he abandoned her slamming her back to the present even as she recognised her father's tones and Lord Coopley's growling bass.

'Th-thank you,' she stuttered, raising shaking hands to straighten her bodice and smooth her disordered curls.

Seconds later, the two men entered the library, stopping short when they saw she wasn't alone. 'Hello, Papa, my lord. Is the group breaking up?' she managed.

'Yes, the others have gone,' her father said, looking curiously between her and Hadley. 'Coopley and I were going to have one last brandy.'

'As you can see, Mr Hadley lingered to thank me for dinner, and I'm afraid I waylaid him with some further conversation, even though he'd informed me he needed to get away to prepare for a meeting tomorrow. But I shall let him go now.'

Whatever her father might be thinking about finding the two of them alone together, he made no comment. 'We will wish you goodnight, then, Mr Hadley. Thank you for attending our little gathering, and I hope we will have the pleasure of your company again soon.'

'The pleasure was certainly mine,' Hadley replied. 'Lady Margaret, Lord Witlow, Lord Coopley.' He bowed, and before she could more than nod, he strode from the room.

'Will you join us, Puss?' her father asked.

The last thing she needed now, with her body in an uproar and her mind in disarray, was to face her father's all-too-perceptive scrutiny. 'No, you'll wish to finish whatever discussion was ongoing, and I don't want to prevent you. I am rather sleepy, so I'll take myself to bed.'

She rose and walked over to give each man a kiss, hoping her father wouldn't notice her breathing was still uneven and her hands were trembling.

At a pace she hoped looked decorous rather than panicked, she exited the library.

The following morning, after tossing and turning for hours, Maggie got up at first light. Too restless, and irritated by her restlessness, to attempt to return to sleep, she decided to go for an early morning gallop. The rush of cold air and exhilaration of a hard ride would settle her, clear her muddled mind, and help her decide what she must do.

She rang for her maid, donned her habit, and as the first grey light broke over city, gathered her horse and a sleepy groom and set out for Hyde Park.

She knew what frustrated desire felt like—she'd experienced it often enough, after friendship with Robbie turned to passion, and before they could be wed. Tiring her body with a strenuous ride would dissipate it. If only it might also dissipate the confusion in her brain, and resolve the tug and pull between the compulsion to pursue a relationship with Hadley, and the caution that warned she had far too little self-control where he was concerned, and ought to avoid him.

Sending her groom home after she made it safely to the park, since the sun would be well up by the time she was ready to return, she urged her mare to gallop. For the next hour, she alternated between riding hard and resting her mount, until her hands ached and her legs were trembling.

But the clamour of her body for more of Hadley's touch had not abated. Not was her mind any clearer than when she'd set out.

Irritated at herself for this unusual inability to make up her mind, she was walking her lathered mare along the path when, rounding a corner, she came upon the cause of her dilemma, trotting on a high-stepping chestnut gelding.

His horse, obviously fresh, reared up, giving Maggie a few seconds to calm the sudden racing of her heart at seeing Giles Hadley again.

He dismounted and walked towards her, his face alight in a smile. 'Lady Margaret! How delightful to see you. Though it is rather early for a ride.'

Oh, how she could lose herself in that smile! It took all her increasingly feeble strength of will to keep herself from running to him and throwing herself in his arms. 'I don't like to waste the morning in bed. At least, not alone.'

Horrified she'd actually said that aloud, her cheeks flamed as, after a shocked moment, he threw back his head and laughed. 'Now, that's a sentiment with which I can heartily concur.'

He fell in step beside her—just a hand's breadth away.

The air between them fairly sparkled with sensual tension. Oh, she wanted…how she *wanted*.

She hadn't felt this powerful an attraction, this irresistible a need, since the early days of her marriage with Robbie. Love might be out of the question…but it was only the matter of the ever-ticking clock before the possibility of passion was lost, too. Could she pass up this chance to feel again its heat and power and fulfilment?

A pied piper to lead her wherever he wished, he looked down at her as he took her hand and kissed it. 'My very dear Lady Margaret.'

Her world narrowed to the wonder of his blue-eyed gaze, the force of the need flowing from her to him, from him to her, in that simple clasp of fingers.

Before prudence had a chance to try to wrestle will back under control, she blurted, 'I'm about to be very unladylike. But as I discovered some years ago, one cannot depend on the future; if one sees something one wants, one should seize it while one can.'

His eyes searched her face. 'And you see something you want?' he asked softly.

'You,' she whispered. And then sucked in a panicked breath, terrified, once the word had been spoken and couldn't be taken back, that her brazenness would shock or offend him, that he would utter some blighting word and walk away. Would he be gentleman enough not to make her a laughingstock at his clubs? she wondered, light-headed at the risk she'd just taken.

Never taking his eyes from hers, he shook his head a little. 'Excuse me, Lady Margaret. Did you just suggest what I think you did?'

'Yes,' she said tartly, her face burning now with heat of another sort, 'and I do wish you would answer, instead of staring at me in that confounding way. If you intend to refuse, please do so, and let me bid you good day and quit the park before I expire of mortification.'

'You must know I'm not about to refuse!' With a laugh, he lifted the hand she'd almost forgotten he still held and brought it to his lips. 'You must excuse my shock; I've never been offered *carte blanche* by a lady before. But now that I've recovered, I have only two questions: Where? When?'

She better do this immediately, before she lost her nerve. 'My house—Upper Brook Street, Number Four. Now. The elderly cousin who lives with me for form's sake is very deaf, and never rises before noon. Come by way of the mews. I'll tell the grooms to admit you.'

He nodded, and without waiting for anything more— she was now so agitated, she couldn't have stood still a moment longer in any event—Maggie tugged on the reins and led her horse away.

Giles stared after the retreating form of Lady Margaret, still not sure he'd heard her correctly. Rapidly he replayed the conversation in his mind: yes, it had not been just wishful imagining. She really had invited him to become her lover.

Now.

Hell and damnation, what was he doing just standing here?

With a joyful laugh, he tugged on the reins to bring his horse close, then threw himself into the saddle. After one reckless, whooping delight of a gallop around the deserted Rotten Row, startling milkmaids and scattering cows, he pulled up, laughing.

He still couldn't believe it. After the suspicion in the eyes of her father when he caught them in library last night—after kissing her with wanton abandon on the sofa in her father's library, the door open, a roomful of guests only a few doors away, any one of whom could have walked in and discovered them, he'd thought he'd be lucky if she even spoke to him again.

He'd come to the park to ride before his meetings this morning, to clear from his mind the fog of last night's brandy and to work out how best to apologise. He couldn't explain it to himself—how he couldn't be near her without wanting to touch her, couldn't touch her without wanting the feel of her body pressed against his, his mouth on hers...

Instead of being forced to grovel for forgiveness for his effrontery, after three short meetings, she was inviting him into her arms. He shook his head, marvelling. The progression towards that invitation was like no path of seduction he'd ever trod before. There'd been virtually no flirting, no exchange of remarks laden with suggestive *double entendres*, no meaningful glances, no surreptitious touches in public, heightening desire by inciting it when it could not be sated.

Just a great deal of conversation centred on politics, sensual tension ever humming between them, and one sanity-robbing, blazing inferno of a kiss.

Lord bless a lady who knew her own mind! The connection must be as powerful for her as was for him.

He took another circuit around the park, letting the gelding walk off the heat of the gallop, until he judged the lady would have had enough time to return home and prepare herself. The thought of her removing her habit, brushing out her hair, waiting for him, naked under her dressing gown, tightened his chest and hardened other things until, almost dizzy with desire, he could scarcely breathe.

His mouth dry, his member throbbing, he imagined

that first touch. He'd worship her with hands and mouth before the first possession. Giddy with delight, on fire with need.

As for the committee meeting to begin soon, he dismissed it without a second thought. The Whigs had been trying to pummel through a Reform Bill for almost ten years; this one could wait a few hours for his attention.

He—and Lady Margaret—could not.

Grinning, he turned his mount towards Upper Brook Street.

Chapter Eight

By the time Maggie reached her town house, the heat of the ride had evaporated, leaving second thoughts to ambush her with the ferocity of a Reform zealot decrying a rotten borough. As she turned her horse over to the groom, she opened her mouth to tell him a gentleman would be coming for whom he must unlock the gate… but the words died on her lips.

She took the stairs to her bedchamber, directing a passing housemaid to go for hot water and another to help her out of habit and into a morning gown. Although she did keep clothing in both locations, since she was to spend several days at her father's town house, her lady's maid would be awaiting her there. Polly would think her mad when she turned up later, saying she'd inexplicably changed her mind and decided to go to her own home after her ride to bathe and change.

Not as mad as Mr Hadley would think her, when he arrived shortly to discover she'd changed her mind about an affair.

Oh, why could she not have reined in her raging desire before she blurted out that ill-judged invitation? She'd rather walk through the House of Lords in her shift than suffer through the interview she was about to have with her erstwhile lover.

He was almost certain to be angry, and with good cause. At best, he would think her a featherhead who didn't know her own mind; at worst, he'd accuse her of being a tease—or a wanton. It made her sick to think of forfeiting his respect and friendship.

She took a deep breath to settle the nausea. There were worse things. She could weather this loss.

Yet another loss.

Steeling herself for the uncomfortable interview to come, she walked down to the parlour to await Giles Hadley.

She was pacing restlessly when he arrived, some fifteen minutes later. After a knock at the door, a puzzled footman showed him in, and he came over to take her hand and kiss it. 'I'm afraid the groom forgot to leave the gate unlocked,' he said, squeezing her fingers. 'I had to bang and shout before I attracted attention, and he let me in and took my horse. I hope I didn't keep you waiting too long.'

He looked down at her face as he said that, and his smile faded. 'What's wrong?' he asked, his eyes narrowing in concern. 'What happened?'

She pulled her hand free, the nausea returning with her nervousness. 'Nothing—except I'm an idiot. I'm very sorry, Mr Hadley—'

'Giles. I think it's past time for you to call me Giles, don't you?'

Ignoring that, she began again. 'I'm very sorry, and I know I'm acting like a perfect ninny, but…but I'm going to have to rescind my offer. I…I can't do this.'

'I see.' He took a step back, studying her face. 'You… no longer want me?'

'No, that's not it at all! Surely you know how much I want you—I promise you, I've never before in my life propositioned a gentleman! It was entirely the unprecedented strength of the attraction between us that drove me to it. That, and the bitter knowledge that the intimacy that brings such joy is precious, and often fleeting, meant to be seized and appreciated while we can. But I can't risk it.'

Too agitated to remain still, she took to pacing the room, looking back at him as she spoke. 'I'll be indelicately blunt. Unlike most matrons who indulge in a tryst, I don't have a husband who could cover up any…unfortunate consequences. I couldn't bear to shame my father, and it would kill me to bear a child that I had to give up and could never acknowledge. And before you say anything, neither would I want to drag you into "doing the honourable thing"—forcing us into a marriage neither of us is prepared for.'

Sighing, she came back to stand beside him and looked up to meet his sombre gaze. 'Yes, I still *want*—more than you can imagine. But for so many compelling reasons, I cannot *have*. I am so sorry.' She swallowed hard, fighting back the humiliation of tears. 'I…hope you will not think too badly of me.'

She tried to look away, but he took her chin and tilted it back to face him. To her surprise, his expression seemed…tender, rather than aggrieved. 'I don't think badly of you at all. Rather the opposite! After what my mother suffered, I understand only too well the penalty imposed upon a woman for a dalliance that a man enjoys with no risk of retribution. To deny what one so strongly desires, in order to not shame family or harm innocents, is an honourable act. But a *carte blanche* doesn't have to be completely blank. One can write a few rules upon it.'

She shook her head. 'I don't understand.'

'Do you not?' At her puzzled look, he laughed softly. 'As I'm sure you know, there are many delightful ways to pleasure other than the…consummation that could put you at risk.'

She thought of how, after a long time apart, Robbie had been able to bring her to her peak with just a kiss, while he stroked and fondled. How at any time, his mouth and fingers could tease her closer and closer to that summit, close enough that she might have reached completion, even had he not claimed her.

But what of *his* pleasure? 'Do you mean you could be satisfied with…less than full possession?'

In answer, he bent down and captured her mouth. Her lips acutely sensitive after her hasty journey from arousal to frustration to excitement to disappointment, Maggie moaned, his lips coaxing her immediately to response.

'You see,' he murmured, breaking the kiss. 'So many delightful roads to pleasure. If a sensible caution is all that holds you back, you need resist no longer.'

'But what if I…want more?' she asked, by no means sure that, under the mind-numbing drug of passion, she'd have the will to restrain herself.

He chuckled again. 'I'll just have to refuse you. For protection's sake, I shall retain the most essential part of my clothing. But do not worry, my sweet. I shall very much enjoy removing all of yours.'

It was a dangerous, outrageous suggestion—but she so wanted to believe it possible. The consequences for failure, however, would be dire.

Her conflict must have been written on her face, for he said, 'Shall we try?' Dropping her hand, he went to the hearth and plucked a poker from the fireplace. 'If I should forget my resolve, use this.'

'What if I forget?'

'When you are satisfied, there will be nothing to forget.'

A tremor went through her at the thought. 'And what of your…satisfaction?'

His eyes lit, the smouldering blue light irresistible. 'I can show you the ways. Shall I? Now?'

He bent and kissed her again, unabashedly seductive, his tongue insinuating itself into her mouth, stroking, teasing, advancing and withdrawing. Dizzy, she clung to him, pressing against him, taking the kiss deeper, until they were both panting for breath.

She would burn to a cinder if she didn't have this. 'Now,' she said. Knocking the poker aside, she took his hand and led him to her bedchamber.

Once inside the room, she pulled him to her. Angling her head up, she wrapped her his arms around neck and brought her lips to his for another sweet, drugging kiss meant to banish every possibility of misgivings or regret. But as they stumbled towards the bed, she realised muzzily that she wasn't sure what should happen next, if the usual progression from kissing to completion was to be avoided.

Uncertain, she halted, and broke the kiss. His breathing ragged, he looked down at her, ran a finger gently over her cheek. 'What is it? More doubts?'

'Just…I'm not sure what to do…now.' She waved towards the bed. 'Perhaps better not to go there?'

'How about here?' He urged her to the end of the bed, sat her down and took a step back. 'Now, you tell me what you want.'

'What I want?' she repeated stupidly.

'Yes. How do I pleasure you best, my sweet lady?'

At the idea of boldly stating aloud how she wanted him to make love to her, she flushed scarlet. 'I d-don't know if I can,' she stuttered, need warring with embarrassment. 'I've…never done this before.'

He must have sensed she was on the brink of another panicked retreat, for he said quickly, 'Let me imagine, then. If I do something you don't want, just stop me.'

Before she could stutter out a reply, he sat beside her, wrapped his arms around her and leaned her back against him. Acutely sensitive to his touch, she jumped with surprise when, instead of the more intimate caress she anticipated, he began to massage her shoulders.

It felt heavenly, though, so good it quieted, for the moment, the shrill voice of passion that wanted more. After a moment, with a sigh, she relaxed against him, leaning back into the soothing ministration of his hands.

'Yes, relax, my sweet,' he murmured against her ear. 'This is for you, only for you. At your pace, according to your desires. Only yours.'

Like water dripping off a roof after rain, she felt doubt and tension slide away, one small drip at a time, until at last she was emptied of all worry. As those turbulent emotions exited, need moved in to fill the space, until her whole body was smouldering in slow, sweet arousal.

As if sensing she was ready for more, he bent down to nuzzle her neck, then sucked and nipped his way towards her ear. She shuddered as he reached the sensitive spot below the lobe, then licked and suckled the edge. 'Do you like that?' his whisper rasped in her ear.

'Yes,' she breathed, squirming to turn so she might meet his lips.

But gently, holding her in place, he massaged from her

shoulder down her arms and under, stroking along her ribs. With a whimper, she arched her back, straining to bring his caressing fingers up to her breasts.

Seeming to understand, he halted, lifting his hands up to cup her breasts. A long shuddering sigh escaped her as he rubbed his thumbs over each peaked nipple.

'Do you want this?' he whispered.

'Yes!'

'Tell me,' he urged. 'Tell me what you want.'

'I want you to…to caress my breasts,' she got out, finding it easier this time to voice the need.

She felt his hardness surge against her, and she realised, in a little flash of awe and gratification, that it aroused him to hear her say the words aloud. Emboldened by the knowledge, she said, 'I want to feel your hands on my naked breasts.'

Ah, once again she felt that delicious hardness press more firmly against her as he bent to place a long, nibbling kiss on the nape of her neck. 'Gladly.'

The drum of her heart accelerated as he moved away a bit, and she felt his hands unfastening the tapes at the back of her gown. 'Hurry!' she urged, increasingly impatient, now that she'd envisioned it, to feel that intimate touch.

He worked the bodice free, and she helped him shrug it off, but the skirt still held shift and stays in place. 'Females,' he said, kissing the bit more of her back bared by the removal of the bodice, 'wear entirely too many garments.'

Murmuring agreement, she wriggled on the bed, expecting him to unlace and remove the restricting skirt. Instead, he reached up to grab a pillow, dragged it down and leaned her back against it.

As she lay back, the stays beneath her breasts pulled

the fine linen of her shift tight across her nipples. Before she could think what he was doing, Giles took nipple, fabric and all into his mouth and suckled.

The heat and wetness of his mouth, the friction of the fabric created a sensation both similar, and entirely different, from anything she'd experienced before, when loving had begun only after she'd been completely undressed. The friction sparked a tremor that seemed to go straight to her core, sparking there a similar reaction of warmth, wetness, and tightening the spiral of desire.

His mouth moved to her other breast, bringing the magic of moisture and friction to that nipple while his thumb circled over and rubbed the wet fabric. Tension coiled tighter as the fire within built and built, until she was straining towards the peak.

Her skin flushed with heat, she tossed her head restlessly, tilting her hips, instinctively trying to move in the familiar, rhythmic pattern. As she writhed beside him, he moved his mouth to claim hers, his lips demanding entry, his tongue sweeping in to lave and dominate. At the same time, he swept an arm down under her skirts.

She kissed him back just as fiercely, seeking out his tongue, darting with hers to explore and lave each corner of his mouth. Then gasped, as his hand beneath her skirts caressed and squeezed in a slow ascent…his whole hand surrounding her ankle…two fingers tracing the delicate skin behind her knee…a single finger tracing the top edge of her stocking, sliding under and out, under and out. And finally, finally, while she whimpered her need, he moved the hand up and cupped her.

She wiggled beneath it, wanting him to go further, but for a maddening few moments, he simply rubbed that mound with his whole hand. Finally, when she thought she would shatter if he delayed any longer, he slid two fingers down to caress the tiny bud at her centre.

After so many years of abstinence, it took only this single touch to send her spiralling into the abyss. Crying out, she tensed as pleasure ignited, sending sweet fulfilment rushing outward in waves from her centre through her body to the very tips of her fingers, her toes, her earlobes.

A few mindless moments later, as the tremors faded, she sagged back, replete. In the vastness of the ocean of contentment, one small worry floated forth as, finally conscious of his rapid breaths and the still-hard member pressed against her, she realised he had not yet had his satisfaction.

Before she had recovered enough for speech, he bent to kiss her again, this time light and tender. Murmuring, she opened her mouth to him. But after a minute of gentle caresses, his tongue grew bolder, laving hers, teasing the tip. A spark of arousal flamed up out of the ashes of fulfilment.

Within a few moments, her heartbeat accelerated and she felt the pulse begin to pound in her ears again. And then, he moved his fingers from her little nub and nudged them at the entrance to her passage.

She gasped, arousal building in one giant leap, and pushed against him, wanting the exquisite caress of those fingers to slide deeper, to the very core of her.

But he took his time, progressing deeper ever so slowly, each minute a new bit of flesh igniting as he touched it. When at least he'd penetrated to the depths of her and began a slow advance and withdrawal, advance and withdrawal, she was sobbing with arousal.

But he would not be hurried. Only gradually did he increase the rhythm, and when his thrusting fingers finally reached a rapid tempo, she shattered in a climax so intense, she lost all sense of who and where she was.

When the earth had settled, the stars realigned, and the ability to breathe and speak returned, Maggie gazed up to see Giles watching her, a slight smile on his lips.

She smiled back, tried to lift a finger to trace his lips, and couldn't quite manage it. He caught her hand and kissed it.

'That was—glorious,' she told him. 'Thank you.'

His smile widened and he made her a little bow. 'Your humble servant is pleased to serve.'

She shook her head at him. 'But it's not right.'

His smile vanished. 'What do you mean?'

'That was the most erotic experience of my life—and you are still completely clothed.'

He grinned again. 'What would you have me remove?'

'Nothing! Not yet. But if you will pour me some restorative wine—there should be a decanter on the table over there—I will endeavour to do the removing.'

'I like the sound of that. But remember—the breeches stay on.'

She gave him a long, slow smile. 'So did my shift.'

She saw him catch her meaning in the widening of his eyes and sharp intake of breath. Bounding up, he soon located decanter and glass, poured a generous amount, and offered it to her.

She sat up and took a long swallow, then handed him the glass. She could see the erection straining against his trouser flap as he carried the glass back to the table, and another spiral of anticipation and delight whirled through her.

She stood, unhooking her skirt, stepping out of it and tossing it away; she didn't want its clinging length to get in the way of what she planned. When he came back to the bed, she motioned to the place she'd been seated and said, 'Sit, please.'

He promptly complied, then looked up at her. She could see the rapid pulse beating at his temples and smiled, pleased at this evidence of his heightened desire.

She stood before him and began untying his cravat, slowly unwinding and removing the broad band of linen, then folding it neatly. He wasn't the only one who knew how to heighten anticipation with delay. After flicking back the edges of his shirt, she moved her hands to massage his shoulders and bent to kiss his bared throat.

He sighed when her lips contacted the rough skin, then groaned as she licked her way to the hollow where the pulse beat strongly. Massaging still, she kissed up his throat to nibble his jaw, evading his mouth when he tried to meet her lips, and continuing to lick and nip from the jawline up to his ears, his cheekbones, across his closed eyes, to his brow and into the hairline.

Reaching down, she lifted his arms and pulled the shirt over his head. She stepped back a moment to admire him, all muscled shoulder and strong arms and broad chest, where the flat nipples puckered.

He hissed between his teeth as she slowly ran a fingernail over each one.

Lifting her skirts, she bared herself to the waist, watching his face as he watched her. He opened his lips, an inarticulate mumble, and she placed a finger over his mouth to forestall any protest. Then she sat down on his lap and straddled him, her naked torso pressed against his trousers.

She felt his member leap as she wound her legs around his back and rocked her hot, moist, naked centre against his fettered erection. With a gasp, he cupped her bare bottom and pulled her closer. Wrapping her arms around him, she kissed him hard, rubbing her breasts against his bare chest while he picked up the rhythm, thrusting against her.

He must have been as ready as she had been, for after half-a-dozen such thrusts, he turned rigid in her arms, gasping into her mouth as his completion swept over him. Kissing him still, she followed him down as he collapsed back on to the bed, his chest drenched in sweat, his breathing ragged.

Rolling over to cuddle beside him, she pushed the moist hair off his brow and stroked it, waiting for his breathing to steady and slow, aglow with more peace and contentment than she'd felt since… She pushed her mind back from the thought. This moment was for enjoying now, without tarnishing it with sadness from the past.

At length, with a groan, he pushed himself up on his elbows. 'Thank you, my sweet. Although if we hadn't made this…unusual bargain, I should have to apologise for…reaching the finish line so quickly.'

'No matter. Shall we rub down the horse and prepare him to race again?'

His eyes lit. 'Absolutely. Although for safety's sake, I should do the "rubbing".'

'Absolutely not. When I serve, my service is complete.'

She walked over to the dressing table, poured water in the washbasin and returned with it and a soft rag. He stayed her hands when she attempted to unbutton the trouser flat.

'It will be all right,' she told him, going down before him. 'I promise, my knees shall not leave the floor.'

'If you're certain.'

'I am.' Pushing his hands aside, she plucked open the buttons and pulled the flap free, exposing his spent member. Gently and carefully she washed it with the rag, then the upper part of his legs and his belly. Once he'd been cleansed, she began pulling the rag slowly over the exposed skin. She bent down and blew a breath over the dampness, watching as he shivered, the little hairs on his stomach standing on end.

Pleased, she moved the damp cloth back to his now-stirring member. Up and down she stroked, alternating the soft caress of the rag with a long exhale over the tightening skin, bending closer each time, until her lips were almost but not quite touching him.

She looked up, into blue eyes locked upon her. 'Does this please you?' she whispered.

'Yes.'

'Tell me. Tell me what you like.'

He smiled slightly, picking up the game. 'I like having you stroke me. I like feeling your warm breath on my cock.'

At the words, she felt her own nipples tighten and the moist heat build between her legs. She bent and licked the hard velvet tip, which jerked under her ministrations. He gasped, his hands clutching the bedclothes, his arms rigid.

'Do you like that?'

'Yes. I love having your tongue on my cock.'

'Good.' She bent forward again and grasped him with one hand, holding him steady as she took him in her mouth, slid him in and back out.

'Do you like that?'

'Devil's breath, yes! I could live for ever inside your mouth.'

She leaned forward to suckle him again. Oh, what a wonder he was, all hardness and sinew, silky tip and satin shaft. She loved the taste and feel of him, loved the groans she elicited as she licked and suckled, laved and stroked. After a few moments, he dropped the bed-clothes and clutched her shoulders, thrusting with her as she took him to completion.

As he fell back on to the bed, limp, she returned the basin and refreshed the wine glass. She was sitting be-side him, sipping from it, marvelling at the power and beauty of sensual pleasure, when he stirred and opened those incredible blue eyes.

And smiled at her.

Her foolish heart expanded and she smiled back, a smile of pure joy and contentment. Oh, how easily she could become accustomed to this loving—and this man!

'That was beyond words glorious,' he told her, sitting up to accept the wine glass and take a long sip. 'But it wasn't right.'

'No?' she said with a chuckle. 'You didn't seem to complain at the time.'

'Ah, but that's because I knew I would insist on hav-ing my turn.'

Her simmering senses sparked as the meaning of those words penetrated. Before she could respond, though, he continued. 'I believe a little more undressing is called for, once we finish this wine.'

'If you wish.'

He gave her a long, slow, heated scrutiny. Her skin prickled as his gaze passed over it, as if she could literally feel his touch as his eyes inspected her. 'Oh, I wish—to touch *everything.*'

They shared the glass, then Hadley returned it to the table and came back to the bed. She looked up at him, little eddies of excitement swirling in her stomach, and all her nerves once again primed for his touch.

'First, this.' he said, and began raking the pins from

her hair, until the heavy mass fell to her shoulders and down her back.

'If you only knew how often I dreamed of doing this,' he murmured as he continued to comb his fingers through her hair until he'd winnowed out all the pins. Then he arranged the waves over her shoulders, down her back, and around her breasts. Hands on her shoulders, he took a step back, once again studying her.

'Glorious,' he pronounced, and kissed her.

She murmured in protest when he broke the kiss, and he chuckled. 'Do not fret, my sweet. There will be more of that, soon enough.' Urging her to stand, he unlaced her underskirt, pulled it down, and helped her step out of it. He stood up and drew her close, kissing her again, light and gentle, then deeper and penetrating. While he drugged her with his mouth, he slowly raised the hem of her shift, until he could reach her garters. After unhooking her stocking, he urged her to sit.

He knelt before her, slowly rolling down the stocking, and kissing the skin of her leg as he bared it: inner thigh, knee and the soft skin behind it, along the shin, around the fullness of calf, across the smooth arch of the foot, until he pulled it free from her foot and suckled each toe in turn.

Glad she was seated, for she would have been too dizzy to stand, she braced herself on the bed as he started on the remaining garter and leg. Once he had her barelegged, he stood her up, unlaced and tossed away her stays, then pulled the shift over her head.

She stood before him completely naked now, but so sensitised by his touch that she felt no embarrassment. Only an exuberant confidence, from seeing the need blazing in his gaze, that he found her desirable, and anticipation for what he would do next.

In answer, he eased her on to the bed and against the pillows. 'Close your eyes, my sweet, and just *feel*,' he murmured.

And so she did. He began at her temples, kissing and stroking lightly, over her cheeks and lips, her ears and chin. He fisted his hands in her hair, then brushed the silky strands against her shoulders, her arms before he nibbled and kissed them. Slowly he progressed lower, teasing with the satin brush of her hair, tantalising with the soft pressure of his mouth and the wetness of his tongue.

She was breathing hard again, feeling the climax building, by the time he reached her waist, her hipbones, the round of belly. But to her dismay, he bypassed her aching centre, instead moving down her legs, her knees, her ankles and toes.

She pulled at his hands, trying to urge him higher, but he would not be hurried. Gently detaching himself, he returned to his slow transit up and around her legs, setting off delicious vibrations in nerves she didn't know she possessed.

And then, finally, his mouth moved to the tender skin of her inner thighs. At his urging, she let her legs fall open, giving him full access to the most intimate part of her. When she thought she could stand the wait no longer, he at last moved his mouth to her.

He parted the nether lips and licked delicately at the little bud within. Frantic, she twisted her head from side to side, lifting her hips to bring him closer. Then, with tongue and fingers, he traced the path into her slick passage.

So near to the precipice was she that only a few strokes would have been enough to send her spinning into the free fall of climax. But this time, she wanted them to reach that pinnacle together. Rolling away from him, she sat up, then pulled him to lie down beside her, his head towards the bottom of the bed, then lay back down with her own head on the pillow.

Understanding her intent, he eagerly returned to tasting her, while she slid her hand under the waistband of his breeches to clasp the erection now within her reach. Stroking him while he laved her, the two of them mingled their cries as they reached the summit together.

For a long, sweet time, they lay panting, spent. Recovering more quickly than Maggie, Giles crawled up to lay on the pillow, then repositioned her with her head resting on his shoulder, her arm across his bare chest, and her leg wrapped around his. After tossing the rumpled blanket over her nakedness, he kissed the tip of her nose and promptly fell asleep.

Lying in his arms watching him, content, replete, Maggie realised she was feeling…happy. Something she hadn't experienced in so long, she'd almost forgotten what it was like.

That realisation should have terrified her, and maybe it would, later. But for this glorious moment, in the wondrous present, she would simply enjoy it as a gift.

All too soon, Giles stirred. She held her breath as his sleepy eyes opened—would he shatter this magic by tossing back the covers, throwing on his clothes and bidding her a cheery goodbye as he hustled out to his meetings?

She saw that moment recognition of time, place—and his companion—register in those bright blue eyes. Which then widened, as a smile warmed a face alight with what she didn't dare call tenderness.

'My sweet lady,' he murmured. 'My very dear Lady Margaret.'

Despite her efforts to restrain it, her own heart swelled

with an answering emotion. 'After this morning, I think it should be "Maggie", don't you?'

'My very dear Maggie,' he repeated, and pulled her head down for a kiss—gentle, caressing almost—cherishing. As he released her, he said, 'I wish we'd awakened in the Outer Hebrides.'

Puzzled, she angled her head at him. 'You have a fondness for cold Scottish islands?'

He chuckled. 'No, my love! But if we were in the Hebrides, I could resume the delightful business that has occupied us this morning. Since we are unfortunately in London, I suppose I must finally bow to my responsibilities and get back to work. I can only hope Davie hasn't already sent out a search party, certain he's going to discover my cold, dead body in some dark alley somewhere.'

'You seldom miss meetings?' she guessed.

'I'm normally the first to arrive and the last to leave. But this morning I had a more pressing engagement. Although, to make up, I probably will be the last to leave.'

Reluctantly, she slid away and off the bed. Now that the loving was over, she should feel awkward, standing completely naked before a man she knew so slightly.

But he had loved her so well and so tenderly, all she felt was warmth and gratitude.

Tracking down his shirt, she brought it over to the bed, while he moved to sit up and lifted his arms for her to slip it back over his head. 'The cravat is probably hopeless,' he advised as she brought that over. 'I'll have to stop by my rooms to change out of riding gear anyway, before I go to Parliament. Though I heartily approve of my valet's current uniform,' he said, leaning forward to press a quick kiss on each bare nipple. 'Can I help you, or would you rather call your maid?'

'I'd appreciate the help. I'm sure the staff already has

an accurate notion of how we spent the morning, but I'd rather be dressed when I face them. My lady's maid, who's been with me for years, would probably freeze any gossip, were she here, but unfortunately she's at my father's house. And incidentally, since I left to ride at dawn, *she's* probably wondering if she should send out a search party to look for my cold, dead body.'

As she talked, she tossed on her shift, gathered up stays and stockings, and went to the clothes press to extract her habit, and Giles stepped closer to help her into them. He made an excellent lady's maid; Maggie refused to let herself speculate how he'd become so skilled.

Once she was dressed, he took one hand and kissed it. '*Will* the servants gossip?'

'I don't think so. They've all of them been with me a long time, and I like to think they are fond of me. Besides, if it comes to it, I'm a woman of age with my own household. I'm not accountable to anyone for my conduct.'

'I'd prefer there weren't any salacious talk, though.'

'No, I wouldn't imagine that titterings about a tryst with a woman from the wrong party would help the image of—'

'I don't care about me!' he interrupted. 'But I should definitely take exception if anyone were to malign *your* reputation.'

'Thank you, that is kind.' The euphoria was slipping away, and much as she didn't want it to end, she had to ask. 'Will I...be seeing you again?'

His expression turned incredulous. 'Did you truly think one time would be enough?'

His reassurance delighted her much more than it should. 'I didn't know. As I told you, I've never done this before. I didn't know whether, once the...novelty was over, you would want to...continue.'

He shook his head disbelievingly. 'I cannot wait to touch you again. When can I return?'

She laughed. 'I don't know. I'll have to check my schedule, as I imagine you will need to consult yours. Truly, I didn't plan for this to happen today.'

'I heartily approve of your spontaneous idea.'

'Not totally spontaneous. Following through on the desire was, perhaps. But I'd been thinking about it for a long time—probably from the first moment I met you. I tried to talk myself into being prudent and responsible, but every time I see you, prudence and responsibility seem to fly out the window—and in flies this great, fierce bird of need that grips me in its claws and won't let go.'

He leaned over to kiss her again. 'Here's to great, fierce birds. I hope you keep a whole flock of them.'

She shook her head. 'You must think me absurd.'

He cupped her face in his hands. 'I think you delightful. Whimsical. Fascinating. The most glorious lover who has ever touched me. But now I must go. Do check your schedule and send me a note. Number Six, Albany. And make it *soon*.'

'Number Six, Albany,' she repeated.

He pulled her to him and gave her one last kiss, deep, cherishing, possessive, powerful. 'Oh, yes—soon!' she said, and let him go.

Chapter Nine

Maggie stood in the doorframe, watching Giles as he descended the stairs, then walked back into the bedchamber to pour herself another glass of wine.

Goodness, two glasses of wine before luncheon! But then, the occasion deserved it. She'd just propositioned a man she knew very little, had him come to her house in broad daylight, and spent the morning making love to him while the staff went about their duties and her cousin snored, blissfully unaware, in a nearby bedchamber.

What had come over her?

She'd known Robbie all her life, the transition from best friends to lovers as natural and gradual as growing older. She'd known Sir Francis for several years, been engaged for several months, and even then, only succumbed to his urgings when the protection of a wedding ring loomed. Now, she'd just taken to her bed, if not to ultimate surrender, a man she'd met…three times?

Maggie shuddered. By the world's measure, she'd be judged a woman of easy virtue, even a harlot. And yet… and yet.

It was more than just the powerful physical connection. Something about him, his passionate support of the causes he found important, and his willingness to devote his life to them, seemed to mesh so well with her ideals of sacrifice and service, making him seem like a friend of long acquaintance, rather than a man she'd barely met. It felt right and natural to sit across the table from him and debate politics; to lie in his arms and thrill to his caresses; to pleasure him and bring him to bliss.

She wanted to do all those things again and again.

A little chill of foreboding cooled the euphoria of satiation. This could end very badly. There was no question Giles Hadley saw this as a pleasant but temporary, short-term liaison. It would be all too easy for her to want much more.

She didn't dare let herself want more.

What was it that sailors had once said about voyaging towards the edge of the known world—'beyond here be dragons'? Having dared to venture into something she'd never experienced, behaving in a way she wouldn't previously have considered possible, she might well learn the bitter truth of that maxim.

But having had just one taste of Giles Hadley, she was not about to stop now.

An hour later, properly garbed in her habit, Maggie rode back to her father's town house, trying out, during the transit, various explanations for her very tardy return.

A wasted effort, as it turned out. Her maid sat in her bedchamber, bent over some needlework, but before she could utter a syllable, Polly looked up and exclaimed, 'Lord and stars, missy, what do you think you're doing?'

Damning the guilty flush heating her face, Maggie gazed at the maid who'd been with her since she was a child at Huntsford and Polly a junior nursemaid. No point trying to deny what the maid already knew, not that she had intended to waste any effort trying to conceal an affair that was probably already the focus of speculation below stairs at Upper Brook Street. 'I didn't imagine I could hide anything from you,' she said with a rueful laugh. 'But I didn't expect you'd find out this soon. Who told you?'

The maid raised her eyebrows. 'You leave at dawn for a ride that normally takes you an hour, and are gone four. Don't you think I sent that worthless groom back to look for you, and with a flea in his ear for leaving you alone? When he didn't find you, he stopped by Upper Brook Street—doubtless to delay having to return and report you missing! They told him you were...entertaining a gentleman. Now, you needn't be worrying the news will get out anywhere but this room and Number Four! We've all of us seen you go through more heartache than one body should have to bear, and we'd none of us add to it by tarnishing your name. But gracious, child, what are you thinking?'

'I suppose you want me to tell you I *wasn't* thinking, but that's not exactly true.'

With her own mother ill for much of Maggie's life, confiding in Polly had become a childhood habit she'd never outgrown; the wise but sharp-tongued woman had been her supporter and comforter from the days of scraped knees to times of devastating loss. As Maggie trusted she would be now, whether or not she approved of her rash actions.

'Oh, Polly, I've missed Robbie for so long and so keenly. In some ways, Mr Hadley couldn't be more different than the quiet country gentleman I meant to spend my life with. But he does make me...*feel* again! The same sort of excitement and delight in life that Robbie did. And the passion. I don't expect to find again a love like ours, but can't I enjoy myself a little, before I dwindle into an old widow?'

'I've no objection to you finding pleasure—who deserves it more? But there's no reason you couldn't "enjoy yourself" by choosing another fine gentleman to marry—' She held up a hand, forestalling Maggie's protest. 'I know, I know. But even if the husband wasn't the equal of your Robbie, he could provide you with the passion you seek—*safely*. How can you even think of risking—?'

'I'm not! I'm hardly likely to forget what the consequences would be for conceiving a child out of wedlock, and I have no more desire to disappoint Papa and tarnish my name than you would have to see it. I *was* intimate with Mr Hadley, but in a…controlled way. We'll not do anything that will risk my becoming with child.'

The maid shook her head. 'I've heard of them "French letters", or whatever it is the apothecaries call what decent people ought not to use, but nothing will truly stop a babe. I don't doubt this Mr Hadley is as charming as the devil himself, but it's still not worth the risk, child.'

'We're not using a "French letter". We are…limiting our intimacy to include only what will avoid any chance of conception,' Maggie explained, her face flaming, unable to describe it any more plainly even to a woman who knew every mishap she'd ever suffered and every mistake she'd ever made.

It took a minute for Polly to puzzle it out. 'You mean you're not letting him—'

'No. As long as I avoid the ultimate act, why shouldn't I take some pleasure, when, after so long alone, I've discovered a man who intrigues me, whom I intrigue in turn?'

'I don't like it, Miss Maggie,' Polly said, shaking her

head. 'He might be a fine gentleman, and if you like him this much, I'm sure he must be. And he might tell you now that what-all you're doing is enough for him. But a man's a man, and sooner or later, he'll want more, you take my word on it. And then what?'

'Actually, I think it's more likely I will want more,' Maggie admitted. 'But knowing the consequences, I think I can manage to be at least that prudent—although you would say,' she continued, watching the expression on Polly's face, 'that I am not being prudent at all.'

'Ah, child, you know I only want what's best for you. To see you happy and well loved and settled in your own home again, as you were with your Robbie. But you'll not be finding that if you're giving away your favours to "intriguing" gentlemen, without benefit of your wedding lines.'

That cut a bit too close to the bone, even coming from Polly. 'I don't *want* any wedding lines!' she snapped back. 'Much better to enjoy passion and part when passion cools, than to be yoked for life to a man who no longer interests me.' *Or love again and risk a loss that might drive me to madness.*

Though she didn't imagine the fire of attraction she felt for Giles Hadley would be banked for a long time. Nor, unfortunately, could she honestly claim that she believed she would find life with him tedious, once satiation had honed the sharp edge off appetite.

It was far more likely she'd find living with him very much to her taste.

But it was too late to back away now, nor did she want to. Like a troublesome filly who'd got the bit between her teeth, she would run as far and fast as she could—probably until Giles Hadley tired of the arrangement. She'd just have to restrain her enthusiasm by remembering Hadley expected a short, idyllic interlude, remind herself that was what she wanted, too, and be prepared to send him away at the first sign that he was ready to end it.

If she had any regrets afterward, she would deal with them.

She would certainly never regret the passion.

She came back to herself to discover Polly shaking her head, her expression concerned. 'Lost as a maid gazing at the moon, dreaming of her lover. Don't look to me like you're about to lose interest in this gentleman.'

Probably true. But she wasn't going to spoil the days ahead worrying about that. 'What I'm interested in at the moment is changing my gown. I've got the household accounts to review, and I'm afraid today is an at-home afternoon.'

And while she was reviewing accounts, she could also review her calendar…and figure out how soon she could see Giles Hadley again.

A short drive away, Giles strode into the entrance to Parliament, a spring in his step. Whistling a merry tune, he headed towards the committee rooms, absently nodding a greeting to the men he passed.

A dawn gallop in the fresh air—and then one of the most sensual experiences of his life. Had any man ever had a more glorious morning?

He'd known from his first glimpse of her that Lady Margaret attracted him. From the first discussion at the inn in Chellingham, her understanding of Parliament and political theory had intrigued him. But never in his fondest imaginings had he anticipated what a skilled, sensual and inventive lover she would be.

Though she was a paradox, he thought with a chuckle.

Initially tentative and uncertain, shy as a fawn in a meadow and as ready to bolt. Unable at first to voice what she wanted without blushing…then later, when he put himself literally into her hands, pleasuring him with boldness and skill.

He couldn't remember being this relaxed, refreshed and…*happy* for a long time—if ever. If this was bewitchment, he wanted more of it!

It had all happened too fast; his senses and mind were still too stunned in the brilliant, lingering afterglow for him to understand yet the full significance of what they'd done. Or how they would navigate the tricky waters of an intimate relationship and avoid compromising her reputation.

Somehow, they would. Where exactly they might be going, he wasn't sure. All he did know was he had to have her, and they *must* go forward.

Secure in that conclusion, he entered the committee room, still humming. Looking up from a stack of papers, Davie exclaimed, 'Giles, at last! I was beginning to think you'd been abducted.'

'No, just some…unexpected business I had to take care of.' Oh, how lustily he had cared for it, he thought with a private smile.

Ben looked him up and down. 'Business, eh? Humming a tune, smile on his face and a spring in his step? Looks to me like a man who's been well satisfied. What do you think, Christopher?'

Glancing up from the document he was drafting, Christopher's eyes widened and he grinned. 'My, my, my. Madame Seraphene must have been unusually skilled last night! About time! With all the impediments keeping the bill from passage last session, you've been as grumpy as a hen who'd lost her last chick.'

'Have you ever!' Ben said with a laugh. 'So, Giles, *did* she try something new? The intimate details, please!'

'Find a lady of your own, and make your own details,' Giles threw back, irritated that the source of his well-being had been so transparent. Though he was confident his friends would cease bantering and be as discreet as nuns were he to reveal the truth, they'd also want to know—since he never trifled with ladies—exactly what his intentions were.

Giles had as yet no answer to that question.

'Maybe your luscious Madame Seraphene has a recommendation?' Christopher said.

'Do your own committee work,' he shot back. 'Or ask Ben to advise you. He's familiar with every bordello in London.'

As Giles had hoped, that was enough to set the two friends off trading good-natured insults over their relative familiarity with the pleasure houses of the capital. Relieved to be free of their scrutiny, he sat down at the table—to face Davie's curious gaze.

'You do seem unusually—blithe,' his friend remarked, studying Giles. 'Nor do you usually visit Madame when there is another woman in your sights.'

The last thing he needed was a grilling by the most perceptive member of their group. 'Later,' he told Davie, and opened the dossier of papers.

The rest of the day passed in a blur, Giles unable to recall by nightfall either what he'd read of the bill or any of the notes he'd scrawled in the margins. His friends swept him off to dinner, their animated chatter covering his unusual reticence, with only Davie—of course, Davie—occasionally glancing over with a look that said he *had* noticed it.

He'd have to tell Davie something, eventually. Fortunately, Davie would wait for him to speak in his own time, rather than hound him for immediate answers.

Returning to their rooms after dinner, he'd gone through the correspondence with eagerness—to find no missive from Lady Margaret. Disappointed, he tried to tell himself that she would have been late returning to her father's, probably had many duties to attend to, and wouldn't have had time to consult her schedule.

Surely she would bid him visit her again soon.

The book he chose did not engage, nor, when he gave up in disgust and sought his bed, did he find oblivion in sleep. He tossed and turned before giving up to indulge himself, now that he was alone, in reviewing every detail of that wondrous morning.

After falling asleep late, he awoke in the faint predawn light, impatient and dissatisfied—until it occurred to him to wonder whether Lady Margaret rode every morning. His rueful smile at having fallen into intimacy with a woman about whom he knew so little, not even her usual routine, was lost in excitement as a new possibility occurred.

If he were to go to Hyde Park now, might she turn up?

Once the idea was envisioned, there could be no return to sleep. Despite the few hours of rest he'd obtained, Giles scrambled up, pulled on his riding gear, and sent for his horse.

A short time later, he trotted his mount into Hyde Park. A low fog veiled the landscape, obscuring everything at a distance, blurring into hazy outlines the objects nearby. Restless, eager, Giles signalled his horse to a trot, hoping that around this bend or the next, Lady Margaret might materialise out of the mist.

He'd rounded the last curve and was regretfully directing his horse towards the exit gates when he suddenly came upon the slender figure of Lady Margaret mounted on her grey mare, a ray of just-emerging sun burnishing her auburn hair to flame. Excitement and pure gladness swelled his chest.

A moment later, she saw him and pulled up, the groom following her halting as well. Startled to see the servant, Giles was forced to abandon the greeting he'd intended, scrambling instead to come up with a form of address appropriate for a lady who was merely an acquaintance.

'How nice to see you, Lady Margaret.' *So much for your vaunted eloquence, Hadley,* he thought with disgust.

'And you, Mr Hadley. Peters,' she said, addressing the groom, 'I shall stop at Upper Brook Street before I return to the Square. I'm sure I can trust Mr Hadley to escort me there safely, so you may go. Oh—and tell Polly she need not worry, I will be fine.'

Grinning, the groom bowed. 'I'll be sure to tell her, your ladyship. Right tore a strip off me yesterday, she did, for coming home without you!'

'Your hide will be safe today,' Lady Margaret promised. At her nod of dismissal, the groom trotted off.

Once the man was out of earshot, Giles said, 'My very dear Lady Margaret, I am enchanted to see you! Though I must say, I hoped to have had a note from you earlier.'

'Oh, that.' She coloured a little. 'It's just…when I sat down to write one, I didn't know what to say. And then to have to ask a footman, or my maid, to carry it to Albany for me…' Her blush deepened. 'In any event, I wasn't sure you'd want to…return so soon.'

'Not return? Last night would have been better—or yesterday afternoon. I was useless at the committee meeting; all I could think about was you, and our morning together.'

'Then, you'd like to go there with me…now?'

His heart—and other things—leapt. 'More than anything. Shall I give you a few moments to ride there first?'

She laughed ruefully. 'Since my whole staff knows what's going on—indeed, my maid has already taken me to task for it—I suppose we could arrive together and boldly enter the front door! But on the chance that not all of London yet knows about us…yes, give me a few moments.'

Concerned, he rode over to catch at her reins. 'Your maid has taken you to task! Devil's teeth, what effrontery! Would you rather I not visit you? I don't want to make life…uncomfortable for you!' *Though it would kill me to stay away.*

'No, I want you to come! Surely you know how much,' she replied, looking up at him, the banked passion in her green eyes immediately raising the level of his desire. 'Polly's looked after me all my life. She just doesn't want me to do something foolish that might get me hurt.'

'I wouldn't want to do anything that would hurt you, either.'

In the flash of an instant, her troubled expression turned provocative. 'What you do to me definitely doesn't hurt. I've lain awake most of the night, impatient for you to do it again.'

'Then let us go now, while we still have most of the morning! How late does your cousin sleep?'

'Until noon. But don't worry. Timid little thing, she is so grateful to have food, lodging, and the leisure to pursue her own interests, I could probably ride naked down

St James's, like Lady Godiva, and she'd not reprove my behaviour.'

'I would. I insist that all naked riding be done with me.'

Her smile heated and she licked her lips. 'I look forward to it.'

'Not half so much as I do.' With that promise, he slapped the mare on her rump and set horse and rider off towards the park gates.

One slow circuit of the park, and he would head after her. He spent that transit in glorious anticipation, recalling the taste of her mouth, the pebbled softness of her nipples under his tongue, the satin of the skin beneath her ears, behind her knees, the responses he drew from her as he laved her passage and the tight bud hidden above it. And what she did to him...

He recalled Ben's comment about inventiveness, and his chest tightened, until it was difficult to breathe.

Would she have some new clever technique to pleasure him? He couldn't wait to find out.

Chapter Ten

Maggie returned from Upper Brook Street to her father's house the following morning in a glow of satiated satisfaction. Having the previous day agreed with Giles that they would meet every morning, unless one or the other had a commitment that precluded it, she could look forward to each new day with an anticipation she hadn't felt in years.

Ah, what a new day! Her well-pleasured body tingled at the memory.

She felt reasonably sure she was proceeding with sufficient discretion. Papa was used to her coming and going between their two dwellings, and would be unlikely to question her; most of the *ton* was abed until afternoon, so the chance of anyone discovering their crack-of-dawn assignations was slim, and she felt secure about the discretion of servants who had watched over her since childhood. In addition to which, she had no doubt that Polly had warned all the staff that if the merest whisper escaped either dwelling, the offender would be turned off without a character.

The only concern that might trouble her happiness—and she refused to spoil the idyll of the present with worry—was the possibility of Giles Hadley deciding he was ready to end the arrangement.

If that happened, so be it. In the interim, she intended to suck from the liaison every possible morsel of joy—an emotion she'd had experienced too seldom these last few years.

As she walked in, the butler came over to meet her. 'Lady Margaret, I thought you'd wish to know that Mr Hadley—Mr *George* Hadley,' he clarified, not looking her in the eye, 'has called upon your papa. They are in his study.'

That announcement was enough to dissipate her cloud of euphoria. Remembering what Giles had told her about how vindictive his half-brother could be when denied what he wished, Maggie felt a niggle of foreboding.

'Thank you, Rains. After I change, I'll be in the morning room, if Papa wants me to join them.'

Had George come to ask her father for her hand, as Giles had told her he intended? Maggie wondered as she went up to her bedchamber. If he were rushing his fences with a proposal, she was going to have to reject him—and deal with what might be unpleasant consequences.

If she must, she would, she told herself philosophically. Were a proposal in the offing, she'd just as soon get it—and any unpleasant consequences—over with, so that possibility wouldn't cloud a future now brilliant with the promised pleasures of her association with George's much more compelling brother.

She walked in to find Polly with needle in hand and her morning gown draped across the bed.

The older woman looked up to study her face. Maggie tried, unsuccessfully, not to blush. 'What lovely needlework,' she observed, gesturing towards the tambour frame the maid had set aside.

Predictably ignoring Maggie's attempt to divert her, Polly said, 'You don't look so over the moon this morning. Having second thoughts already?'

'No,' Maggie snapped, irritated at having another bucket of cold water dumped on the lingering warmth of her morning tryst. 'I shall probably ride and then stop at Upper Brook Street every morning for the foreseeable future. I will notify you when that changes.'

Rather than being chastened by the rebuke, Polly merely chuckled as she helped Maggie out of her habit. 'You should know by now that toplofty tone won't discourage me from speaking my mind, if it's something I think you need to hear.'

'Please, do not let me hear anything! Rains already told me Mr George Hadley has called on Papa, which is dispiriting enough for one morning. Help me into that gown, please, in case Papa needs me to join them.'

'At least that's a gentleman who might do the proper thing, and ask for your hand,' Polly observed as she settled the garment around Maggie.

Maggie repressed a shudder. 'If you knew the gentleman better, you'd find the idea of a proposal from him more appalling than appealing. George Hadley is interested only in George Hadley, and what a wife can do for *him*. Specifically, a wife with the correct political connections and a handsome portion.'

'Isn't that what all gentlemen want?'

'Which is why I haven't married again,' Maggie retorted. Turning so the maid could finish the ties at the back, she said, 'If you want to do me a good turn, pray that this Mr Hadley did *not* come to ask Papa for my hand.'

A short time later, Maggie descended to the small back parlour. In truth, she *was* curious why George Hadley was closeted with her father. Since he would not be serving in the next Parliament—unless his father had found him another pocket borough to represent—he wouldn't be part of Papa's caucus. Perhaps he intended to get himself returned for the following session, and wanted to tap her father's expertise in planning his strategy.

She only hoped his reasons were political. In any event, if she were not summoned to join them, Papa would doubtless tell her later what they had discussed.

Her thoughts had drifted back to the delightful interlude with Giles when a current of cool air alerted her that the parlour door had been opened. But instead of her father, the man striding into the room with the familiarity of a family member was George Hadley.

Before she could wonder what had happened to the servant who should have announced the guest, Hadley swept her a bow. 'My dear Lady Margaret! I'm so pleased to find you alone.'

Not at all pleased, she said, 'Mr Hadley, what a surprise! I thought you had called upon my father.' She looked pointedly towards the door. 'He did not accompany you?'

'No, he knew I had a matter of some…delicacy to discuss with you.'

Was it the proposal she'd dreaded? Drat Papa for not warning him off! Although the man was so self-absorbed, he was probably oblivious to hints, even active discouragement. Incapable of believing she'd refuse him, unless the rejection came from her own lips.

Well, it was going to—unless she could head him off. 'I cannot imagine a matter so delicate you would not wish to discuss it with Papa present. As political friends and allies, we've spent many an evening talking over policy.'

'A modest observation,' he noted with an approval that

made her grit her teeth. 'Quite proper that a lady not be so forward as to anticipate more—though you cannot be totally unaware of my admiration for you.'

Your admiration for Papa's power and my money, you mean. 'As I admire all those who dedicate themselves to serving their country. We share that esteem; anything *more* would be out of the question. I am quite content in my position as hostess and companion to my father, and have no wish to be anything else.'

She could hardly make it plainer. But as she feared, he was not to be deterred.

'Ah, but you could be so much more! A wife and mother, a helpmate to a man of rising prominence and power who could secure your position well into the future. Which, you must allow, a man of your father's advancing years cannot. My dear Lady Margaret, becoming my wife would bring us both such advantages!'

So after reminding her of her father's eventual demise, and without any declaration of tender emotion— not that she would welcome or believe one—she was to accept his hand?

'Sir, I pray you will not continue in this manner!' she cried, exasperated. Catching him by the arm before he could go down on one knee, she said, 'There is no need to say more. Though fully aware of the honour of the offer you were about to make, I cannot accept.'

He patted her hand before she snatched it away. 'Your father warned me you might have some missish reservations about a change in your position. But only consider the benefits! You would be allying yourself, not with a mere baron, but with the scion of a noble family of impeccable lineage, whom you could assist in continuing the important political work so cherished by your esteemed sire. Allying yourself to a man of youth and vigour, who can give you the children so necessary to the happiness of any woman. A man of means, who would maintain you in the style appropriate to your station. Nor do I have any objections to your continuing to call yourself "Lady Margaret."

She wagered he would not, since the title indicated he'd snagged a wife of higher birth than his own. And he might be a 'man of means' now, but when his father died and Giles inherited, gaining control over the income from the estate currently being lavished on the second son, he'd be using *her* funds to buy his hunters, pay his tailor, and maintain the household.

Though she would like to tear him limb from limb for referring to her darling Robbie as 'merely a baron', she made herself say in a civil tone, 'Benefits indeed, had I a desire to remarry. But I have not.'

When that statement finally penetrated, he stared at her. 'Not remarry? How could you not wish to? Even with a woman's limited wit, you must realise how imperative it is for a lady of your…mature years to get herself settled while it is still possible.'

'My "wit" is not so limited that I do not know my own mind,' she snapped, struggling to keep her temper under control. 'Beyond politics, we have little in common, Mr Hadley. I am convinced we would not suit, and I would appreciate it if you cease importuning me and accept my decision.'

He finally seemed to understand what she was saying, for his smile faded. 'You truly mean to refuse me—you, who have been on the shelf for six years? You may be a marquess's daughter, but at your advanced age, you are unlikely to receive a better offer. Unless…'

His eyes narrowed and his expression turned hostile. 'You cannot believe that my *half-brother* would propose to you? I'm sorry to disillusion you, but I must warn you that though he *trifles* with widows, he doesn't marry them. I heard about your little *tête-à-tête* in Chellingham! I would have thought your father would forbid your associating with a jumped-up soldier's bastard, who has neither the training nor the breeding to assume a more elevated role!'

'If he has not the training, that is more the fault of his father, the earl, than it is his,' she flung back.

'His father, the *earl*?' he scoffed. 'So he *has* drawn you in! I would urge you to stay away from him! Giles Hadley spoils and destroys everything he touches, and has from the moment of his birth. You must have heard how he ruined his mother's life, turning her into an outcast shunned by all good society.'

'*He* ruined her?' Maggie shook her head, hardly able to believe she was hearing him correctly. 'That's ridiculous! He was only a babe, hardly responsible for the behaviour of the adults involved!'

'Indeed?' he said with a sneer. 'I would have credited you with more wit than to accept his Banbury tales!'

The wit you have already disparaged? she thought, incensed. 'Enough! I will not be drawn into the quarrel between you and your half-brother. Since I have refused your most obliging offer, there is nothing left to say. Good day, Mr Hadley.'

'You think to dismiss me like some…*lackey*?' he cried, his handsome face distorting with anger. 'I will not be treated thus by a mere female! You would do well to remember that what I want, I obtain, and woe to those who stand in my way! If you choose to ally yourself with Giles Hadley, you thrust yourself into more danger than you could possibly imagine.'

'Put myself in danger?' she echoed, her hands shaking from the effort to refrain from slapping him. 'Surely you are not trying to *threaten* me?'

'Warn, only,' he temporised, and then summoned a smile. 'Any danger would be swiftly dissipated, once you were sensible enough to accept my hand. What an outstanding team we would make!'

Flabbergasted that he had the audacity to berate her in one breath and renew his suit in the next, she said, 'I believe I have already made clear there is no chance of that. Now, once again, Mr Hadley, I must insist that you leave.'

'A command that I second,' came her father's voice from the doorway. 'Did my daughter not just order you to go?' The marquess crossed the room to stand protectively beside her. 'Then get you gone, sirrah—or do I need to summon a footman to assist you?'

His expression transitioning rapidly from surprise, to incredulity, to the petulant frown of a child denied a treat he expects as his due, Hadley bowed stiffly. 'As you wish, my lord, Lady Margaret.' Straightening his shoulders, with an air of injured dignity, he walked out.

Once the door closed behind him, her father gave her a quick hug. 'Are you all right?'

'Quite fine—if a little out of temper.'

'As well you might be!' The marquess shook his head. 'I could scarcely believe it, when Rains came to tell me Hadley was closeted with you.'

'I do wish you had not inflicted him on me,' she said ruefully.

'I certainly did not intend to! You'd already made your feelings clear, so when he broached the reason for his visit, I told him quite plainly that you would not consider accepting his offer. I suppose I can't blame an ardent suitor for wanting to confirm that disappointing news with the object of his affection, but from what I overheard just now, it appeared he did not want to accept the truth from you, either. You had to ask him more than once to leave? I only wish I had come down sooner!'

She considered telling her father he'd also threatened her, but Papa was angry enough already. 'Thank you, but I had the situation in hand.'

'I have no doubt!' her father said with a laugh as he ushered her to the sofa. 'I am disappointed in Hadley, though. I knew he'd been much indulged, but I still expected him to be a gentleman.'

'Hardly a gentleman! More like a spoiled child.'

Her father gave her a penetrating look. 'Are you sure knowing Giles Hadley is worth it?'

Startled, she looked at him, trying to keep her expression bland. Just how much did he know about her relationship with the fascinating Giles? Not that he had any say in her behaviour—but she wouldn't want to disappoint her father.

'What has that to do with George Hadley's offer?'

'He gave me quite a harangue about making sure you were protected from his half-brother's "evil influences"— at least until he could wed you and assume the vigil. I imagine he would be even more incensed if he were to hear that after thwarting his hopes, you continued to associate with his detested brother.'

'Surely you're not suggesting that I terminate my friendship with Giles Hadley,' she said, choosing her words carefully, 'because he has the misfortune to be related to a man who acts like a wilful child? Besides, would not my cutting his half-brother just encourage a bully?'

'Perhaps, but it's my daughter he's bullying.'

'Don't worry, Papa,' she told him, giving his arm a

squeeze. 'Remember, you taught me how to aim at vermin and shoot straight.'

Her father laughed. 'True, but I never intended you to have to use that skill on vermin the size of the Honourable George Hadley.'

'Who turned out to be not so honourable,' she said with a sigh.

'Indeed. I shall write to his father, and ask that he be summoned home—as a favour to me. That should be enough to remind the earl that since his precious second son is not a peer and no longer sits in Parliament, he *can* be arrested. I won't have him harassing my daughter.'

'Thank you, Papa. But it's late, and if I don't consult with Cook soon, we'll have no supper tonight.'

'Goodness, can't have you dwindle away to nothing, my sweet. Don't worry your pretty head about any more unpleasantness with George Hadley. A word to his father, and we'll table that bill before it leaves committee.'

'I would appreciate that!' Relieved to be able to transfer the problem of George Hadley to her father, she gave him a kiss and stood up. 'Now, to order your dinner!'

'Make it a good one! I'm going to study some notes Bathhurst made about the Reform Bill that's nearly certain to pass. I'll need something to cheer me.'

'Cheering it is,' she said, and walked out. She felt cheered herself, knowing that George Hadley would disturb her no more.

Now, she could concentrate on the much more enjoyable prospect of her mornings with his half-brother.

Chapter Eleven

Later that afternoon, Giles had returned to his rooms at Albany to pick up some documents when he heard a knock at the door. Opening it, he found the porter on his doorstep.

'There's a gentleman to see you, Mr Hadley,' the man said. 'A Mr Angleton, from Romesly. He said you wouldn't know him, but he's from the county your half-brother used to represent in Parliament.'

Wondering why the gentleman would seek him out at his lodgings, rather than at Parliament, Giles said, 'Tell him I cannot spare much time, as I'm already overdue at committee, but I will see him.'

Curious why someone from Hampshire would want to consult him, Giles waited impatiently until the porter escorted in a short, spare man dressed in the plain but well-made attire of a prosperous merchant or tradesman.

The man made him a bow. 'Thank you for seeing me uninvited, Lord Lyndlington. As I told your man, I'm James Angleton, of Romesly—a village within Abbots-weal, your father, Lord Telbridge's, estate.'

'Good to meet you, Mr Angleton,' Giles replied, swiftly deciding it would be too much trouble to object to the use of his courtesy title by this man who'd probably never heard him called anything else. 'What can I do for you?'

'I—and the other electors in the county—need your help.'

'I shall help if I can,' Giles said, motioning the visitor to a seat. 'But if this concerns Abbotsweal, you should rather address yourself to Lord Telbridge. As you must know if you live near the estate, I have no power there, and no influence whatsoever in the running of it.'

'Aye, that's true—for now. But as the heir, you will have both, one day.'

Resistant as always to even thinking of a life beyond his duties in the Commons, Giles said, 'Although the earl and I are estranged, I bear him no ill will.' Which was not exactly true, but he didn't intend to air his dirty laundry before a stranger. 'I have every expectation that he will continue to direct Abbotsweal for many years to come.'

'We, too, hope he continues in health and vigour. But in the interim, Lord Lyndlington, the electors in the county have a problem. As you doubtless have heard, we chose not to return your half-brother to Parliament. He…has never had much interest in the common folk, and displayed little knowledge of the needs of either tradesmen or farmers. I imagine the fact that we elected another man, rather than the earl's son, came as an unpleasant shock. I very much doubt Mr Hadley will forget or forgive the slight, nor, I expect, is the earl very happy about it.'

'Probably not,' Giles replied. 'But my acquaintance with the earl is slight—' *more like non-existent* '—so my opinion about his reaction is no more informed than yours.'

'Though you've not resided on the estate since you were a child, knowing you would one day inherit, we in

Romesly have followed your career with great interest. We're impressed and encouraged by your ideals, and your dedication in working to implement them. So, with the prospect of reform upon us, we decided to take a great risk, and throw in our lot with you.'

'Throw in your lot with me?' Giles repeated. 'I'm sorry, but I don't understand. I represent Danford. What can I do that affects you?'

'You represent Danford now, but when you inherit, you will represent *us*. In rejecting Telbridge's son, we've effectively burned our bridges with the earl. There will probably be retribution, although it's too early to tell yet what form that will take. The other electors nominated me to call on you and beg you not to wait until you inherit to come to Abbotsweal and get to know the district and its people. We are most anxious to introduce you around the area, so you can become familiar with it, and with us and our needs. If Lord Telbridge knows you are active on our behalf, it might blunt whatever retribution he might be contemplating against us.'

'Would not having me tromping about the village and the surrounding countryside incense the earl even more? It might appear to him that you—and I—are anticipating his demise.'

'Perhaps,' Mr Angleton allowed. 'But in the end, we agreed the benefit of having you up to snuff about the estate from the moment you receive your inheritance outweighed the possibility of further offending the earl. Besides, since you *are* going to inherit, there is nothing unreasonable about you visiting the village and freeholders thereabouts. Were you and your father not estranged, you would have been doing so since you came out of short pants.'

'Probably,' Giles admitted. 'However, it doesn't seem

proper for me to be poking about Abbotsweal without having been invited by the earl, or at least informing him of my intent.'

'You can certainly inform the earl if you wish, though we don't consider it necessary. Lord Telbridge may own the land, but he doesn't own *us*. Every farmer and merchant and tenant has the right to look out for his own interests, and to invite whomever he chooses into his home or shop. If we choose to invite *you*, that's none of the earl's business. I won't press you now, Lord Lyndlington. But won't you at least consider it?'

Troubled, Giles got up and paced the room. With everything in him, he resisted the very idea of reaching out to the earl, and despite the townsman's assertion, he didn't see how he could visit the estate without at least informing Telbridge of his intent. He turned back to Mr Angleton, intending to give him a regretful but firm refusal, and met a glance of such hopeful entreaty the words withered on his lips.

Even the idea of 'Abbotsweal' burned in his gut like acid. But, sent by his anxious neighbours, the man had come all the way to London to see him. He could at least let them down more gently.

Though let them down he would. Never while the earl still breathed would he set foot on the land from which Telbridge had cast out his mother.

Maybe not even then.

'Very well, Mr Angleton. I make no promises, but I will consider it.'

The man broke into a relieved smile. 'Thank you, Lord Lydley! I have other business in London that should me take a week or so. May I call upon you before I leave for your answer?'

'Yes. Send me a note here to arrange a time.'

'Good day, then, my lord. And may I add, I do hope we will see you at Romesly in the near future!'

A vain hope, that, Giles thought as he ushered the man out. But he needn't consider the disturbing matter any more right now—he had an important piece of legislation to draft. Putting the earl and his visitor out of mind, he packed up his papers and set off for the committee room.

The following morning, too filled with anticipation to sleep any longer, Giles Hadley rose before dawn and called for his horse. Tiptoeing through the common area of the rooms he shared with Davie, he sent a rueful glance towards the chamber where his friend dozed peacefully. Although Giles often rode early, normally he returned to breakfast with Davie and discuss the work they'd be engaged upon that day. Though his friend had as yet said nothing to him, it would take a man far less perceptive than Davie not to notice Giles's continuing absence at breakfast and his repeated late arrivals in the committee room.

Although Davie would bide his time, waiting for Giles to speak when he was ready, Ben and Christopher had surely noticed his tardiness, too. Sooner rather than later, they would take him to task for it. He really needed to figure out what to tell them.

But he wasn't going to waste a particle of energy this morning worrying about that, he told himself as he strode down the steps and back towards the mews. Not with the glorious prospect ahead of a hard ride, and then a sweet session with his delightful, sensual Maggie.

He'd felt a niggle of unease when he impulsively proposed their bargain, worried that he'd grow frustrated with less than a full possession. And though he certainly would prefer to make Maggie completely his, so sensitive was he to her touch, and so inventive the ways and places she came up with to touch him, that he now had no doubt he'd be intrigued by the arrangement for the indefinite future.

Which was even more exceptional, when he considered that they were meeting daily, something he'd seldom done with his previous amours, when the press of political obligations often occupied him far into the night. Perhaps it was the happy circumstance of trysting first thing in the morning, before he became caught up in business…but he didn't think so.

Nor could he remember being this excited, this energised, this…*happy* in any previous arrangement. Perhaps not since the end of his carefree childhood in that little cottage with his mother.

But enough analysing, he thought as he took the reins from the groom and threw himself up on his mount. Maggie would be racing her mare in the park, awaiting him. He meant to speed to her side and treasure every moment of their precious morning together.

A heavy, swirling mist veiled the park as Giles rode in, impatient to see Maggie again and frustrated at having to proceed slowly in the limited visibility. He turned his mount into Rotten Row, straining his ears over the sound of his own horse's hoofbeats, listening for the muffled trot of another rider.

Several rode past before he saw Maggie, emerging ghost-like out of the fog in a dark habit on her grey mare. Delight bubbled up like champagne uncorked, fizzing over into anticipation that tingled in all his nerves.

Mindful that in the cloaking fog, there might be unseen listeners, he called out a prosaic 'Good morning, Lady Margaret. Not so auspicious a day for riding.'

'Yes, I'm thinking a short ride would be desirable this morning. Won't you walk your horse beside mine?'

She'd never before asked to *ride* with him before setting off for their morning interlude, he thought with a stab of alarm. Surely she couldn't have developed misgivings, and want to end this?

A panicked feeling he didn't want to examine too closely flashed through him at the thought. Squelching it, he said, 'What is your pleasure, my lady?'

'You will find that out soon enough,' she replied, pitching her voice to reach him alone.

Relief coursed through him along with a thrill of expectation. 'I cannot wait.'

'But you will, for a bit. I thought you would want to know that I received a most…interesting call yesterday. From your half-brother.'

Nothing like the mention of that name to cast a fog-damp blanket over his enthusiasm. 'From George? What did he want?'

'He first sought out my father to ask for my hand. Since you'd warned me he might do so, I'd already spoken with Papa and let him know I would never countenance such a match. Which he informed your brother. Apparently unable to take Papa's word for it, George then sought me out, first trying to point out the advantages of a speedy marriage for a—' she gave a rueful chuckle '—woman of my "advanced age" who'd been six years on the shelf and might not receive another such attractive offer.'

'The devil he did!' Giles exclaimed. 'I knew he was maladroit, but that beggars belief!'

'Belief was an article in short supply,' she agreed. 'Particularly after, with what I thought was saintly restraint, I replied in quite a civil tone that though cognisant of the honour of his offer, I could not accept it. He tried to convince me to change my mind, and when I wouldn't, he warned me about you.'

'I can only imagine what he said on that front,' Giles muttered, angry and irritated that Maggie had been subjected to his brother's ill humour—on his behalf.

'He said—well, let's simply say he was not complimentary. In fact, I am glad you warned me how... unpleasant he can become when he is thwarted, else I might have been ill prepared for what happened next. I'd just asked him to leave a second time when, having no idea that he had not left the house after their interview, my father was informed of his presence and came to rescue me. Though your half-brother wasn't ready to follow my orders, he acquiesced readily enough to Papa's command that he leave.'

'I am certain he did. Damnation!' Giles swore, swatting into the air with his riding crop. 'Excuse my language, but I am so sorry that you had to suffer through that. George knew you were seeing me?'

'He knew about Chellingham. I don't think he knows about...this.'

'There's no guarantee he won't find out,' Giles said grimly. 'And if he does...he could be even more unpleasant. It makes no difference to me—our encounters are always bitter. But I'd not for the world cause you any further difficulties.' Hardly able to get his mouth to form the words, he forced himself to add, 'If...if you think it wise, we could...discontinue our meetings.'

'What, allow your spoiled child of a half-brother to dictate our actions? Certainly not! I thought we'd agreed on that point before.'

Relieved, Giles still felt it necessary to offer her one more chance to reconsider. 'You *are* sure?'

'I am. I only told you about the episode so you would

be on your guard, and not be caught unaware if your brother seeks you out to complain about my rejection, or hold you accountable for it.'

'Thank you for the warning! He might well try to take me to task, but that's nothing out of the ordinary. I learned long ago how to handle George.'

'The thing is,' she said, her voice tentative, 'I don't want to make a bad situation worse. Knowing he will probably hold you responsible for the disappointment, are you sure *you* want to continue the relationship?'

'There is nothing I desire more! I told you before we began, I want never to cause you any anxiety. Only to bring you pleasure.'

She smiled at him, her eyes lighting with a heat that fanned the banked flames of his desire. 'Then why are we still riding in the park?'

'I'll see you soon,' he promised, his excitement and anticipation rekindling as she kicked her mare to a trot and disappeared into the mist.

The shock of learning of George's harassment and its threat to disrupt their arrangement must have added an extra edge to his impatience, for the time necessary to complete a full transit of the still-foggy park seemed an eternity to Giles. He was itching with impatience and breathless with desire by the time he was finally able to bound up the stairs to Maggie's bedchamber.

He entered upon his knock, to find her still fully clothed in her habit, and smiled. He never knew how he would find her—fully dressed, in her shift, and once, delectably, completely nude beneath a gentleman's banyan.

'So, are we to have a slow undressing?' he asked, striding over to give her a kiss.

Which she ducked to avoid. 'No. I was thinking of what might happen, if I were never to see you here again.'

His eyes widened in alarm and panic tightened his gut. 'I thought we'd agreed—'

'Oh, we did. But then I thought how it might be, if we had decided it would be wiser to terminate our arrangement. What might happen, if we were to meet later, by chance, perhaps at the house of a mutual friend. How, despite our best efforts, we could not keep from succumbing to a taste of the forbidden.'

'I like the sound of that,' he said, reaching for the buttons of her jacket.

'No, you mustn't!' she warned, batting his hand away. 'You cannot remove any of my garments, nor can I remove any of yours.'

He shook his head, mystified. 'Then—what? Are we to have only conversation? If so, I shall do my best… though with you so near, I can't vouch for how coherent I will be.'

'Conversation…of a sort,' she replied with a wicked little smile that stiffened his flagging hopes. 'Sit here.' She gestured towards the foot of the bed. 'Talk if you like, but you may not touch me.'

That sounded more promising, as he couldn't imagine a conversation with Maggie taking place on a bed that wouldn't lead to some sort of thrilling consummation.

'Let's pretend,' she murmured, sitting beside him, 'that we've just encountered each other at Sir James Graham's salon. Our host has invited us to walk in the garden, while he speaks with other guests. We find a bench—secluded, but still near the house. We chat for a while, until…I cannot resist doing this.'

He sucked in a breath as she leaned over to trace her tongue along his neck, just above the starched cravat, from beneath his ear to the base of his throat. His hands tightening into fists, he leaned his head back to give her fuller access, and with an approving murmur, she licked and sucked at the skin beneath his chin.

His breathing was already erratic when she abandoned that to nibble and nuzzle his earlobe, then lick inside the shell of his ear while she combed her fingernails through his hair, massaging the scalp in rhythm with her stroking tongue.

Suddenly she pushed him away and sat back up. 'Someone is coming along the pathway,' she whispered. 'We turn and smile and greet them, and after speaking with us, they walk back towards the house. We are alone again—for the moment.'

This time she ran just the very tips of her fingers over his face, caressing his forehead, his brow, his nose, his cheekbones with the lightest of touches. She ended by outlining his lips with a fingertip.

He opened his mouth and sucked the finger in greedily, laving it with his tongue until she pulled it free and traced his lips again with the wetness.

Every nerve of his body vibrated with tension and anticipation. Incredibly, after so little contact, he felt himself begin to spiral towards his peak, and instinctively reached for her. She held him off, hissing a warning. 'Someone else is walking this way. We rise, and smile, and chat with them. Ah, now they are returning to the house, and the bench is ours again. For the moment.'

She lifted his hand to her lips and began to nibble and lick each finger in turn. He heard his heartbeat thundering in his ears, and felt almost dizzy, trying to sit upright. A groan tore itself from his throat when she took his thumb in her mouth and sucked on it, then bit down on the tender pad.

'Night is falling,' she whispered. 'Now, with darkness our ally, we can dare to do more.'

With that, she kissed him, pulling his hand to her breast while she slid her other one beneath the waistband of his trousers, where his erection throbbed. She whimpered when he insinuated his fingers beneath the jacket of her habit, pushing aside the bodice so he could caress a nipple, rigid beneath her shift.

The kiss went deeper, wilder, a clash of tongues and teeth, ardent, impassioned, striving for the peak. She clasped her hand around his swollen length, stroking him, rubbing her wetted thumb against the sensitive tip, until he felt the convulsions carry him away to bliss.

He was lying flat on the bed when he came to himself again, still panting and dizzy. 'I think I just fell off the bench.'

Laughing, she leaned down to kiss him. 'It is my aim to make you fall off benches—often.'

'A laudable aim. First, however...' he pulled her down in an embrace and slowly began pushing up her skirts '...it's my turn to make *you* fall off.'

Chapter Twelve

Later, after Giles had pleasured her fully dressed and then both of them again, not so fully dressed, they reclined on the sofa sipping wine, languid and satisfied.

'I suppose you must leave soon,' Maggie said regretfully, giving him a lingering wine-flavoured kiss.

'As I'm sure you must as well. Sometimes I wish there were no world beyond the doors of this chamber.'

A little thrill of surprise and pleasure ran through her to hear him express what she'd been feeling. 'So do I.'

'I hope at least this made up for the unpleasantness with George.'

At his mention of George, something disturbing about that interview recurred to her. She opened her lips to ask him about it, then shut them. Their intimacy was increasing daily, but he might not appreciate her enquiring into a matter as sensitive as his mother.

'What is it?' When she hesitated again, he said, 'Go ahead, say it! Surely you trust enough in our friendship, that you can speak your mind to me.'

Yes, *friendship*. She reminded herself she wanted to share that, and passion, and nothing more. 'Very well. Your brother told me something rather strange when he was railing against you—that you'd destroyed your mother. It sounded like an oft-repeated taunt, even though the very idea is ridiculous.'

Seeing something like a shadow pass over his eyes, she said, 'Surely *you* don't believe that?'

For a moment, he gazed into the distance, and Maggie sensed his thoughts were far away. Then he looked back at her, a slight smile on his face. 'My earliest memory of her was of standing in what must have been her bedchamber, watching as someone—her maid, probably—fixed a diamond necklace around her neck. Her black hair was an intricate mass of curls, and she wore a silky gown of bright blue—the colour of her eyes.'

Like yours, Maggie thought.

'From a child's perspective, the room was incredibly large, with long blue hangings at the windows, gilded furniture, an impossibly high poster bed. Mama sat upon a stool covered in white satin. She looked like a princess—I thought she *was* a princess. But in the cottage where I grew up, she wore her hair in a simple chignon, dressed in plain kerseymere, and lived in a few bare rooms with scuffed wooden furniture, eating off earthenware instead of china and drinking from a wooden cup instead of a crystal goblet. Because of me.'

Maggie's heart contracted with a sympathetic pain at the sorrow on Giles's face. 'Surely *she* never reproached you for it!'

'No, never! There was always a sadness about her, though she did all in her power to see that I felt loved and happy. For years I thought the memory of her dressed in silk was only a dream. I didn't find out what had happened until much later, after my aunt—my mother's sister—took me away to school.' His face hardened. 'It was at Eton that I first met George. He quickly made sure that I knew every detail of my mother's disgrace—and that the other boys knew that, despite my reputed title, I was in truth a bastard.'

'He's been trying to make your life miserable for that long?'

He nodded. 'Growing up wild on the Hampshire downs, milling about with the local children, made me a better fighter than George. He had to get someone else to hold me off when he taunted me. Or when one of his toadies maligned my mother.' He laughed shortly. 'Since I wasn't afraid to take on even the biggest of them, it's a good thing that Christopher Lattimar turned up to watch my back.'

'Did you not go back to see your mother on school holidays?'

'By the time I was allowed to leave on holiday, she wasn't there to go back to. By then, I knew why there had always been an air of melancholy about her, and a sense of…patient expectation. Much as I know she loved me, I think she *was* waiting—for Major Richard Kensworthy, the man she loved, to return from India and claim her. While I was away at school, she got a letter informing her that he'd been killed in a skirmish. Apparently distraught, she took a walk over the downs in the midst of a storm. Our maid-of-all-work told my aunt that she came back soaked to the skin and shaking with chills. She developed an inflammation of the lungs, and before they could fetch me from school, she died.'

Maggie could hardly imagine how awful it must have been—torn from his beloved mother, bullied and taunted at school and forced to endure hearing her maligned as an adulteress, then losing her without even the chance to say goodbye. 'I'm so sorry,' she whispered, laying a hand on his cheek.

He took and kissed it. 'Thank you. It's a very old wound, and mostly healed.'

'Mostly,' she noted.

'I told myself that later, when…I came into enough funds, I would buy the cottage where I'd been so happy. When I made enquiries about it recently, I was told it was part of a large estate, and the owner had no wish to sell. Perhaps he will, some day; I will certainly continue to pursue it. Her grave is there.'

Once again, his eyes went unfocused, and she could almost feel him being pulled into the past. Then he shook his head and looked back at her. 'But I'm not the only one to have suffered a loss. Despite my half-brother's ridiculous words about your "advanced years", I've no doubt you could have remarried any time you wished, which makes me believe you did not wish to. Because your first husband was so compelling, you didn't believe anyone else would ever compare?'

So he remembered that she'd told him Robbie had been the love of her life. 'Compelling, definitely!' she said with a smile. 'Robbie and I grew up together—his estate, an ancient barony even older than my father's titles, borders ours. He and my brother Julian and I roamed the countryside, and of course, I wanted to do whatever they did. As you may remember, my mother lost two babes, and never truly recovered her health. After I'd scared off my third governess, overseeing me was turned over to a junior housemaid—Polly—who became maid, friend, and confidante, and who was not nearly as strict as Mama would have been about confining me to proper maidenly activities. If I hadn't been so mad about politics and desperate to have Papa's ear on his visits home, I might have grown up an untutored savage.'

'Instead, you studied philosophy and literature,' he guessed.

'Languages, too. I cajoled Julian into letting me share

his tutor. Boys are always taught so many more interesting subjects than girls! With Mama ill much of the time, I did learn to run a household, though I'm hopeless at needlework or sketching. Robbie didn't care about things like that. He thought it splendid that I could climb trees and shoot straight and catch more fish than he did.' Her smile softened at the memory. 'When he came back from university, so handsome and serious and yet still so dear a friend, I'd put up my hair and let down my skirts. Falling in love came as naturally as breathing. Despite my interest in politics, after the Season my great-aunt Lilly insisted I have, I expected to marry him and spend the rest of my life at Raven's Cliff, only a few miles from where I was born. But then came the carriage accident.'

'His death devastated you.'

Even after so many years, her throat closed and tears threatened. 'Yes,' she whispered, unable to say more. He wrapped his arms around her and pulled her against his chest, hugging her close in wordless sympathy.

Releasing her a moment later, he said, 'Then I'm mistaken in thinking I'd heard you'd been engaged again, several years ago?'

Sir Francis Mowbrey was a topic almost as unpleasant as Robbie's death, and one, despite their growing friendship, she had no intention of discussing. 'Yes, briefly. We decided we should not suit. Have you never been back to your father's estate since you left with your mother as a child?'

'No, nor have I any wish to see my father. If he is my father. The way my half-brother tells it, I'm the brat of a younger son who died obscurely in a battle half a world away.'

'But you were born within the confines of marriage, which makes you the earl's heir, regardless of the feelings between you. Knowing you will eventually inherit, surely at some point he will summon you and begin to acquaint you with the duties you will one day have to take over.'

Giles shrugged, his gaze hardening again. 'I make no such assumption.'

'Does your father manage Abbotsweal himself? Or does he use an agent?'

'As I haven't been there since I was too young to notice such a thing, I have no idea.'

She probably shouldn't press the point, but she felt so strongly, she couldn't help herself. 'But you need to have an idea—more than an idea. You need to *know* the land and the people who work it, intimately! Your Radicals talk about reforming government, giving every man his say. Perhaps you will go as far as the French, confiscate the land people like my father have managed for centuries and parcel it out to tenants, or anyone greedy enough to hold out their hand. But for now, the health of the land and the well-being of those who live on it depend on the man who owns it—the man who bears the title. He likely serves as magistrate for the county, director of the parish poor house, and supports the livings of the pastors who minister to its people. Directs which fields will be planted with what crops, provides updated tools to farm the land, keeps his tenants' cottages in repair, sees to the care of their elderly and to those who are sick or in need. Would you know which curate to give which living on your father's land? Who to appoint as judge? Who to sit on the poorhouse committee?'

'Of course not,' he replied, impatience and irritation clearly written on his face.

Since he was already angry, she might as well finish. 'I know it's not my place to harangue you about this, but only think, Giles! When your father—when the earl—

dies, and Parliament sends you the writ of summons to the Lords, you can ignore it. Refuse to serve. Never visit the estate. But then the people there will have no voice. You are responsible for them, even more so than for the people who voted you to represent them in the Commons. *They* can elect someone else, should they be unhappy with your service. The villagers and tenants and farmers and householders of Abbotsweal cannot. Would you leave them at the mercy of some hireling, or even worse, with no oversight at all?'

Making no answer, he pushed away and sat glaring at her, arms folded.

'Very well, I'm done. I imagine you are now quite impatient to get on your way,' she added ruefully.

Still silent, he stood, adjusted his clothing, and turned to stride out. At the doorway, he halted. 'You really are brave, you know. Few of my friends dare speak of my mother, and none of them—no one—has the audacity to take me to task about fulfilling my "duty".'

'It needed to be said, little as you wished to hear it.' She gave him a gallows grin. 'And I didn't think you'd strike a lady. In truth, though, you *should* get to know the people and the land. Do not make all those who depend upon Abbotsweal suffer for the enmity between yourself and the earl. Please, Giles, at least consider it.'

He stared at her for a long moment, his face grim and shuttered. And then, most unexpectedly, he threw back his head and laughed. 'You don't happen to know a tradesman named "Angleton" from the town of Romesley, do you?'

Relieved that he no longer seemed so angry, she said, 'I don't believe so. Should I?'

'If I didn't know better, I would swear you coached him up and sent him to my rooms yesterday. Apparently delegated by the town and county that chose not to re-elect George, he called on me to urge that I visit Abbotsweal and become acquainted with its people. As you have just done.'

'How wonderful that they are eager to meet you!' she cried. Then, reminding herself that *he* was the one who had to become convinced such a visit represented a price-less opportunity, she damped down her enthusiasm. 'Will you?' she asked quietly.

To her dismay, his expression hardened again. 'I don't know. As I told him, I will…*consider* it.'

With that, he walked out the door.

With a sigh, Maggie watched him go. Would he come back again, or had her plain speaking alienated him for good? Something twisted in her chest at the idea that he might never visit her at Upper Brook Street again, should the pleasures of intimacy not be sufficient to overcome the anger she'd aroused by badgering him about his duty.

But if there could not be an honest exchange of opin-ion between them, nothing more than a temporary lust would be possible anyway.

She drew herself up short at the direction that thought was headed. There wasn't *supposed* to be anything more between them beyond a temporary lust—and, if she were wise and lucky, a lasting friendship.

Still, what kind of friend would she be, if, without a word of caution, she let him continue down a path that seemed so clearly to her to be one of disaster for him and those who would depend on him?

Not her father's daughter, who'd been raised to love and care for the land and its people.

Sighing again, Maggie straightened her habit and pre-pared to return to Cavendish Square. Though the very thought of not seeing Giles again sliced like a knife to the bone, she couldn't regret forcing him to listen to her views. She only hoped he would honour his word, and consider them.

A disgruntled Giles returned to his rooms at Albany to change and ready himself for Parliament, glad that Davie had already departed for the committee rooms. He couldn't believe, after opening himself up to discuss his memories of his mother—something he did very rarely— Maggie had blindsided him with her insistence that he think more carefully about his eventual inheritance.

After avoiding, as a rule, thinking about the earldom at all, to be harangued about it twice in the space of two days seemed incredible.

He could still remember the confusion he'd felt, when a woman he'd never met invaded their cottage to demand that his mother let her take him away to school. The hurt and sense of betrayal when his mother, instead of laughing in the woman's face, had *thanked* her—and turned him over without even a token protest. The shock and disbelief of learning during their travel to Eton that, not only did he have a father he didn't remember, the man was still living and was wealthier and more prominent than he could imagine. The soul-deep anger that smouldered still over how that father had spurned and humiliated his wife and abandoned his son.

The vastness of his shame and guilt at discovering he'd been responsible for his mother's banishment and anguish.

He felt an almost violent aversion to accepting anything that came from the earl, who had chosen to do nothing to assist him or his mother during the poverty of his childhood, or at any time since as he grew to manhood. Somehow, it seemed a travesty to be forced to accept a largesse that would never be offered, if the law didn't require it.

And so, all these years, he'd put the succession and what it would mean for him out of mind. Distancing himself from the society in which his father moved, despite his uncle's and Davie's increasingly frequent hints that he needed to become familiar with the world and the duties that would eventually be his. Stubbornly holding himself apart from his heritage, ignorant of the scope and range of responsibilities that would fall to him sooner or later, when the earl died.

As they both grew older, that hour would come sooner rather than later.

Much as he hated to admit it, Maggie was right; it probably *was* time for him face up to the future he could not avoid.

Mr Angleton's invitation provided an excellent opportunity to begin.

As he shrugged on his coat, Giles thought ruefully that, much as he'd castigated George for being spoiled and self-absorbed, on this matter, he'd been just as immature. He'd excused himself for ignoring the problem, citing the important national issues in Parliament that demanded his immediate attention, while this 'other matter' was distant enough to be put off. But in reality, he'd been metaphorically sucking his thumb in the corner like a resentful child, refusing to prepare for his future out of spite for the father who'd rejected him.

The realisation was sobering, and he didn't much like the picture it painted of him.

Then he smiled, recalling Maggie's passionate conviction as she championed the cause of the tenants and villagers. Ignoring every warning sign that normally silenced Davie or anyone else who dared to mention forbidden topics, she'd forged ahead in the teeth of his angry resistance. So convinced that he must recognise the truth of what she said, and so sure that he would do what was right, once he did.

Do not make all those who depend upon Abbotsweal suffer for the enmity between yourself and the earl. If he did not take up the invitation from the Romesly electors and intervene to ally himself with these people, would he be doing just that?

You are responsible for them... But that wasn't quite fair. He hadn't asked the Romesly voters not to support George. Though, he admitted with a sigh, given an alternative, how could anyone of sense *not* have voted George out of office? Still, it had taken courage for the electors to reject the choice of the most powerful man in the county.

Encouraged by the principles he'd avowed over his years in Parliament, the electors had counted on him to stand by them when they did so. How could he let them down?

How could he force himself to return to the land from which he and his mother had been evicted all those years ago? Where the father he wouldn't even recognise still lived?

Conflicted, and irritated by his indecision, he threw on his greatcoat and prepared to join his friends in the committee room. Mr Angleton had told him he'd be in London for some time; Giles didn't need to make a final decision now.

But the spectre of becoming Earl of Telbridge seemed to loom much closer.

Early that evening, throwing down his pen in disgust, Giles rose from the table in the committee room. He'd had difficulty concentrating all day, the questions about the future raised by Maggie and the elector from Romesly affecting his ability to hammer out policy in the present.

'I've had enough for today,' he told Davie, who'd gazed over at him as he stood up, a question in his eyes. 'Let's begin again tomorrow.'

'Early tomorrow?' Ben asked, giving him a pointed look.

To his annoyance, Giles felt his face redden. 'Early enough.'

'Shall I save a place for you at the Quill and Gavel?' Davie asked.

'Yes, I've some matters to attend to, but I'll meet you there later for supper.'

'Perhaps I can help you work out that point of law.'

Giles knew Davie meant far more than the minutiae of the language for the Reform Bill. Maybe it was time to confide in his friend. 'Perhaps. I'll see you later.'

Having considered and rejected and reconsidered the idea several times over the course of the afternoon, Giles ordered a hackney and set out for Cavendish Square. His friends knew all about Parliament, crafting laws and getting out the vote. But none of them knew anything about managing an estate.

He knew only one person who did. And if he intended to begin preparing for the responsibilities that would inevitably become his, he at least needed to know what to look for when he accepted Mr Angleton's offer to visit Romesly.

Which, he realised, some time over the course of the day, he'd decided to do.

Fortunately, since he wasn't exactly sure how he would have explained the reason for his call to Lord Witlow, the butler informed him that Lady Margaret was at home. Leading Giles into another elegantly appointed room done in the Adams style, all classical pilasters and pale plaster, the butler went off to commune with his mistress.

Giles found himself pacing impatiently, though had little doubt that, once informed of the identity of the caller, curiosity alone would prompt Maggie to receive him.

As he expected, after only a brief wait, the butler ushered her in. Just the sight of her, her auburn hair glowing in the candlelight above a green gown that accented her eyes and flattered her slender figure, warmed his heart and smoothed the hard edges off his urgency.

'Mr Hadley, what a pleasant surprise!' she said, giving him her hand. 'Will you take some refreshment?'

'That would be much appreciated.'

'Please, do be seated, and tell me how I may assist you. Rains, will you bring wine?'

As soon as the butler exited, he gave her hand a lingering kiss. 'How lovely you look tonight! I find myself wishing we were at Upper Brook Street.'

'You look quite delicious yourself,' she replied, smiling at him before giving her lips a naughty lick that made him want to consign his serious errand to perdition and carry her off where they might indulge in activities not prudent to perform in Cavendish Square.

'But alas,' she continued, putting a halt to his lascivious imagining, 'I know you wouldn't come to Cavendish Square with trysting in mind.' The sparkle faded from her eyes and a look of distress creased her brow. 'Particularly if you are still so angry about my outspokenness this morning that you intend to…terminate our arrangement.'

'Terminate it!' he cried, astounded that she might imagine that to be the reason for his visit here. 'Of course not! How could you even think that?'

'You were quite angry when you left. I did insist on meddling in what is none of my business.'

He'd spent so much of the day pondering what to do, he'd completely forgotten that he had, in fact, initially been irritated by her persistence. 'I'm not angry any more. Although what we were discussing *is* the reason for my visit tonight.'

Understanding immediately what he meant, she said, 'You've come to a decision, then. Are you going to accept Mr Angleton's offer?'

'I think I must. As you pointed out so persuasively, whether I like it or not, the earldom will one day be mine, and with it, the responsibility for managing the land and caring for its people. The responsibility is vast, and so is my ignorance. I cannot afford too long a visit to Abbotsweal now, when I need to help prepare the bill for its first reading, but even a short trip could begin to chip away at that mountain of ignorance.'

'I'm so pleased!' she exclaimed, her enthusiasm making him feel even better about the decision. 'I knew, if you could just be brought to think rationally about it, you would embrace the task. You need only the proper training to become an effective guardian and advocate for Abbotsweal.'

'I certainly need that. In fact, I was hoping that you and your father might offer me some suggestions about what to look for and ask about when I visit Romesly, so I might take the fullest advantage of the trip.'

'I'm sure Papa would be happy to! Let me have Rains see if he can join us.'

After sending the butler off in pursuit of her father, she looked at him thoughtfully. 'We can both make suggestions for what you might explore during your visit. But if you'd like my opinion…'

'On a matter about which you feel so strongly,' he

said with a grin, 'I expect I shall have it, whether I want it or not.'

'How very unhandsome—if, alas, also true!' she replied with a laugh. 'It occurred to me that, although you *should* visit the village and speak with the farmers, those enquiries alone will not give you an accurate picture of an earl's job, which is the co-ordination and management of a rather vast enterprise. The only way to learn about that task is to watch someone performing it. Do you think you could spare a few days to visit Huntsford? My brother Julian is an excellent manager, trained since childhood for the task. I know he would be happy to take you around the estate and show you the duties involved in running it.'

'Would you escort me to Huntsford?' he asked, surprising himself with the question.

Initially looking startled, she quickly recovered. 'If you wish me to.'

The prospect of spending unhurried time with her, seeing the world that had moulded her into the fascinating creature she'd become, the world he must one day inhabit, sent a thrill of anticipation through him.

There might even be a few discreet opportunities for intimacy.

'I can think of nothing that would give me more pleasure. Well, I can think of a few things, but not anything we dare do in your father's front parlour.'

To his delight, she was blushing when the door opened.

'Good evening, Mr Hadley,' the marquess said as he strode in. 'Now, what's this mysterious purpose Rains tells me my daughter has summoned me to consult with you about?'

'Really, Papa, it was hardly a summons!' Lady Margaret protested as she walked over to give him a kiss. 'I'll let Mr Hadley tell you about it himself.'

Giles gave her a rueful smile. 'If I'm about to embark on this endeavour, I suppose I ought to call myself "Lyndlington".'

Lord Witlow raised an eyebrow. 'Your father has invited you to Abbotsweal to begin learning about the estate?'

'No, not Telbridge. Surprisingly, a request was made by some of Abbotsweal's merchants and farmers for me to visit Romesly, one of the villages on the estate, and the surrounding area.'

Witlow gave a huff of impatience. 'That business with your mother happened over twenty years ago. It's long past time for the earl to have got over his injured dignity and look to the future of his heritage, by training his heir to manage it. Well, visiting Romesly is a start.'

'Yes, but it won't show him what is actually involved in managing an estate,' Lady Margaret said. 'I thought perhaps I could take him to Huntsford and let him go about with Julian for a few days.'

'An excellent idea!' the marquess replied, and then chortled. 'If it gets back to Telbridge, which doubtless it will, perhaps it will shame him into finally doing *his* duty.'

'I thought you would approve,' Lady Margaret said.

'Otherwise you'd not have invited my opinion, eh, Puss?' he teased, tweaking one of her auburn curls.

'You know I value your advice—even when it conflicts with my desires,' she replied, giving him a hug.

Giles watched them, startled at first by their open display of affection. Suddenly his mind was filled with a vision of himself as a youngster, returning to the cottage after fishing with some of the boys from the neighbouring farm. Mama had met him on the porch with a kiss, and invited the boys to linger for a mug of water and a slice of bread. While they ate, she stood behind him, her arms draped loosely about his shoulders, listening attentively as he nattered on about every small detail of his fishing expedition.

A profound sense of sadness struck him, part grief at his mother's passing, part longing for the joyous intimacy that Lady Margaret shared with her father, the warmth and comfort of close family he had not experienced since childhood.

Thankfully, he had his friends, who were almost as good as family.

Almost.

'You shall have to watch out for my "managing" daughter, Lyndlington,' the marquess said, recalling him. 'She'll have you out riding the acreage and tending crops and calling on tenants before you know what's happening.'

'Those all sound like things I need to learn to do,' Giles replied.

'Indeed. If I do say so myself, Esterbrook makes an excellent estate manager—which is my only solace for having a son so uninterested in politics. I wish I could accompany you, but with your forces marshalling against us, I must be here to prepare for the assault.'

'As one who will be assisting with the marshalling, I won't be able to stay long at Huntsford, but I appreciate your lending me your son's expertise. And your knowledgeable daughter's assistance as well.'

'The latter I shall surely miss, so mind you don't linger at Huntsford too long, Puss. I shall write Julian tonight, Lyndlington. We may have opposing views, but I admire the vigour of your intellect and the passion of your opinions.' The marquess chuckled. 'I shall look forward to the day you take your place in the Lords! But for now, I must return to work.'

'Shall I have Cook prepare a tray for you, Papa, or will we dine as usual?'

'I'd like to see your smiling face at the table—after which I shall have to repair to Brooks's for a tiresome meeting.'

'I must be off to dinner and some tiresome meetings as well,' Giles said. 'Lady Margaret, please send me a note when you're ready for the excursion to Huntsford. I'll delay my visit to Romesly until afterwards—when hopefully I'll have a better notion of what I should be looking for.'

'Send you a…note?' she repeated, raising an eyebrow in query.

Did she fear that, now that they would be seen associating openly, he might cease his clandestine visits?

Did she really think he could stay away?

'Yes, a note. In the interim, I shall follow my usual routine. *All* of my usual routine.'

'Very good,' she said, looking relieved. 'I expect it should take about a week to arrange—if that will be agreeable?'

'I am at your disposal,' he replied with a wink. Turning to the marquess, he said, 'Thank you again, my lord, for your advice and your invitation. I shall look forward to meeting your son.'

The two men bowed, and Lady Margaret walked them to the door. 'Papa, I'll see you later. I shall look forward to showing you Huntsford, Mr Hadley.'

'I shall look forward to seeing it with you,' he replied, letting a glance convey what he could not say out loud in her father's presence: how much he hoped that during their journey, she'd be sharing with him more than just her ancestral home.

Feeling as if he'd had a burden lifted, Giles walked out to hail a hackney. It wasn't until he was seated in the vehicle, bowling along towards dinner with his friends at the Quill and Gavel, that it struck him how easy and natural it had seemed to consult Maggie.

Normally, he hated asking for help, working twice as hard as he might otherwise have to in order to sort out problems on his own. The lingering effects, he supposed, of having to stand alone against the world during his early days at Eton.

Even more ironic, he was actually *anticipating*, rather than dreading, his upcoming journey into a life he'd never wanted.

Because Lady Margaret would accompany him, easing the transition, as she eased the tension in his body and carried him to delight?

Better not study too closely the implications of that fact. And simply focus, for now, on the satisfaction of having taken the first step towards accepting his destiny.

Chapter Thirteen

The next afternoon, Maggie was attending to the myriad of details that would keep her father's household running smoothly during her absence when Rains appeared in the small back parlour she used as her office. 'The Dowager Countess of Sayleford to see you, Lady Margaret.'

'How lovely,' Maggie said, feeling guilty for not having made time to see her elderly great-aunt since her initial call, when she'd gone trolling for information. 'You've shown her into the Blue Salon?'

'Yes, ma'am. Lady Sayleford has already ordered refreshments,' he added.

Trust Aunt Lilly to have no compunction about issuing commands in her nephew's house. 'What are we having?'

'Tea and cakes, Lady Margaret,' the butler replied, trying to hide his smile.

Maggie chuckled. 'Tell her I'll join her directly.'

After washing the ink off her hands and tidying her gown, Maggie hurried to the salon, wondering what might have prompted her great-aunt to seek her out, rather than issuing a summons for her to call at Grosvenor Square. Some delicious piece of gossip she couldn't wait to share?

A moment later, she walked into the Blue Salon and gave her visitor a kiss. 'Aunt Lilly, what a delightful surprise!'

'If my great-niece saw fit to call upon her old great-aunt occasionally, it wouldn't be such a surprise,' that lady returned tartly.

Trust Aunt Lilly to go straight to the point, without wasting any time on the social niceties. 'You are quite right, Aunt, and I should apologise. With Parliament convening again and the hubbub over the efforts to push through the Reform Bill, Papa has been busier than ever with his political dinners, which means I have, too. But that's no excuse for neglecting you.'

'It certainly is not,' the dowager agreed. 'I have heard you've been exceptionally busy. Particularly after your early morning ride.'

Maggie froze, shocked into silence. Could her great-aunt know about her morning rendezvous—and if so, how had she found out?

By the time she'd gathered enough wit to search for a reply, she realised her obvious chagrin at the pronouncement would make it rather difficult to fob it off. Before she could give it a try, her great-aunt shook a finger at her.

'No point trying to tell me you have no idea what I mean, missy. Guilt is painted all over your face! Besides, you could never tell a convincing lie, and you know it. But I didn't come to take you to task, though I probably should.'

'You didn't?' Maggie said, still trying to wrap her mind around the horrifying news that her great-aunt knew she'd been trysting with Giles Hadley.

'No.' Her great-aunt chuckled. 'That would be rather hypocritical, after I'd practically urged you to take a lover. And if I were angling for one myself, Giles Hadley would certainly catch my eye!'

'Indeed,' Maggie said faintly.

'Thank heavens that monster Napoleon no longer terrorises Europe! I've not been abroad for ages, and a nice long sojourn on the coast of Italy during a chilly English winter and spring would be just the tonic. So I wanted to tell you that I stand ready to assist if any little…consequences develop.'

Maggie felt her cheeks flame, while sickness at the very thought of such a catastrophe made her stomach churn. 'We've…arranged things to make sure nothing like that ever happens.' She shook her head, still a little stunned. 'I can't believe I'm talking to you about this.'

'I would have hoped you'd have your mama to talk with about whatever most concerns you. Sadly, Ophelia hasn't been strong enough to fill that role for years. I want you to know in your present…circumstances, you'd have someone sensible to protect you, if protection should be needed.'

'Protection rather than chiding?'

Her great-aunt reached over to take her hand. 'How could I chide you for doing something that makes you happy, child? It broke my heart to see how devastated you were after you lost your Robbie. You've been simply *existing* for too long! How could I not rejoice to see the bloom back in your cheeks, that long-absent sparkle in your smile, the bounce back in your step? I noticed the difference in you the moment you entered the room! All I ask is that you be as prudent as you can—and relish every moment of joy. One never knows when there will be another.'

'Of that, I'm well aware,' Maggie said.

'You don't envision anything…longer term?'

'Probably not. I don't think so—oh, I don't know! Since *I* effectively propositioned *him*, there has been no discussion of his expectations.'

'You propositioned him? Bravo!' her great-aunt said, with an approving nod. 'I wouldn't have thought you'd have the gumption.'

'Or the foolhardiness,' Maggie said.

'Why, are you already regretting it?'

'Oh, no! It's been…wonderful. I'd forgotten just how wonderful it can be between a man and a maid. I shall be grateful to him for ever, just to have once again tasted that sublime pleasure.'

Her great-aunt raised an eyebrow at her tone, which was perhaps too enthusiastic. 'Are you sure you're not beginning to want something more?'

Maggie snuffed out the flicker of hope before it could catch fire. 'I can't, Aunt Lilly. I don't think I could bear loving like that again. I admit, this is the first time since Robbie that any man has interested me enough for the thought to enter my mind. But we didn't begin the affair with any intention of it being more than a mutually enjoyable interlude. I intend to continue considering it only that.'

'Probably wise for you to tread carefully, my sweet. One broken heart is enough for a lifetime.'

'With that, I can certainly agree. But—Aunt Lilly, how did you find out?' The idea that, even as they sat here drinking tea, the tantalising *on dit* about aloof Lady Margaret dallying with a lover might be blazing through the *ton* like wildfire across dry grass, made her feel ill.

'Don't worry, my dear, I haven't heard a whisper of gossip—yet. It probably will get out sooner than later, by the way, a fact for which you should prepare yourself. In the meantime, I have my sources,' she ended, looking smug.

'Your sources? But if there's not gossip, you must mean…from within my own *household*?' Maggie cried.

'Don't get your feathers ruffled,' her great-aunt said, patting her hand. 'After your mama was so ill for so long, and your father off at Parliament, how else was I to learn how you were getting on? I needed to have some way of knowing if anything were amiss, in case you required someone to step in and assist. And with your mother unable to fill the role, *you* needed someone who could be a companion.'

It took only a moment for Maggie to piece it all together. *'Polly?'* she gasped.

'How else would a junior housemaid suddenly get herself advanced to being the maid and companion of the daughter of the house? I'd had my eye on her for some time, and when I was sure she might be the one, broached the possibility to her. She was quite enthusiastic, and it was the trick of a moment to get your father to agree.'

'I can hardly believe it. Polly, *spying* on me all these years?'

'I'd hardly call it "spying"!' the dowager objected. 'Has she not always been a friend, confidante and supporter when you needed one? Looked out for your welfare, rejoiced with you in your happiness, sustained you in your sorrow?'

'Yes,' Maggie admitted.

'Well, then. Heavens, child, it wasn't as if I'd been paying her to report back to me! All I did was obtain her the position, and tell her to call on me if circumstances developed she thought you might not be able to manage alone.'

'Like the repercussions of taking a lover,' Maggie muttered.

'Very true. Polly might sympathise, but she hasn't the resources to assist you, should assistance of that sort become necessary. So, of course, she told me about it.'

'I still can't believe it.'

'You might rather thank me for being such a good judge of character. I think she has served you well.'

Aunt Lilly was right; it was silly to cling to her outrage over having a loving relative place a concerned individual to guard her, with instructions to call for assistance if the need arose. 'She has served me well,' Maggie admitted. 'But I do wish you'd told me about the arrangement sooner.'

'Well, now I have. I understand you are taking Hadley to Huntsford?'

'Yes,' she replied, no longer surprised that her great-aunt seemed to know all her plans. 'He has finally decided he must face the future he's avoided all these years. Although, I'm sorry to say, not because he reconciled with his father. A delegation from the townspeople in one of the villages on the estate begged him to start becoming involved with their community.'

Aunt Lilly nodded approvingly. 'About time he started acting like Viscount Lyndlington. Since his attics-to-let father refuses to see to teaching him how to run an estate, someone must. Julian will set him an excellent example.' The dowager raised an eyebrow. 'You had some hand in this decision, I'm sure. Well done of you! I hope he appreciates it.'

Maggie chuckled. 'He certainly didn't at first! I did rather lecture him about it, though, which he was kind enough to forgive. Of course, I can't wait to show off Huntsford.'

'I'll leave you to your preparations,' the dowager said,

setting down her teacup. 'Just remember, I'm here to help, should you need it.'

Maggie walked her to the door and gave her a hug. 'Dearest Aunt Lilly! What would I do without you?'

'Heaven knows, child,' her great-aunt said with a chuckle. 'I won't tell you not to do anything I wouldn't, for that would give you far too much leeway.' With a little wave, she allowed Rains to escort her down the hallway.

Smiling, Maggie climbed the stairs back to her chamber to instruct Polly in some packing. And put a word in her ear!

She had to marvel again at her great-aunt putting in place someone to watch over and guard her, a fact which still touched, gratified and outraged her. She felt the world somehow tilted: her great-aunt knew of and approved her having a lover, would help her should there be any consequences—heaven forbid!—and had been a secret presence, watching over her most of her life.

While she'd thought she had been fending for herself.

Shaking her head, she entered her bedchamber, where Polly was spreading layers of tissue paper over her gowns. Halting, she stared at the woman until the maid looked up, a question in her eyes.

'You might have told me.'

Predictably, Polly showed neither surprise nor remorse, her expression more the patience of a mother trying to quiet a troublesome child, than guilt for having reported on her mistress for years.

'Tell you what—that her ladyship obtained me this position? That she begged me to let her know if a child who was virtually motherless and fatherless needed help? I'll not apologise for that, missy!'

'How often did you call upon her?'

'Only once—when your Robbie died. I knew to survive that, you'd need all the loving arms you could get surrounding you. I considered telling her about that last… incident, but that resolved itself before any intervention was necessary. This time, with no wedding ring in the offing, I wanted her prepared to help, in a way I cannot.'

Polly rose and came over and touched Maggie's cheek. 'My dear Lady Maggie,' she said softly, 'don't you know I would do anything in my power to keep you safe and happy?'

It might have been a conspiracy, but it had been one of love and concern. Blinking back tears, Maggie gave the maid a hug. 'Very well,' she conceded, letting go the last of her anger. 'But no contacting her in future, without letting me know first!'

'As long as you're doing what's best for you,' Polly replied.

'In whose opinion?' Maggie muttered, knowing that half-concession was the best she'd get from her independent, irrepressible, but loving caretaker. 'Very well, let's get the packing finished. I can't wait to get to Huntsford!'

'Or get Mr Handsome to Huntsford,' Polly said. 'Remember, those are country folk. Promise me you won't scandalise them by carrying on while you're in the neighbourhood.'

'Under the eyes of my mother and brother?' Maggie replied. 'I haven't a discreetly hidden away house of my own to use there, you know.'

'You have Raven's Cliff.'

Maggie froze, the sudden pain so intense, it robbed her of breath. 'I couldn't go there,' she said when she could speak again. 'And I could never take…anyone else there.'

Polly looked at her, an echoing sorrow in her eyes. 'Then I am sorry to have mentioned it.' She pressed Maggie's hand, then returned to the gowns. 'You'll need to see to your papa's dinner soon. How many are to dine tonight?'

Whether she'd meant to or not, the maid's mention of her home with Robbie and the immediate anguish of remembering his loss had a cautionary effect, underscoring Aunt Lilly's warning.

She must be careful not to let herself get too close to the far-too-charming Giles Hadley. Even if she had begun to suspect he might be a man who could keep her intrigued—and tantalised—for a very long time, she couldn't bear to open herself again to the prospect of such pain.

As Aunt Lilly had said, one broken heart was enough for a lifetime.

Chapter Fourteen

A week later, anticipation buoying her up like a boat on a wave crest, Maggie sat beside Giles in the post chaise for the final leg of their journey to Huntsford. Protesting that he didn't like being cooped up in a vehicle, he had ridden most of the way beside the carriage, keeping pace by her window. But with the prospect of seeing her beloved home soon, she'd asked him to stay in the carriage, so she might point out aspects of the view as they neared the house.

He was an excellent rider, with an easy command of his various mounts, she'd noted—so not just a park-strutter, who could maintain his seat well enough to walk a job horse around Hyde Park during the fashionable hour. Although they had met in the park several times, they had never actually ridden together, so until this journey, she hadn't known what his level of horsemanship might be.

Maggie wondered whether he'd been put on his first pony before he and his mother were exiled from Abbotsweal, or whether the uncle who had sponsored him had taught him equitation, as one of the skills required of a gentleman. It had to be one or the other; an exiled woman living in a simple cottage wouldn't have possessed the means to keep a riding horse.

Not until they began the journey had she wondered whether returning to a great landed estate would be painful for him, even though Huntsford was probably quite different from Abbotsweal, nor would visiting it require meeting the estranged father who had rejected him. Amiable but rather reticent during the transit, Giles had given her no clue to his feelings.

Perhaps he was normally a quiet man, when he wasn't debating political issues. Their few long conversations had focused on that topic, and at Upper Brook Street, their time was mostly spent in conversation of a different sort. Just as she'd not known until the drive here how good a rider Giles was, she had to smile again at how ignorant she was about the man with whom she'd become so quickly intimate.

But she would not have postponed intimacy for an instant in order to get to know him better.

A dearly familiar stretch of road outside the carriage window brought her back to the present. A few moments later, the carriage passed through Huntsford's elaborate iron gates and entered the Long Drive through the parkland.

Maggie clutched Giles's sleeve. 'Watch, now,' she said, pointing out the window on his side of the carriage. 'As soon as we round the next curve, you'll have a view of Huntsford in the distance.'

Almost as she spoke, peering around his shoulder as he turned to the window, she made out the brick-gabled outline of her beloved family home. As they did every time she returned, no matter how short her time away, her spirits soared with a thrill of gladness.

'Tudor brick work, isn't it?' Giles asked, watching the

vista pass before them, before the road took them back into the shelter of the Home Woods.

'Yes, an ancestor who was one of Queen Elizabeth's courtiers gave it that Tudor façade, but inside, it's a hodge-podge—medieval Great Hall, Tudor antechambers, and a new wing behind the façade added by my grandfather in the Georgian style, rooms with larger windows and French doors that open to the garden.'

'It sounds quite impressive. You'll have to lend me a footman for a guide, so I don't get lost on my way from my bedchamber to breakfast.' He turned back to gaze at her. 'Unless, by happy chance, our bedchambers are adjacent?'

Oh, that they might be! But to be safe, she'd instructed the staff to assign him a chamber that was a temptation-resistant distance from the family wing. 'Regretfully, no. I'm afraid we'll both have to be on our best behaviour for the duration.'

'A pity. Then I must seize what might be my last opportunity.'

With that, he tilted her chin up and claimed her mouth.

Ah, how well she knew him now, the contours of his chin and face under her exploring fingers, the wine-sweet taste of his mouth, the raspy softness of his tongue stroking hers. With the sudden realisation that it might be their last moment of privacy, by wordless consent they deepened the kiss, Maggie moving his hand to caress her breast while she dropped hers to trace the length of him, rigid under her fingertips.

And then, before she could reconsider what she was doing, Maggie slid to her knees in the cramped carriage, popped open the buttons on his trouser flap, and took him into her mouth.

Giles uttered a garbled sound and batted at her shoulder. But any motion towards stopping her quickly ceased, and a moment later, he arched his back against the cushions, giving her full access.

With the plethora of detail needing to be accomplished before he could leave London, Giles had cried off their last two mornings, and was obviously as starved as Maggie to savour the explosive attraction between them. For though she prided herself on having learned the range of touch and pressure that brought him the greatest pleasure, she needed none of that expertise for him to swiftly reach his peak.

As he subsided against the cushions, gasping, she crawled back up beside him, shaky herself with unsatisfied desire. 'No,' she whispered when his vision cleared and his eyes refocused on her. 'Don't even think of returning the favour. We're much too close to the house now.'

'What, leave you unfulfilled when you have just pleased me so thoroughly?'

'There's no time to undo my bodice, and I can't—'

Stopping her words with a kiss, Giles coaxed her lips open and began an assault on her tongue, sending her quickly back to full arousal. While she whimpered against his mouth, he laid her back on to the seat.

Kissing her still, he threaded a hand under her skirts and began caressing her leg slowly, from ankle, to knee, to thigh.

He spent a maddeningly long time running his fingers along the tender junction between leg and torso, flicking a fingertip just to the edge of her nether lips, until she was on fire and desperate for him to finally caress her there.

Squirming under him, she moved her hips, trying to bring his stroking fingers closer to the centre of her desires, aware in the dim recesses of her mind that within moments they'd be arriving at the house, a footman running up to open the carriage door…

Finally, finally, Giles eased his fingers to her slick centre. He must have been studying her, too, for he stroked right to the most sensitive place along the little nub, then into her passage, then back, until she convulsed against him.

He pulled her up into his arms, cradling her against him while her heart tried to beat its way out of her chest. Chuckling, he placed little butterfly-light kisses over her nose, her eyes, her chin, while she struggled to control her breathing and recover some semblance of wit.

A few moments later, he eased her upright on her seat, gave her a critical inspection and straightened her bonnet. 'Well, my sweet love, it appears we are about to arrive at Huntsford.'

He peered out the coach window, then pulled out his small travelling flask and offered it to her. 'Have a quick sip to settle your nerves. If my assessment of the lady's appearance is correct, I'm about to meet your mother.'

To her surprise, standing beside her brother Julian on the entry steps to welcome them was Lady Witlow. Joy—mingled with a bit of alarm—filled her at the sight of that dear face. Just what message had Papa sent to Julian, that the lady who seldom ventured further from her chamber than the morning room or its adjacent parlour had been prompted to come greet her?

And her charming guest.

Hoping Papa wasn't reading too much into her friendship with Giles, Maggie let the footman hand her out.

Julian bounded up to wrap her in a hug as Giles exited behind her. Pulling away, Maggie said, 'Lord Lyndlington, may I present my brother Julian, Lord Esterbrook.'

The two men bowed, then walked with her to where her mother awaited them on the doorstep. 'How sweet of you to greet me,' Maggie said, giving her mother a kiss, then stepping back to inspect her. 'You're looking very well, Mama. Are you feeling better?'

'How could I not feel splendid, when my dearest daughter has come for a visit? Bringing such a handsome escort, too,' she said, as Giles bowed to her.

Isn't he? Maggie thought. *And, oh, so clever with his hands.*

Gesturing to Giles, she said, 'Mama, may I present Giles Hadley, Lord Lyndlington. My mother, the Marchioness of Witlow.'

'A great pleasure, Lady Witlow. Thank you for allowing me to visit your magnificent home.'

Knowing how much the walk must have strained her mother's fragile strength, Maggie said, 'Shall we go to the morning room? Breakfast at Maidstone was hours ago! I could use some refreshment, and I dare say Lord Lyndlington could as well.'

Giles looked at her and grinned. 'It was a very... taxing journey.'

Giving him a frown, she tucked her arm in her mother's and steered her in the direction of the morning room. 'Did you stop at The Soldier's Rest?' her mother was asking Giles. 'We always found it a most excellent coaching inn.'

'Is that where you stayed when you accompanied Lord Witlow to London?' Giles asked.

With a few more questions, Giles engaged her mother in a conversation about inns, travelling, and the delights of returning home. Maggie smiled approvingly; Mama could be reticent with strangers, but Giles was doing an excellent job at drawing her out.

Her suspicion that her mother had pushed herself to

her limit was confirmed by the ever-increasing weight that lady put on her arm as they progressed. A little anxious, Maggie hurried to seat her mother on the sofa, brought a shawl for her shoulders and hunted for her favourite footstool.

'Don't fuss, Maggie,' her mother scolded gently. 'I'll be quite restored, once we have some tea. Lord Lyndlington, I understand that Julian is to show you around Huntsford and give you an idea of the workings of a large estate, such as you will manage once you inherit Abbotsweal?'

'Yes, ma'am. I'm going to Romesly later, my first visit to any part of the estate since I left it as a child.' Maggie noted how smoothly he passed over the circumstances of that departure. 'Lady Margaret was kind enough to suggest that I visit your estate and observe first-hand the most important tasks in its management, so that I can be evaluating those aspects of Abbotsweal during my visit.'

'You haven't reconciled with…'

'Regrettably, no,' Giles answered, his expression bland.

Maggie wondered at the pain, resentment and anguish that must hide behind that carefully emotionless façade. A simmering resentment of her own bubbled up that the earl couldn't have shown himself more a *man*, getting over his pique and stepping forward to heal the breach with the child who deserved no part of the blame for the estrangement of his parents.

'Are you too taxed from the journey to ride this afternoon?' Julian asked.

Avoiding Maggie's gaze, Giles said, 'I believe a bit of tea will be sufficient to revive me. We travelled all the way to Maidstone yesterday, so there would be daylight enough to see some of Huntsford after our arrival. As much as I would enjoy a longer visit, I can't afford to be gone from London more than a few days.'

'Excellent! Maggie, I thought we would ride out first to the Home Farm and show Lyndlington the cattle barns and sheep pens, then back through the oak forest. Tomorrow we can drive by some of the tenant farms, the church at Wexford and Tarney Village.'

'An excellent plan. After tea, I'll change into my habit and join you.'

So, for the next few days, Julian showed their visitor around Huntsford, explaining the purposes of different types of cattle and sheep, looking over the Home Wood's supply of oak and walnut that was harvested for building and furniture making, and explaining the crops grown on the farms. They stopped by several, Maggie greeting by name the tenants who hurried over. While the men talked of ploughs and grain and crop rotation, she enquired about the health of the family, complimented mothers on new babies, and teased children who'd grown several inches since she'd seen them the previous autumn.

After passing through hop gardens and fields of barley, past oast houses where the grains were malted for making ale and beer, they called on the vicar of the Wexford church, a Romanesque building dating from ancient times. Julian ended their tour at the village of Tarney, where they lifted a mug of home brew at the Lamb and Calf.

As her brother walked off to consult with the innkeeper, Giles raised his mug to him.

'Huntsford is a vast enterprise indeed, yet Esterbrook seems to have every detail in hand.'

'He has been working at it all his life. If you can write

and steer a complex bill though Parliament, you can master this,' she assured him.

'I don't doubt I can—eventually. But it will take time to learn it all. In the interim, I don't want to make mistakes that might injure the people I'm supposed to protect. Not to mention, I know nothing about cattle or sheep.'

'The men who tend them will know. Or you might ask your Whig colleague, Mr Coke of Norfolk—it's said he's the foremost expert on sheep breeding in England.'

'I'd heard he's a great agriculturalist. All our previous conversations have centred around politics; he's been a Foxite Whig and supporter of Parliamentary reform for years. Very well, I shall ask him.'

'So you see now why it is so important to have a skilled manager tend the land, someone who loves and is invested in it, who can oversee and co-ordinate the whole? Maybe you will be not quite so radical a Republican, ready to take it all away from the owners and distribute it to the masses.'

'A skilled manager is necessary, yes; but if the man who owns it isn't knowledgeable, or doesn't care about the welfare of his people, they might be better off if it were confiscated and parcelled out to the masses,' he countered.

Maggie shook her head and laughed. 'I don't suppose we will ever agree on that.'

Julian paced back to rejoin them. 'Maggie, would you mind if I turn you over to Lyndlington to escort you home? The village solicitor has obtained deeds for land whose ownership is being disputed by two neighbours. I should look at them.'

'Of course, Julian, I'll be fine.'

'Thank you, Esterbrook,' Giles said, shaking her brother's hand. 'These last two days have been…illuminating.'

Her brother chuckled. 'Not fair to give it all to you in one big swallow. It's much easier to take, I promise, when you can gnaw at it a bite at a time.'

'I'll keep that in mind.'

'I'll see you at dinner. Don't worry, Lyndlington— Maggie still knows the way home.' Giving her arm a pat, Julian nodded to Giles and walked off.

Their ale drunk and the afternoon light beginning to fade, Maggie headed them back to Huntsford Manor on a less-travelled route that wandered in and out of the Home Woods. They emerged a second time into the sunlight near a field of barley.

An elderly farmer hoeing at the edge of the field looked up, then trotted to the fence, hat in hand. 'Mistress Maggie, it's good to see you!'

'And you, Mr Grey! The field looks in excellent form.'

'Yes, if the weather holds fair, we should have a bountiful crop.'

'Won't you welcome Lord Lyndlington, a family friend who's come to consult with my brother? We've been riding him about Huntsford today.'

'Welcome, my lord,' Grey said. 'Will you be taking the gentleman to see your land, too, mistress?'

She closed her eyes at the sudden, sharp pain in her chest. 'Maybe on another visit,' she said after a moment. 'Lord Lyndlington's time here is rather short.

'Can you stop for some home brew?'

'Thank you, but we've just had a pint at the Lamb and Calf. If I have any more, I won't stay in the saddle long enough to make it home.'

'As you wish, mistress! Though I'd stake you in the saddle against anyone, whatever you've drunk. All those times you and the boys raced across these fields! Well,

God's blessing on you both,' the man said, doffing his cap before turning back to his hoe.

As they rode away, Giles said, 'Mr Grey treated you with surprising familiarity. Sure you're not secretly a Republican at heart?'

'Hardly! Farmer Grey has known me since I was a tot, mounted in front of Papa as he rode about visiting the tenants.' Maggie laughed. 'I had to get you away before he recounted any embarrassing episodes from my misspent youth.'

'Riding *ventre à terre* with your boys.'

'Among other things I don't intend to confess.'

'What did he mean, "your land"?'

They'd surmounted the crest of a hill that gave a wide view over the fields and farms, strips of velvet green and burnished gold divided by the deeper hue of hedgerows and the green-shaded mix of woodland. Dismounting, Maggie dropped her reins to let the horse graze and walked to the edge of the summit, Giles following behind her.

She pointed across the valley to a hill in the far distance, where one could make out the outline of a stone manor surrounded by an embrace of woods.

'That is mine. Or rather, Robbie's—my late husband's. His father died when he was quite young, naming my father as guardian and steward over the land. We grew up together. These last few years, Julian has watched over the property for me. I haven't been able to go back since I left after Robbie's death.'

Giles stood quietly, watching her, and she made herself go on. 'They brought him back to the manor after... after the carriage accident.' She closed her eyes, trying to shut out the memory of the bloody, mangled body that had been her last glimpse of him.

'His injuries were…'

'Catastrophic.'

'I'm so sorry. Bad enough to lose him, but like that—'

She nodded. 'I felt as if someone had tried to rip my heart out through my throat. There was such a weight on my chest, I couldn't breathe. Even thinking of going back to that house, where we were so happy—the old sensation returns, and I can't force any air into my lungs.' She laughed shortly and shook her head. 'Silly, I know, but there it is.'

'It never gets much easier, does it? When one loses… someone dear, one goes through life as if walking through London on a foggy morning—the shapes and patterns recognisable, familiar, and yet somehow…distant.'

She nodded. 'One goes through the motions of life, without ever feeling a part of it.' She looked up to catch his gaze. 'Except with you. That's the gift you given me, even greater than the pleasure, which has been treasure enough. When you touch me, for the first time in a long time, I feel fully alive. Thank you for that.'

He reached over to take her hand and kissed it.

'It's a gift you've returned in full measure.'

He looked for a moment as if he would say more. Maggie held her breath, waiting, but when he said nothing further, she chastised herself for a fool.

He didn't need to say anything more. She wouldn't really want to hear it.

'Even when I chide you about matters that are none of my business?' she asked at last.

'Even then. I needed to be chided, whether or not I appreciated it at the time.'

'What will you do now?'

'I'm not sure. This visit has certainly shown I need to learn a great deal more about Abbotsweal, and to do that, I must spend time there. If I nose about Hampshire without calling on the earl, it will look like I'm sneaking behind his back, afraid of him, or trying to tweak his nose by inserting myself into estate business before I have the right. I'm not afraid of Telbridge, but neither have I any desire to meet with him. However, it looks more and more like I must.'

Maggie nodded, pleased that he'd come to the conclusion she'd reached at the outset. 'Can you be civil?'

Giles laughed. 'Davie says I have the hottest temper of all the Hellions, and I'm afraid he's right. But I'll do my best.'

Maggie bit her tongue on an offer to accompany him. How she wanted him to learn and love the land that was to be his! But it wasn't her place to go with him as peacemaker; there was nothing official between them that gave her such a right, much as she might wish to help smooth things over.

She needed to stop thinking herself into his life, and limit herself to the friendship they shared. 'Maybe you should ask Davie to go with you.'

'I'd prefer to take someone else,' he said, giving her a significant look, 'but doing so would occasion too much comment. I might consider asking Davie—if it wouldn't make things worse with the earl from the outset, my bringing with me as advocate to the mighty earl's house the humble son of a farmer.'

'The earl need only know he's a standing member of Parliament,' Maggie replied. 'But the sun's nearly down; we should get back. I shall need to wash and change, and if I'm late for dinner, I'll earn one of Polly's scolds.'

'Your maid again? She sounds like a tyrant!'

'Definitely. She's been with me since I was so young, she's used to ruling with an iron fist.' Maggie paused, thinking ruefully of the discovery she'd made the week before. 'But I can't resent it—she truly does look out for my good. It was Polly who insisted I come back to London and start running Papa's household again after… after Robbie died. She practically dragged me back into life single-handedly.'

'If she had not, I would never have met you. I must leave her a generous vail.'

Leading their mounts, they walked back to the trail. As Giles paused to help her remount, she spied a clump of her favourite wildflowers on the verge. 'The first rose campion of the season! I must bring some home.'

'Did you pick your mama posies as a child?' he asked.

'Of course! Didn't you?'

'Always.'

While Giles held the reins of her mount, Maggie bent down to pluck a handful of stems. An instant later, she heard the blast of a pistol shot, a fiery whoosh of air right above her head, and a soft thud as the ball buried itself in the tree behind her.

Chapter Fifteen

Watching with horror as a shot streaked through the air where Maggie's head had just been, Giles dropped the reins of the startled, rearing horses, grabbed Maggie and dragged her into the woodland, pushing her down behind the trunk of an ancient oak and covering her with his body. His heart racing, he peered around the tree in the direction of the shot.

He saw and heard nothing—no thrashing and snap of branches, no swaying of tree limbs as someone pushed their way back into the undergrowth.

'What could that have been?' he whispered. 'A poacher?'

'I don't think so,' she replied as softly, squirming to a sitting position behind his protective body. 'It was a pistol shot, wasn't it?'

'Yes.'

'A poacher's mainstay is lairs and traps. A pistol would be too expensive for a farmer or cottager to own.'

'You're right,' he realised suddenly. 'None of the families on the downs where I grew up had one. Ben, who served with the army, told me his rifles were all hand-made, the best from a skilled gunsmith who left his mark, and quite expensive. But if it wasn't a poacher... Stay here and stay down!' he commanded.

He darted across the trail and into the woods in the direction from which the shot had come. This time, he heard a faint rustling in the far distance, and stealthily made his way towards the sound. If the weapon had been a pistol, it couldn't have been fired from very far away.

Almost at once, he came upon a place where the branches had been bent back, the ferns on the ground trampled. Looking back towards the trail, he had a clear line of sight to where he and Maggie had been standing.

A shiver running through him at the implications, he looked all around, trying to find the perpetrator's trail. Studying the ground closely, he found a trace of boot prints, and followed them onward...to a series of shallow and then deeply cut hoofprints that showed a horse had set off at a gallop in the direction from which it had come.

He'd never be able to catch up to them on foot. Convinced that whoever had fired on them was now far away, Giles abandoned any attempt at concealment. Picking up his pace, he continuing past where the deeper fresh prints cut out of the woods to follow the shallower hoofprints—which showed that the rider had been shadowing them along the trail, keeping just out of sight under the cover of the trees.

Having learned all he was going to, Giles retraced his steps. To his exasperation, if not surprise, when he emerged from the woods, he saw Maggie waiting on the opposite verge, the reins of their mounts in hand.

At his raised eyebrows, she explained, 'I thought it would be better to track down the horses, in case we needed to get away quickly. They did run in the opposite direction from which the shot came.'

'Unless the shooter had gone in the direction they fled.'

She shook her head, unwilling to concede the point. 'Then the horses would have run another way. Horses are intelligent like that. Besides, a pistol only holds one shot.'

'And can be reloaded.'

'I ran. And I didn't run in a straight line. Robbie always told me it's hard to hit a moving target. But will you stop arguing, and tell me what you discovered?'

Giving up the point, he said, 'It appears someone was following us.'

She paled as the implications registered. 'But who, why? I can't imagine anyone wishing to do me harm.'

Giles chuckled. 'You did just refuse George's suit, didn't you?

Instead of laughing at his joke, her face clouded.

'What?' he asked sharply.

'Well…' she said slowly, 'He did threaten me when I refused him.'

'He *threatened* you?' Giles echoed, incredulous.

'Yes,' she admitted. 'When I gave him his *congé*, he was…quite ugly, as you'd warned me he might be. He went so far as to say that if I allied myself with you, I would put myself in danger.'

Remorse, chagrin, fury and shame churned in him. 'Why did you never tell me?'

She shrugged. 'I thought it the rant of a spoiled child denied his sweetmeat. But you can't really think…?'

'I would hate to think it! But neither can we afford to rule it out.' Sickened by the possibility, he tried to push it out of his mind and concentrate on what must be done. 'A man with pistol would have to be hired; he would likely not be local, and therefore he might be traced. But first, we must get you safely back to the manor and keep you there. No more riding out in the open.'

'You can't mean to keep me trapped in my own house!'

He held out his hands to give her a leg up. 'We can debate that later. Now, let's get back to Huntsford.'

He threw her into the saddle and remounted. 'Take us back the fastest way, at the fastest pace possible.'

'There's a path down this trail that goes straight back to the stables. Can't do more than a trot on that.'

'Lead the way.'

The pound of cantering hoofs and then the necessity of going single file on the path put an end to any further conversation.

Not until they'd turned their horses over to a groom, did Maggie speak again.

'You're going to tell my brother, aren't you?'

'I think we have to, though we will spare your mother, if you wish. I'd like Esterbrook's assistance in deciding how best to protect you while we try to figure out who did this.'

Maggie sighed. 'So I'm to be hidden away like a bottle of laudanum concealed in the pantry, while you two figure it out?'

'You can certainly help with the figuring, but it would be foolish for you to go about, putting yourself at risk. I'm sure your Polly will agree.'

Maggie shuddered. 'If Polly finds out, she'll lock me in my chamber and sit at my door with a kitchen knife. But promise me, no conferring about all this without me in attendance. I'm not some package for you men to dispose of.'

Giles stopped and looked at her. Could she even imagine how precious she was to him? 'Hardly a package,' he replied gruffly. 'But consider how I feel! Just the possibility that George might be behind the attack sickens me. I castigate myself for arrogance and selfishness in casually dismissing his malice, so I could do what I wanted. Have what I wanted. You, regardless of the consequences.'

'It was what I wanted, too,' she answered softly. 'If it *is* George—still a very large "if", you must concede—we will face those consequences together.'

Hearing her repeat the possibility out loud just hung another leaden weight of guilt on him. His chest tight with the anger and remorse, he said, 'I should have broken with you the night he accosted me at Brooks's.'

'Then I would have had to track you down and seduce you in your rooms. Where Davie would have discovered us, and only think what a scandal that would have been!'

When he could not make himself respond to her attempt at lightness, she tilted his chin down until she could look him in the eye. 'Giles, I'm a part of this, too. It's not all your responsibility.'

'You didn't know how vicious he can be.'

'You don't know for sure he's involved.'

Giles shook his head. 'No. But I've got a bad feeling in my gut.'

'Whatever the cause, we'll find out and put a stop to it. I'm not about to meekly submit to coercion and give up the best thing that's come my way since…for a very long time, because of your idiot of a brother. Not unless or until you tell me you don't want it any more.'

Caution, regret and his sense of responsibility urged him to say just that. 'Would you believe it if I told you so?'

She shook her head. 'Not now. At this moment, I would only think you were being stupidly chivalrous and annoyingly high-handed, making that decision "for my own good". For however long we both want to be together, we will *be* together.' She held out her hand. 'Agreed?'

Suddenly it struck him that after being fired upon and learning the attack was probably deliberate, most females would have swooned or dissolved into hysterics. His fierce Maggie looked angry, annoyed, and ready to ride down the perpetrator all by herself.

'What a marvel you are,' he murmured, and seized her for a kiss.

He let her go after the merest brush of their lips— they were much too close to the house for more—but that fleeting taste left him ravenous.

No, he wasn't ready, either, to bow to coercion and give her up.

As long as he could keep her safe.

For now, there would be no more tasting. Not until he figured out what was going on—and, he hoped with all his soul, confirmed that it was not because of him that she'd come into danger.

He couldn't bear the thought he might be responsible for bringing harm to yet another woman he cared for.

In a sombre mood, they returned to the house. As soon as he reached his bedchamber, Giles penned a note to his host, asking that they meet before dinner to discuss an urgent matter. When the footman he'd dispatched to deliver it returned with a reply, inviting him for a brandy in the Blue Parlour as soon as he was dressed for dinner, he wrote another to Maggie, informing her about the rendezvous.

She was already in the parlour with her brother when a footman guided him there. 'Maggie told me what happened,' Esterbrook said as he handed Giles a brandy, his expression troubled. 'I've agreed it's unlikely the assailant could have been a poacher with bad aim. If he wasn't from the county—and I can't imagine anyone around Huntsford being persuaded to fire at Maggie, regardless of how lucrative the inducement—someone probably will have noticed him. Strangers are pretty rare, here in the country. I'll ride out to the farms and villages tomorrow and send messengers to all those I can't reach, asking if anyone has seen someone lurking about.'

'If I ride south, across the downs, while you ride north through the forested part, we could cover more ground,' Maggie said, holding up a hand to forestall the men's instantaneous protest. 'Giles, you admitted yourself that a pistol would have to be fired at close range, and the fields there are very open. I'd be able to see anyone in the area while still well out of range.'

'Out of the question!' Giles replied. 'Just because the shooter used a pistol today doesn't mean he might not also have a rifle.'

'Then I'll bring along some of the dogs. If there's anyone within a thousand yards, they'll sniff him out and give the alarm. Surely that's far enough away for me to be safe.'

When he and Julian looked at each other and gave their heads a negative shake, Maggie said with exasperation, 'You can't expect me to just sit here cooped up and do nothing! Besides, how are you going to explain to Mama that you two went out riding, and I decided to stay at Huntsford? She'll never believe I suddenly developed a taste for sewing samplers! And I absolutely don't want her worried about this.'

'Couldn't you say you needed to—oh, I don't know, inspect the still room or something?' Julian said.

'Why would I need to look at the still room, or the silver, or the attics, during a visit that is only supposed to last a few days? And you know I'm a terrible liar.'

Julian sighed. 'That's true enough. I'm not much better at it—not with Mama. It probably would be wise to keep you away from her.'

'You could ride with me, Giles,' Maggie said, with a look of appeal. 'The shooter must know that after the failed attempt, we will be looking for him. If he's a stranger, he must also know he will stand out. My guess is that he won't chance making another try. It's just too risky—even the attempt is a hanging offence, after all. If you consider the circumstances dispassionately, the danger to me is small.'

'I would prefer the danger to be "zero",' Giles said flatly.

Maggie shook her head. 'Life itself makes that impossible! I could be thrown by a spooked horse, or hit by a falling tree limb, or trip on the stairs. Be reasonable!'

'And do it your way?' Julian said wryly. 'I have to admit, Lyndlington, what Maggie says is probably true. If I were the miscreant, I'd be halfway to London or Dover by now.'

'So we'll ride out tomorrow, together, with the dogs?' Maggie asked.

Julian looked at him. Giles wanted to insist she stay home—he'd like to lock her in a windowless inner room with three stout footmen outside to guard the door, until they learned who had fired at her today and why. But if her brother, who knew the countryside and its residents much better than he did, agreed the risk of her riding out was acceptable, he supposed he'd have to bow to their wishes.

There was the problem of keeping the incident from her mother, which, he conceded, would be rather difficult if she were locked in a room with footmen guarding the door.

'Very well,' he said at last. 'I still don't like it. You'd better tell all your outriders, if anyone she doesn't recognise even looks like they are riding in her direction, I'm going to blow a hole through them first and ask questions later.'

Maggie shook her head at him. 'Very well, we'll send out a warning. Just don't shoot one of my dogs.'

That settled, they went into dinner, a tense affair for Giles as he tried to respond with appropriate lightness to the banter she and her brother maintained to avoid having Lady Witlow sense that something was wrong. To his relief, the ladies left them to their brandy immediately after the sweet course, and he could finally relax.

He and Julian shared another brandy in solemn silence. 'You're sure she won't be in danger tomorrow?' Giles asked.

'Sure enough not to try to stop Maggie doing what she wants,' Esterbrook said. 'Besides, I know how I'd feel, left to twiddle my thumbs, and there is the matter of concealing things from Mama. Maggie so rarely comes to Huntsford while Parliament is in session, Mama would find it very odd for us not to spend the day together, if she doesn't ride out. Dinner tonight was enough of a strain; I'd not ask Maggie to have to prevaricate for the entire day. If I'm wrong…' He shuddered. 'I don't even want to contemplate being wrong.'

'Nor do I,' Giles said sombrely. Especially since, if anything did happen to her, it would almost certainly be his fault.

Chapter Sixteen

The skies dawned clear the next morning, with an excellent visibility that made Giles feel a bit better. At least he'd not need to worry about fog or mist veiling a miscreant. They breakfasted early, since there was a great deal of territory to cover, agreeing to meet before supper at the Lamb and Calf in Tarney to share what they'd discovered.

Maggie seemed entirely unconcerned as they rode out, calling to the dogs and laughing at their high-spirited antics. She sat relaxed in the saddle as they rode across the open downs, identifying the first farmer they encountered from far enough away that Giles relaxed the hand he'd been keeping on his pistol.

They waited for the man to approach, and after a warm exchange of greetings—it appeared she *did* know every farmer, tradesman and tenant at Huntsford by name—she related the story they'd invented about a problem with a poacher shooting birds in the marsh.

The farmer frowned. 'Don't see why there'd be poaching, mistress. Lord Esterbrook is always good about giving permission, if anyone wants to go out after birds. Besides, none I know but the squire, and such gentry as his lordship invites, go out with guns.'

Maggie nodded. 'Yes, we're pretty sure whoever it is doesn't live on Huntsford land. You haven't seen any strangers about, have you? Asking directions to the village, or for a drink of water on his journey?'

'We get a few pilgrims from time to time, lost or misdirected on their way to Canterbury, but nobody in the last several months. Sorry I can't help, Lady Margaret. Don't need nobody out there, shooting willy-nilly.'

'We certainly do not! Thank you, and please do keep an eye out.'

The farmer assured them he would, they said their goodbyes, Maggie called the dogs to order and they set off down the road.

They visited half-a-dozen farms that morning, but none of the farmers or their families or labourers had seen anything amiss. After stopping for bread and ale at the inn in the village of Hillendon, they inspected another dozen farms over the afternoon.

Finally, Maggie pulled up her mount, Giles reining in his horse beside her. 'What is it?' he asked, his anxiety instantly ratcheting up.

Obviously reading the tension in his face, she sighed. 'We've found nothing all day, Giles. Couldn't you relax now, and enjoy the ride? We have this very rare chance to spend the whole day together. Don't waste it fretting! I know,' she said, raising a hand to stop him before he could speak. 'You feel somehow responsible for the attack. But you shouldn't. And in any event, by now we can be reasonably sure that whatever danger there might have been, it's now over.'

'You are probably right,' he admitted. 'But as long as there is even a small chance, I can't let down my guard.'

'Would you try, for me?' she coaxed. 'If I did get

shot, I'd hate to think the last day we had together wasn't joyful.'

'Don't even say that!' he snapped, unable to appreciate her attempt at humour.

'Very well. I shouldn't tease you to talk with me. I wondered on the drive down if you were naturally a quiet man, not speaking unless the topic under discussion was a matter about which you are passionate, like your politics. Not that I mind!

'Robbie and I often shared quiet evenings together, reading or playing cards, without the need for constant chatter.'

He laughed. 'I can promise I won't give you that. I spent far too much time alone growing up, with only myself and the dogs for company. Not that *I* minded. There were endless wonders for an inquisitive boy to explore, and I needed nothing more than a pole, some line, and a stream to keep me happy. I do wonder how my mother endured it. She had been raised in a fine house with servants, then married into an even grander one, where family and guests milled about and entertainments went on constantly.'

'Did she like to chat?'

Giles thought back, then shook his head. 'I can hardly remember her having callers, and she certainly never paid calls. She liked to read, and she painted—watercolours. I don't know where she got the books and supplies that sometimes appeared. Perhaps her sister sent them. None of her family ever visited us, though.'

His anger over that slight still smouldered, hotter perhaps because he'd not known he *should* be angry until much later.

'Too intimidated by the earl?' she suggested.

'Or too guilty, after accepting Telbridge's blood money.

My aunt told me the earl settled all the family's extensive debts when they married.' He sighed. 'But I shouldn't castigate them too much. To a small boy too self-absorbed to be inquisitive, Mama seemed happy to me.'

'I'm sure she was. She had her son.'

Something Maggie never had, Giles thought suddenly. It must be a great grief and an added source of regret that the husband she'd loved so deeply had not given her a child.

One of the dogs darted off after a rabbit, and with an apologetic look, Maggie rode off to fetch him.

What would it be like to have a son? he thought curiously at he watched her chase after the hound. Would being with the child of the woman he loved be enough to keep him content, living in a remote cottage on the Hampshire downs?

Maybe—if it were the right woman, he thought, smiling at Maggie, who laughed as she herded the errant pup back to the group.

Though he hardly had the right to consider such a thing, after putting her in danger.

As his very existence had caused his mother's ruin. Maybe George had been right about taunting him after all.

Some hours later, having found out nothing, Giles and Maggie rode into Tarney to meet with Esterbrook at the Lamb and Calf. The excitement in his bearing as they walked in told them immediately that he must have learned something useful.

'What did you discover?' Giles asked as soon as innkeeper moved out of earshot.

'Farmer Adams told us he saw a man he didn't recognise riding back and forth along the section of trail the two of you rode yesterday. Mr Williford, the innkeeper here, says he served a stranger in the taproom day before yesterday. He's given us a description of the man, and the ostler at the stable identified his horse, a black-and-tan gelding. Williford said he returned here in the late afternoon yesterday, in a tearing rush. Declining an offer of supper, he asked for his horse to be rubbed down, then set off.'

'Excellent!' Giles said, both relieved that the man was gone, and anxious to catch up to him. 'Did he mention his destination to anyone?'

'Unfortunately, no. But the ostler said he took the London road. I've already sent one of my grooms after him on my fastest horse, armed with a description of rider and mount, to see if he can pick up the trail.'

'There must be hundreds travelling that road,' Maggie said.

'If someone hired him out of London, he'll most likely return there.'

'Yes,' Maggie said. 'To a metropolis that shelters thousands.'

'True, but finding him might be easier than you'd think,' Giles said. 'He's certainly not gentry, and if he accepted a task like this, he probably resides in one of the shadier parts of the city—Seven Dials, maybe. Even there, he might stand out. He's not just a petty thief or housebreaker—he knows how to ride and can handle a weapon. Might even be a former soldier. I'll contact a friend who has connections with Bow Street; they might suggest someone we could hire to ferret him out. Lady Margaret, it would probably be best if you remain here while we investigate.'

Maggie looked at him in exasperation. 'And just how are we to keep my mother from learning about the incident if I stay at Huntsford? With debate raging over the Reform Bill, and Papa busier than ever with the meetings and dinners, she'd think it extremely odd for me to linger in the country. I won't hear of taxing her limited strength by having her worry about my safety. I shall return to London as planned.'

Neither Giles nor Esterbrook could argue with her desire to protect her mother. 'Maybe you should return to London, to keep from upsetting Mama,' her brother agreed.

'Even so, I don't think it wise for you to resume your hostess duties,' Giles said, conceding reluctantly.

'You think some assassin is going to sneak in with the dinner guests?' Maggie asked with a grin. 'Highly unlikely, I assure you.'

'True, our assassin would never pass as a guest,' Giles replied patiently, 'but he might gain access to the stable or the kitchen by posing as a guest's groom or coachman, or as a lackey from a supplier bringing ices or crab or champagne for a dinner.'

'You're right, Lyndlington,' Esterbrook said, looking troubled. 'Once Papa is acquainted with the circumstances, he'll probably forbid Maggie from acting as hostess anyway.'

'I still can't remain at Huntsford,' Maggie insisted. Then her eyes brightened. 'Why don't I stay with Aunt Lilly? Mama wouldn't have to know I'm not at Papa's. I could still co-ordinate his events from her house, much as it will pain me not to act as hostess. We'd use only our own footmen as messengers back and forth, and all the supplies would be delivered to Cavendish Square.'

'That might work,' Esterbrook said, looking encouraged.

'Aunt Lilly would continue to attend entertainments,' Maggie said. 'She hears all the gossip, so although I still cannot imagine who might wish to do me harm, if someone in the *ton* were behind it, she would be more likely than anyone I know to hear the rumours. Though I warn you, I don't intend to live in isolation for ever, so you'd better figure out what happened quickly! Well?' She looked from her brother to Giles and back.

'It seems as good a plan as any,' Esterbrook said. 'Will it do, Lyndlington?'

Giles still preferred the windowless room with three armed footmen outside...but that was as impractical as letting her remain at Huntsford. 'I wish I could think of something more secure...but I suppose that will have to do until I can. But no going out—not to a *musicale* at a friend's, not to pick up some item for the night's entertainment that Lord Witlow's housekeeper forgot. No morning rides in the park.'

She looked at him, stricken. 'No rides?'

'Certainly not!' her brother said. 'If it's dangerous to ride at Huntsford, it's even more so in the city, where there are buildings and alleyways all along the route to conceal a miscreant!'

'No visits to Upper Brook Street?' she asked, watching Giles.

'Regrettably, that would not be prudent,' he said, only that moment realising the full implications of her confinement.

'That will be a grievous loss indeed,' she said quietly. 'And, I devoutly hope, a temporary one.'

'I hope so, too,' he said fervently.

'I'll ride in the coach with you back to London,' Esterbrook said. 'I can easily find an excuse for the trip that will satisfy Mama. I'll send some of our footmen to Aunt Lilly's, too—I'll tell her Papa needs them. They can provide extra eyes to watch over the stables and the kitchens.'

'I'll ride outside the coach,' Giles said. 'How soon can you leave?'

'Let me check with the estate agent to make sure there is no other pressing business; otherwise, I could be ready day after tomorrow.'

Giles nodded. 'That will give me time to send a note to my friend in London.' He turned to Maggie. 'So we can clear this matter up speedily, and let you return to your normal life.'

'I surely hope so,' she said. 'It will be hard to be away when Papa needs me—and not be able to visit Upper Brook Street.'

It was going to be bitterly difficult for him as well, Giles thought.

Esterbrook finished his ale. 'If we're agreed on the details, I must visit that land agent. Maggie, I'll see you at dinner tonight. Lyndlington, walk with me a moment, won't you?'

Once they were out of the taproom, where his sister could not overhear them, Esterbrook said, 'Whoever had the audacity to target Maggie, I want him found.'

'You can't want that any more than I do,' Giles replied.

'I want him found, and I want to know why—for I find it incomprehensible.'

Unfortunately, Giles knew one possible assailant whose motives were all too understandable.

'It will take a number of men to canvass a city the size of London. I want you to hire as many as Bow Street recommends. I'll transfer funds into an account at my bank for you to draw on—'

'Please, that won't be necessary. I can fund this.'

Esterbrook shook his head. 'I appreciate the offer, but Maggie is my sister—*my* responsibility. Besides, in your present situation, I imagine your funds are more… limited.'

'I still can't allow you—' Giles began.

'But you will,' Esterbrook interrupted, for the first time acting like the landed autocrat he was.

Esterbrook could make funds available. He couldn't make Giles use them. 'Very well.'

'Good.' Esterbrook gazed into Giles's eyes. 'I'm depending on you to keep her safe, Lyndlington.'

'I'd rather die than see her harmed.'

Esterbrook nodded, a glimmer of a smile on his lips. 'I rather thought so. Very well, I'll see you at dinner.'

Soon after, Giles and Maggie collected the dogs from the stables and left the Lamb and Calf. Once they were away from the village, she said, 'Now that we know for certain there's no danger at Huntsford, let's enjoy the ride home—especially,' she added with a grimace, 'since it will apparently be the last ride I have for some time. I don't want to be foolhardy, but being cooped up at Aunt Lilly's will be very difficult.'

'I'll send you some books.'

'You will call, won't you, and keep me informed? Even though we can't…indulge in anything more satisfying than conversation, while I'm stuck under my great-aunt's roof.'

'We won't be indulging in anything more satisfying until this matter is cleared up for good and all,' he said flatly.

Maggie sighed. 'Why is it that while I didn't do anything, I feel like *I'm* the one being punished?'

If it turned out George was responsible, *he* was the one who should be punished—for ignoring the possible danger, and proceeding anyway. 'Try to think of it as safe refuge, rather than punishment. And know that I won't rest until we uncover the truth.'

They rode on in silence, Maggie taking a trail through the forest, rather than proceeding back across the open downs. Once under the cover of the leafy canopy, she pulled up her mount.

Immediately concerned, Giles reined in beside her. 'What is it? Do you hear something?'

'No. The dogs would let us know if anyone or anything were lurking in the woods.' She slid off the saddle and dropped the horse's reins. 'If I'm going to be incarcerated *and* deprived for the indefinite future, with Julian at my side all the way back to London, I at least need one final kiss.'

He was on his feet in an instant, drawing him to her, all his frustration and roiling guilt and worry over her safety intensifying the passion of his kiss. She replied in kind, apparently as voracious and driven as he was.

The dogs milling curiously about their feet, Giles kissed her until they were both panting for breath. 'Curse those hounds!' he gasped.

She chuckled unevenly. 'Bringing them was a good idea at the outset. Now, however... If I tried to do what I'd like to do, they'd be all over me.'

'Or me, I if went down on my knees.'

She turned him so his back was against the trunk of an ancient oak. 'Oh, I wish,' she whispered, looking like temptation itself with her lips red from his kiss, her gaze passionate and her face hot under his caressing fingers.

'What?' he whispered.

'It would be so easy... Unbutton your trouser flap. Pull up my skirts. Have you lean back and pick me up, so I could wrap my legs around your waist and rock into you. Rock you into me.'

Listening to her naughty scenario made his member surge. The idea of taking her, finally tasting full possession, was so intoxicating, it required every bit of self-control he could muster not to urge her to act out what she'd just described.

While he wavered, fighting temptation, he felt her fingers stroking him, tugging at his trouser buttons. Control unravelling, of their own volition his hands reached for her skirts, began shimmying them up her legs.

Then one of the hounds jumped up, knocking her away from him. He steadied her before she fell, both of them gazing at each other, their panting breaths the only sound in the wilderness.

'Faithful, indeed,' she murmured, stepping back to shake out her skirts. 'It's his name,' she explained, rubbing the hound behind his ears. 'Thank heavens he was there to keep me from catastrophe! Now that we are both thoroughly frustrated, we'd better return. It's a feeling we—or at least I—will have to get accustomed to.'

Not sure whether he wanted to toss the hound a bone or shoot him, Giles walked Maggie back to the horses and helped her remount.

'Goodbye, my lover,' she said. 'Please, may it not be long before I can say "hello" again.' With that, she kicked her mare to a trot.

'Amen to that,' Giles muttered, and followed after her.

Chapter Seventeen

In the early evening three days later, after seeing Maggie safely to the door of her great-aunt's town house, Giles returned to his rooms at Albany. Before he bathed and changed, he sent their man-of-all-work to the Quill and Gavel in search of Davie with a note requesting that his friend join him as soon as possible.

By the time he'd washed and dressed, Phillips returned with the welcome news that Mr Smith would follow him directly.

Giles poured himself a brandy and sipped it, pacing impatiently until at last he heard Davie's step in the hallway.

'Welcome back to London,' his friend said, holding out his hand to shake. 'I hope you had an instructive visit to Huntsford. Was this summons designed to avoid, for the present, the ribbing sure to be directed at you by Ben and Christopher for having sojourned at the home of the lovely Lady Margaret?'

Davie's teasing tone faded as he looked up at Giles's face. 'No, I can see it's more serious.'

'Didn't you get my note?' Giles asked.

'No, but frankly, we've been so busy the last few days I've hardly been back to Albany. Shall I look for it?'

'Never mind,' Giles replied, shrugging off his annoyance. Fortunately, he had new information that should make up for the delay in Davie's not having read his earlier missive.

'I'm sorry, Giles. Pour me some of that brandy, and tell me all about it.'

Just the presence of his quiet, meticulous, competent friend lightened Giles's anxiety. If anyone could help him clear the muddy waters of this mystery, it was Davie.

When they were both seated with glasses in hand, Giles said, 'It would have been merely an instructive visit to Huntsford. Except that, while we were out riding, someone took a shot at Lady Margaret—and came within a hair's breadth of hitting her.'

'Hell and the devil!' Davie exclaimed. 'Did you find the man?'

'No,' Giles said grimly. 'I found tracks that indicated he'd been shadowing us for some time, under cover of the woods. When we dismounted, he had a clear line of fire—and took it. By the time I found his trail, he'd galloped off. Lady Margaret, her brother, Lord Esterbrook, and I made an exhaustive canvass of the area the following day, and discovered that a stranger who left by the London road had passed through the local village. Esterbrook sent a groom after him with a description. We learned just as we reached the city tonight that the groom had in fact picked up the trail, and tracked the man back to London.'

'Excellent! Does the groom have any idea where he went after he arrived?'

'The innkeeper where he stopped just outside the city said the man told him he'd send the horse back from the

Green Dragon in Seven Dials. He's been using the name "Teddy Godfrey", by the way. Now we need to find him, and I'm hoping you can direct me to the right people to help me look.'

Davie shook his head. 'Why would anyone want to shoot Lady Margaret? Granted, there have been Swing Riots in the countryside around Manchester, Liverpool and Leeds, even some houses of the aristocracy burned, but nothing in her area. Witlow is known as a fair and concerned landlord who looks after his land and his tenants. Although,' he continued, his voice troubled, 'she has campaigned for Tories in areas that are far more volatile. Still, I can't imagine any radical, no matter how extreme, targeting a *female.*'

'It may be worse than that,' Giles said, guilt and anger scouring him anew. 'After the attack, when I jokingly teased her about having refused George's suit—which, by the way, she did—she told me after she rejected him, he threatened her.'

Davie waved a hand. 'Surely that was just George being George, frustrated at being denied something he wanted. You don't seriously think he would *harm* her for refusing him?'

'I don't know what to think. I certainly hope not. That would make it worse.'

Davie, ever perceptive, understood immediately. 'Yes, I see. Knowing how George can be, you'd feel responsible for not avoiding her after George quarrelled with you over her.'

'It's too late to change that now. All I can do to redeem myself is figure out as quickly as possible who was behind the attack.' He grimaced. 'I would have preferred to incarcerate her in an inner room at Huntsford, but both she and her brother insisted that leaving her there while we deal with the threat would make it impossible to hide the incident from her mother, whom they don't wish to upset—she's in delicate health. As a compromise, Lady Margaret has returned to London, but will remain in seclusion at the home of her great-aunt, Lady Sayleford.'

'At least she'll hear all the latest gossip. How can I help?'

'I remember you told me when you first met your mentor, Sir Edward, in Hazelwick, you helped rescue Lady Greaves—she wasn't Lady Greaves then—from the radical who kidnapped her, working with a prosecutor and a government agent, as well as some men from Bow Street?'

'You want me to look up Mr Albertson, the Home Office man who presented the evidence to the prosecutor,' Davie said, immediately making the connection. 'But that was years ago. He's probably long retired.'

'A mention of his name should get you referred to someone of equal authority, who can recommend some agents to work undercover. We have a name, or at least an alias, an excellent description, and know the general area to which our suspect returned. With that, I'm hopeful we can turn up something.'

Davie nodded. 'There'd be a money trail, too. From what Albertson told me, agitators are usually advanced a sum up front, to fund their activities, but receive the bulk of the payoff after they complete their assignment.'

'If the task was to murder Lady Margaret, he didn't accomplish it. He might not want to meet his employer and admit that.'

'That won't wash,' Davie said, frowning. 'It's extremely unlikely anyone would be foolish enough to agree to murder the daughter of a marquess, no matter how much he was promised! He'd have to know that a person of wealth and position like Lord Witlow would never give up until he found the perpetrator—which would mean the gallows. It would make more sense if the man was only supposed to fire at her.'

'As a warning? But why—and for what? What good is a warning if you don't know what you're being warned about?'

'I didn't say I had the answers,' Davie retorted. 'But you're right; with an alias, a description and a destination, we may well be able to trace the gunman.' He tapped his finger on his glass. 'I believe Albertson's assistant, a Mr Farnworth, still works in the office; I called on him a few years ago to settle a matter for Sir Edward. I'll look for him tonight. Maybe we can get this moving forward immediately.'

Giles clapped him on the shoulder. 'Thank you, Davie. I knew I could count on you.'

His friend smiled. 'I like and admire Lady Margaret. I'm honoured to do all I can to find the man who fired on her. Just one more thing before I go.'

'Yes?'

'Are you having an affair with Lady Margaret?'

Caught off guard, Giles froze, scrambling for an answer.

Before he decided whether to confess or deny it, Davie said, 'You are, aren't you? Everything pointed to your being involved with a lady—the missed meetings, the late mornings—' Davie gave him a smile '—the air of bliss about you. Christopher and Ben are convinced of it, and you may thank me for keeping them from pestering you about it. But…I just couldn't wrap my mind around the idea of your paramour being Lady Margaret. She's always been the very model of propriety, passing up numerous opportunities for dalliance, to say nothing of offers of marriage, since her husband's death. She just…doesn't seem the sort of woman for a casual affair.'

Stung, Giles said, 'Isn't that her business?'

'And yours, not mine,' Davie agreed. 'It does explain why you feel the threat to her safety more keenly. Especially if George is involved. But don't worry, I'm not about to whisper my conclusions into the ear of anyone, even the other Hellions.' He laughed. 'Besides, it's much too amusing to listen to their daily changing theories about who your mystery lady must be.'

'Thank you for your discretion, at least,' Giles said, still irritated.

Davie nodded. 'You're welcome. I'm off to find Farnworth. Are you staying here, or going to the Quill and Gavel?'

'Here, probably. Esterbrook said he'd send word if he heard anything else, and I'm too weary to fend off questions from Ben and Christopher.'

'Probably wise, given that they know you summoned me. At the whiff of mystery, they'd tear into you for answers, like starving hounds with fresh meat.'

'I may involve them, too. Just not tonight.'

'Get some rest. You look exhausted.' Scooping up his greatcoat, Davie headed out the door.

Giles took another deep draught of his brandy. He *was* exhausted—not from the ride, for he'd ridden further, but from the need for constant vigilance that intensified every mile they got closer to London. Scanning each passer-by, rider and coachman, always watching for a hand on a weapon, even though he knew the possibility of encountering danger was slight, had taken its toll physically and mentally.

He resented the hint of disapproval in Davie's tone when he spoke of Giles's relationship with Maggie, even as it smote his conscience. By the stars in Heaven, she wasn't some innocent he'd lured away and debauched! Initially, *she* had propositioned *him*. Though he *had* coaxed her afterward to go through with it, after she'd panicked and withdrawn her offer, he recalled uncomfortably.

Davie was right, though: she wasn't the sort of woman who indulged in casual affairs. Could she be hoping for more? The thought further unsettled him. If so, she'd never even hinted about it.

If he were to marry, he couldn't think of a woman who would make a more interesting, intriguing and passionate partner. But he *wasn't* thinking of it—no matter how special Maggie was. His mother's experience of the institution hadn't inspired in him much enthusiasm or respect for it, or any desire to try it for himself.

Besides, he'd told her from the outset, with his tenuous position and limited income, a union with him could bring her nothing but harm. What a come-down, from daughter of a marquess to wife of a simple Member of Parliament!

Suddenly he recalled the disparaging remarks his half-brother had made about Maggie's age and possibilities when she'd refused his offer. Was their dalliance robbing Maggie of the chance to make an advantageous alliance while she still could, one that would provide her with companionship, passion and protection into a ripe old age?

He certainly didn't want to be the means of destroying her chances, as he had destroyed his mother's.

Even though the idea of her marrying anyone else sparked an immediate sense of outrage.

But no need to think that far ahead. All that was required now was to eliminate the threat to Maggie's safety.

With that conclusion, telling Phillips to wake him if a message came from either Davie or Esterbrook, Giles sought out his bed.

Two days later, Maggie restlessly paced the back parlour Aunt Lilly had given her for an office. She'd dispatched the notes to Papa's housekeeper and Cook about the guest list and menus for tonight's entertainment; supplies had been ordered from their usual providers. The gathering was to be a meeting of her father's closest Tory advisors, which she probably would not have played hostess for anyway.

Still, she chafed at her confinement and struggled to concentrate on the book of travels Giles had sent—reading of someone else's journeys only made her feel more imprisoned. Though she knew it wasn't prudent to risk going out, as the memory of the incident faded, she had a harder and harder time believing someone wished to harm her, and a greater and greater impatience about hiding away as if *she* were the criminal. She wasn't sure how much longer she could stand it, before she rejected all the good advice and returned to Cavendish Square to resume her life.

Would Giles then resume their liaison? She knew even the possibility that his half-brother might have been responsible for the shot fired at her had deeply shaken him. Deeply enough for him to feel he must distance himself from her? Had this unpleasant incident destroyed the sense of magic that had enveloped their relationship, making him ready to move on?

Just thinking about the possibility that he might not visit Upper Brook Street again struck her like a kick to the gut. The blow should be a salutary one, she told herself. It would probably be better if they did end this before she became any more attached—not just to the passion, but to the man.

She'd been woefully naïve in thinking she could become intimate with Giles without also gradually entangling herself deeper into his life and concerns. Wanting to assist and smooth and facilitate, where she had no right and no invitation.

Very well, she conceded, ending it sooner rather than later might be wise.

But she didn't want to end it yet.

On that stubborn resolve, her great-aunt's butler bowed himself in. 'Viscount Lyndlington to see you, Lady Margaret. I've shown him to the Great Parlour.'

Oh, how her heart's leap of gladness ought to alarm her! But too excited about seeing him to spoil the prospect with worry, she said, 'Thank you, Harris. Will you tell him I'll be there directly?'

Rushing to the mirror, she tucked an errant curl back into her *coiffure* and smoothed her gown. Too impatient to bother with any further primping, she hurried to the parlour.

'Giles, what a wonderful surprise! So you've come to check on the inmate?'

At his smile, her stomach did another happy little flip. 'Feeling restricted, are you?'

'"Restricted" hardly describes it! It reminds me of when I was ten, and was caught riding a stallion Papa had forbidden me to go near. He incarcerated me in my room on bread and water for three days.'

'Wanting to make sure you never disobeyed such an order again?'

'I was furious, though secretly I knew he was right. The stallion was a beast, and I was lucky to have made it back to the stables without breaking my neck. However, being cooped up for three days, for someone who rode for miles about the countryside every day, was a torture I've never forgotten.'

She gestured him to the sofa, savouring his closeness as she settled beside him. Oh, how she'd missed him, even more keenly than she missed her freedom!

'You'll be encouraged to learn that we've made enough progress that your liberation may be near. My colleague consulted his Home Office sources, who referred us to several Bow Street operatives. One of them has, we believe, tracked down our man. As we suspected, Godfrey's a former soldier who drifted to London after his family lost their land in the enclosures. He's been hired out on several questionable projects in the past. Hines, our Bow Street man, is going tonight to a tavern in Seven Dials Godfrey is known to frequent.' After a pause, he added, 'I'm going along.'

'You are?' Maggie said with alarm. 'Is that wise? You've no more expertise in dealing with the type of people who frequent Seven Dials than I do. How could you pass unnoticed?'

'Of course, I don't flatter myself that I could handle this on my own—rousting about on the downs as a boy is a far cry from navigating the seamier parts of London unnoticed. But I'll be roughly dressed, and will stay with another of the Bow Street men, who is to provide reinforcements for Hines, if necessary. I want to be near in case we discover…something it would be more proper for me to pursue. Because if we do, I shall pursue it immediately.'

'How I wish I could go, too!' She raised a hand to forestall his protest. 'I know that's not possible—it would be selfish, as well as imprudent, to trail along and end up deflecting Mr Hines from his mission with the need to shield me from danger. But oh, how just *waiting* chafes at me! Promise me you will return and let me know what happened—no matter how late! There's no way I will be able to sleep until I know the outcome. Until I know you are safe.'

He laid his hand over hers, and she closed her eyes, a little sigh of pleasure escaping her lips at even that small measure of contact.

'You mustn't worry, Maggie. If I end up in harm's way, it's no more than I deserve, for placing you in danger.'

'If you feel you deserve retribution for that, only think how I would feel if you were injured, trying to protect me!' she retorted.

He lifted her hand and placed a lingering kiss on it, his gaze as he raised his eyes smouldering enough to dispel her worries that he was ready to end their liaison.

'How I've missed you every morning,' she whispered.

'Not half as much as I've missed you,' he assured her.

'Then may your mission tonight go well, so we may resume our visits to Upper Brook Street.'

'Nothing would give me greater pleasure.'

He stared at her mouth, the intensity of his gaze making her lips tingle and firing her body with need. She closed her eyes and raised her chin, hoping he would follow with his lips the path of his gaze.

She sensed him leaning closer, and her senses exulted. But just as she felt the warmth of his breath and parted her lips to welcome him, he jerked away, cold air replacing that warm promise.

'I'd better go before I do something we'll both regret,' he said, his voice strained.

'Have you taken some sort of holy vow not to kiss me until this quest is completed?' she asked, aware she sounded more than a little sulky. '*You* might regret it. *I* would just enjoy it.'

'Temptress!' he said as he rose from the sofa. 'I will make you pay for teasing me…later.'

'Now that,' she replied, struggling to silence the complaints of her frustrated body, 'sounds a great deal more promising.'

She walked with him to the parlour door. 'You will call later tonight—promise me?'

He nodded. 'I promise.'

With that, she let him go. Tonight, she knew as she walked back to her study, the time would crawl more slowly than ever.

Chapter Eighteen

Maggie tried to stay calm as the night progressed, concentrating on conversing with her great-aunt at dinner, then forcing herself to scan the novel she'd told her great-aunt she intended to read when she'd insisted Aunt Lilly attend her evening entertainments as planned.

By the time her great-aunt returned after midnight, Maggie had become less and less successful at diverting herself. No longer able to concentrate, she abandoned the book to take up some cards. Quickly tiring of playing against herself, she tossed down the pasteboard in frustration and jumped up to pace about the room.

By the time the clock struck one, she was swearing oaths under her breath her great-aunt would have been shocked to discover she knew. If she'd had any idea where Giles could be found, she would have gone out in pursuit.

Finally, as the mantel clock stuck the half past one, a drowsy footman knocked at her door. 'Lady Margaret, there's a gentleman begging to see you. I told him it was—'

'Show him in at once,' she cut the lad off, so relieved she exhaled in a rush that left her dizzy. With her next breath, she vowed she would throttle Giles for making her wait so long.

But the tart words died on her tongue when the door opened to admit, not Giles, but his friend David Tanner Smith.

Fear like an icy hand clutched her heart. 'What happened? Where is Giles?'

'Don't worry!' he assured her. 'He's hurt—but not seriously,' he added at her gasp. 'I'm so sorry you had to wait so long. Apparently after Hines left the inn, Godfrey and some others circled behind them as they made their way out of Seven Dials. Giles sustained a knife wound to his hand, but is otherwise unharmed—he gave as good as he got, he told me. He's already had a doctor clean the wound and bandage it.'

'Thank Heaven for that!' Maggie cried, glad for the doctor's treatment, but not at all reassured that the result would not be serious. A knife puncture could fester, become inflamed...

'Unbeknownst to Giles,' Smith continued, 'the doctor slipped some laudanum in the wine he gave him as a restorative. He'd written you a note—badly, with his left hand—but fell asleep before he could instruct Phillips to deliver it, and only woke up when I came in. Knowing by now you'd probably be frantic, I offered to come in person and reassure you, since a note written in a wobbly hand that admitted he'd been injured might have been alarming. Shall I relate the whole of what happened?'

She tried to tell herself this was Giles, not Robbie. Not the lover who'd been brought back to her broken, battered—and dead.

Trying to stem a rising panic, she said, 'Never mind, I'll ask Giles. I'm coming back with you. I want to see that wound myself.'

Smith stared at her for a moment. 'I don't suppose I need to remind you how…improper it would be for you to visit a gentleman's rooms? Or the result to your reputation, should the visit become known.'

'You do not,' she snapped. Not even to herself could she fully explain the urgent need to fly to him. 'Don't you understand? I must see for myself that he's not in danger! Do you think I care if the ladies of society cut me from their invitation lists or gossip behind my back? I have no desire to remarry, and I doubt my father's political associates care in the least what I do. Papa—well, I can bring him around. And that's only if someone finds out. If I am in and out again before daylight, most likely no one will ever know.'

Her determination must have been written on her face, for after another glance, Mr Smith made no further attempt to dissuade her. 'Then we must see that you are back before dawn.'

She nodded. 'I'll get my cloak.'

A half-hour later, slipping along like proverbial thieves in the night, Mr Smith and a heavily veiled Maggie walked into Albany towards the rooms Giles shared with his friend. Ushering her into the common area, Mr Smith whispered, 'He may be sleeping. I'll be in my chamber. Call if you need anything, and when you're ready to return, let me know.'

Her hands trembling with anxiety, Maggie hurried to the door of the chamber Mr Smith indicated, and quietly let herself in.

A candle burned at his bedside. In the flickering light, Maggie could make out Giles reclining against the pillows, still wearing torn and soiled breeches and a ragged shirt. His hair was dishevelled, cuts and what appeared to be developing bruises shadowed his chin and cheek-bone, and his injured hand, wrapped in a bloodied bandage, lay propped on a pillow.

Despite herself, Maggie uttered an involuntary cry of distress.

Giles opened his eyes to squint up at her. 'Maggie?'

'Yes, Maggie,' she replied, rushing to his side. 'You look a fright! First I shall clean you up, and then I will abuse you for scaring me to death. That was the longest night of my life!'

He seemed to come fully awake then, sucking in a breath with a hiss as he struggled to sit up straight. 'Stars in Heaven, what was Davie thinking? He shouldn't have brought you here!'

'Don't blame him. I would have come on my own, if he hadn't escorted me.'

'But, Maggie—'

'Hush, and don't give me any treckle about propriety. Where can I get clean water?'

'Phillips left some in the basin, there on the dresser. I'd intended to finish washing up, but apparently that damned sawbones drugged my wine.'

'He probably wanted to make sure you rested until the bleeding stopped. And don't get up now, lest you start it again,' she said, putting a hand on his chest to restrain him.

His bare chest, where some of his shirt had been torn away. Despite her anxiety, deep within, a current of response stirred at this touch of flesh on flesh.

For a moment, they both stared at her hand, resting there so intimately.

'Really, sweetheart, I'm not that badly hurt,' he said at last.

'I hope not,' she replied, pulling herself back to her

task. 'But I'll reserve judgement until we get you out of those filthy garments and re-bandage that hand.'

Following his direction, she fetched water, soap, and clean rags. Helping him to sit at the side of the bed, she tugged up the ruined shirt and carefully eased him out of it.

There were cuts and scrapes on his shoulder, but minor enough that he didn't even flinch as she gently washed away the dirt. There was indeed a bruise on his cheek and another on his chin, but the skin was unbroken, nor did he protest when she pressed on them.

'It's been a long time since I've taken a right to the chin,' he said. 'A glancing blow, fortunately.'

'Mr Smith told me your group was attacked. What happened?'

'Hines went to the tavern to find Godfrey, posing as an intermediary for someone who needed a problem "disposed of", and was willing to pay handsomely. Godfrey agreed to consider it, and named a price. But he must have been suspicious to be sought out again so soon after the…incident in Kent. After Hines left, he gathered some mates to follow us. But Hines had warned us about that possibility, so we weren't totally unprepared for the attack. Unluckily for them, all three of us once had aspirations to the fancy, and we weren't the prime pigeons for plucking they must have expected. After a bit of a dust-up, we overcame them and marched them off to the constable. If it hadn't been for Godfrey pulling out a knife at the last, I'd have walked away with nothing more than a few bruises.'

While he talked, Maggie moved her ministrations from his back to his chest and arms, washing off the dirt and patting him dry with the soft cloth. As she stroked over his arms and shoulders, Giles fell silent. 'It's worth a little cut to the hand, to have you do that.'

'We'll see, when I get to the hand! Now, out of those breeches. I'm afraid both they and the shirt are only fit for the rag-and-bone man.'

She tugged at his waistband, urging him to stand long enough for her to peel down the trousers, but he hesitated.

She looked up into his eyes. 'Surely you're not shy! It's not as though I haven't see you—or parts of you—before.'

'True, you've not seen the whole package unwrapped at once,' he said with a chuckle. 'And when you do, you'll know immediately that I find the idea—very arousing.'

Her breath hitched and expectation swirled in the pit of her stomach. But she did need to get him out of his dirty garments and under his blankets, with his bandages changed so he could rest—and she could chastely return to Aunt Lilly's.

'I promise not to stare—more than I have to,' she added.

He stood then, and let her tug the trousers down and pull off the socks. Only then did she raise her eyes—to find him, as he'd hinted, fully erect.

She'd had glancing views of his rigid member as she caressed him within the confines of his breeches, or under and through the linen of his shirt. But to see him completely naked, from toes to collarbone, every hand-some well-made line of him, the curve of calf, strong-muscled thighs, flat belly, broad chest, strong arms and shoulders...

Her mouth dried and her heartbeat galloped. Con-flicted between desire and duty, Maggie tried to remind herself that, no matter how ready he might appear, he'd sustained an injury and needed to avoid any exertion that might start it bleeding again.

He simply stood there watching her, his blue eyes molten in the candlelight, every muscle taut, temptation incarnate, waiting for her to decide.

Near cursing with frustration and regret, she stuttered, 'W-we'd better get you u-under the bedclothes, before you catch a ch-chill.'

He laughed, something between a chuckle and a groan. 'I'm not likely to be chilled any time soon.'

Instead of making her smile, his attempt at humour reminded her of the danger his wound might pose. 'Let's just hope you don't turn feverish, either.'

He let her help him back into bed. She was proud that, though it took gritted teeth and incredible will-power, she managed to keep herself from running her fingers over any of that glorious naked flesh before she hid it under the blankets.

Taking a deep, shuddering breath to refocus her mind, she pulled a chair close to the bed. Bringing the candle nearer to shed the most light on the injury, she gently unwound the bloody bandage.

She gasped, tears starting to her eyes. A long, jagged cut slashed across his palm, biting deep beneath the thumb, where the doctor had closed the gap with tiny stitches. Blood still seeped from the edges, but the wound appeared stable, the skin scraped and reddened, but not warm with fever. Yet, anyway.

'You should sprinkle yarrow powder on it, to keep it from b-bleeding,' she said, a hitch in her voice as she swiped a wrist across her eyes, having unaccountable difficulty trying to stem the trickle of tears.

'Don't worry, sweetheart,' Giles said, his voice tender. 'It was a clean cut, fortunately done after we finished rolling about the alleyway. It's going to pain me for a while, but it will heal.'

Out of memory, the images attacked her. Broken bones that left the limbs at odd, unnatural angles. And blood—blood everywhere.

'I'm sorry—I'm sorry!' she said, trying to hold back the sobs. 'It's just…midnight, shadows, and candlelight, and blood… It b-brings it all back.'

'When they carried your husband home,' he guessed.

'Yes,' she whispered.

'Poor sweetheart,' he murmured. With his good hand, he pulled her up on the bed and hugged her against him.

The frustration of being confined, the strain and worry of waiting, and the nightmare images of blood and injury must have worn her down, for the tears fell harder and faster until she was clinging to Giles, sobbing uncontrollably. He held her tightly, caressing her back and murmuring soothingly.

At last, the tears were spent. 'I'm sorry,' she said again, embarrassed at her lack of control. 'I promise, I'm not usually such a watering-pot.'

'Nor are you often called to tend dirty and bleeding gentlemen in the middle of the night,' he replied. 'You're tired, sweeting. Rest here a bit, and we'll send you home.'

She snuggled against him. But as the misery ebbed and calm returned, she became more and more aware that the arms that cradled her were bare, and the body beneath the bedclothes completely naked.

Little chills chased up and down her arms, and simmering arousal boiled back up. Could she leave without paying homage to that glorious manhood?

'No, I shouldn't,' she murmured, only half-aware she'd spoken the words aloud. 'You need rest, too.'

She looked at him, to see his eyes blazing again with heat and need. 'Thanks to the good doctor, I've already had a rest.'

Wavering, she said, 'I should kiss you goodbye, and go. Your poor hand!'

'I have one good one,' he said, and pulled her to him. His lips met hers—and she was lost.

Their days of separation and abstinence seemed to have created a boiling cauldron of desire that required only that small nudge to spill out of control. She couldn't get enough of the taste of him, thrusting into his mouth, laving tongue against tongue, deep and hard and fast.

While they kissed, she tugged at the bedclothes, until she could reach within and run her hand over the bare flesh, as she'd yearned to since the moment she unclothed him. He caught her hand and brought it down to his erection, guiding her fingers over and around him.

She wanted more, closer. Lifting herself up, still kissing him, she dragged the covers aside, baring his body to her sight as well as her touch. But she craved the feel of skin against skin.

Too impatient for the slow process of undoing all the pins and fastenings of her bodice, she simply pulled up her skirts and lay against him, sighing with delight as she rubbed her bared legs against his.

But that wasn't enough either—she burned to *feel* him, around and within her, inside that aching needy place that had wanted for him for weeks. Rising up on her knees, she parted her legs and straddled him, stroking her hot centre over the slick velvet of his hardness.

He broke the kiss, his eyes wild, half-focused. 'Are you…sure?'

'Yes,' she murmured. 'Yes.'

Clutching his shoulders, she leaned down to kiss him as she thrust down with her hips, and sheathed him within. He pulled her close and she rubbed against him, savouring the delicious stretch and fullness.

Ah, this was paradise, the exquisite feel of him buried deep, pulsing within her. She heard a moan, not sure whether it was his or hers.

He rocked, just a slight movement within her, and suddenly it was impossible to remain still. She thrust down, pulled back, thrust down, the pleasure of it almost unbearably intense. And then they were moving together, one body, one flesh, one need, one purpose, racing each other to glorious completion.

Afterwards, Maggie lay trembling against him, listening to the frantic beat of his heart that echoed her own. An indescribable peace settled over her, satiation and fulfilment and something more, something profound and tender that penetrated to the depths of her soul with a sense of its beauty and rightness.

'Maggie mine,' Giles whispered in her ear. 'What a wonder you are.'

She kissed his neck. 'You're rather wonderful yourself.'

'You'll not think so, if Davie finds you here tomorrow morning.'

Her eyes flew open. Davie! Albany! A midnight misadventure that could end in disaster if she did not get back to Aunt Lilly's before dawn lit the streets.

As she considered the other possible consequences of her rashness this night, panic fluttered up, like a crow flapping its wings to take flight. She pushed the feeling away; time enough, when she was safely back at Grosvenor Square, to sort this out.

Regardless of what rational reflection revealed in the cold light of day, she would never regret this night.

'You're right, I must go,' she said, scooting off the bed. 'Don't get up!' she said as he made motions to follow her. 'Mr Smith told me he'd see me safely home. You should rest—especially after that unintended exertion.'

'I could do with an unlimited amount of that "exertion",' he said, catching her hand and pulling her back for a quick kiss. 'It was…glorious.'

Maggie felt ridiculous tears threaten. 'It was,' she agreed softly. *And it must never happen again.*

Pulling free, she inspected his hand, noting with relief that the bandage appeared dry. 'Heaven be praised, I don't think you re-started the bleeding.'

'You mustn't come here again,' he warned. 'I'll visit you soon in Grosvenor Square and let you know what they learn after they question Godfrey. Hines seemed to think that when they tell him he assaulted a sitting Member of Parliament, he'll sing like a meadowlark. I'm hopeful we'll know the full story soon.'

'It will be good to know the truth at last.' She finished tidying herself and smoothed down her skirts. 'Goodnight—or rather, good morning. Recover quickly, my dear Giles.'

With one last kiss to his forehead, she walked out of his bedchamber.

Chapter Nineteen

Later that same morning, Maggie sat in her bedchamber, sipping coffee. Though she'd not returned until nearly dawn, and despite the peace satiation normally brought, she'd not been able to sleep.

She wasn't too concerned that there would be dire consequences from the previous night's folly. Her courses were due any day, and she was usually quite regular, so the chance that she'd conceived was small enough that she wouldn't worry over the prospect now.

Not when there was a devastating task she must steel herself to perform.

Breaking off her liaison with Giles Hadley.

Last night had proven what she'd secretly known in her heart from the beginning: despite her fine words to the contrary, she couldn't trust herself to be sensible with Giles Hadley. She wanted him too much, and that single taste of completion only whetted her appetite to experience it again and again.

She simply couldn't risk that.

When they'd begun this, she'd hoped that when the end came, they could part as friends. She didn't think that would be possible now—not when the mere thought of him brought a rush of desire and a deep craving to be with him. What she felt for him was too powerful and too all-encompassing to confine within the narrow, polite box of friendship.

Attempting to chat with him over a cup of tea in someone's drawing room would be to sustain a thousand tiny cuts of loss and longing that would bleed for ever. Better one sharp, deep slash to sever the bond cleanly.

No matter how debilitating that single blow was likely to be.

Doing something difficult never got easier by putting it off. Setting down the barely tasted cup of coffee, she drew out a piece of paper, and began to write him a note.

Maggie spent the day gathering her belongings and preparing to return to her father's house in Grosvenor Square; with Godfrey in custody, she intended to resume her usual duties, whether Giles believed it safe or not.

Nor, at the moment, did she particularly care. Why bother worrying about her safety when the man she'd wanted to spend time with when her freedom was restored she must no longer see?

It wasn't until late afternoon that Giles replied to her summons. She'd almost hoped he wouldn't come today, so she might put off the final break. She felt his name like a punch to the gut when Rains announced that Mr Hadley awaited her in the Great Parlour.

Rejecting the impulse to delay, she made herself walk from her study, each footfall like a bell tolling of doom.

The smile that lit his face when she walked in just twisted the knife deeper.

'I'm sorry it took me so long to respond,' he said, coming over to kiss her hand. 'I've been at Bow Street and the magistrate's most of the afternoon.'

Motioning him to sit, she took a chair, rather than a place beside him on the sofa. Might as well begin distancing herself.

'Tell me what you discovered.'

'Godfrey did finally give up the name of the man who contacted and paid him. An intermediary; the Bow Street men are tracing him now, and once they locate him, they are confident they can establish who ordered the attack.'

'So it *was* ordered. I still find it hard to believe.'

'Godfrey claims he was paid just to fire at you, not to hit you. Insists his aim is true enough that if he'd intended to strike you, he would have.'

'What will happen to him?'

'If the charge were attempted murder, he would hang, which is why he tried to silence us all after he left the tavern. Hines subdued him in part by telling him he might get clemency instead of the noose, if he co-operated. That will be up to you and your father.'

Maggie sighed. 'Papa was livid when I told him what happened. He'd probably prefer thumbscrews and the rack, but I'll work on him. How is your hand?'

'Hurts like the very devil, but the wound is dry, with no sign of heat or suppuration.'

'Good. I'll have Rains get you some powdered yarrow from the still room; use it each time you change the bandages.'

'You looked tired, sweetheart—as well you might, after so...vigorous a night. And about that—'

'Please, don't apologise! I couldn't bear that. It might have been regrettable, but I don't regret it at all.'

'Nor do I. Although, I suppose when we begin again, we're going to have to think of some measures to prevent a recurrence of so delightful but dangerous an interlude.'

'I've already given that a great deal of thought.' Forcing herself to say the words, she continued, 'I can't meet you at Upper Brook Street any longer, Giles.'

He recoiled, shock on his face, but she made herself continue, 'I hate to end what we've shared, but last night showed I simply can't trust myself to be prudent. And the consequences of that failure could be catastrophic, for both of us.'

He opened his lips as if to speak, closed them, and sprang up. She watched him pace around the room, drinking in the sight of him, imprinting it on her memory. Even as she died a little with each glance, knowing it was the last time she would see him alone.

He halted in front of her, his face grim. 'I'd like to argue with you, but I cannot. My fault, probably, to think we could place limits on passion, which by its very nature defies limits.'

She shook her head. 'It was just as much my fault as yours. Sadly, wanting something very badly doesn't make it possible. I'd thought to take the coward's way out and send you a note, but then I decided I must tell you face to face. And kiss you goodbye, one final time.'

He seized her as she rose to meet him, crushing her against him with his one good arm, kissing her with intensity and conviction. She kissed back just as fiercely, putting into that final kiss all her passion, love, and regret.

After several moments, his kiss gentled, and ended in a series of gentle brushes of his mouth against her forehead, her eyebrows, her cheeks. He wrapped his arms around her and simply held her, while she battled despair and tears.

'Are you sure?' he whispered against her hair. 'I certainly don't want to give you up! If it is the matter of conception, there are ways…'

'I don't trust them,' she said, slowly detaching from his

embrace, each lost bit of contact—his shoulder, his chest, his hand, and the final release of his fingers—another hammer blow at her heart.

Suddenly it seemed important that he understand how hard this was for her—by knowing the reason she couldn't take even the smallest risk. Before prudence could prevent her from revealing what no one on earth but Polly knew, she said, 'You may think me ridiculously cautious, but I know…I know I could not face the consequences again.'

It took a moment before the meaning of her words registered. 'Again?' he repeated.

Wrapping her arms around herself, she walked to the hearth, facing away from him. 'You asked me once about my being engaged, and I told you we broke it off because I was sure we would not suit. But there was much more.'

'More…what?'

'I suppose, even after Robbie died, I looked at the world with the *naïveté* of a child. Several years had passed since I lost him, and I was lonely. I convinced myself that marrying again might help me finally bury the grief. With Papa's position and my wealth, there were always suitors milling about. Sir Francis Mowbrey was the most persistent and devoted.'

She grimaced, the details humiliating, even at this remove. 'I'd grown up with Robbie, and never doubted his devotion or the sincerity of his love. When Sir Francis gave me the same vows of love and constancy, I accepted them without question, even though I knew that worldly considerations of wealth, position and politics certainly figured into his desire to make me his wife. After I'd accepted his suit and we'd set a wedding date, he…pressed me to become intimate, and I agreed.'

She laughed without humour. 'As I said, I was incredibly naïve! It never occurred to me to wonder why Sir Francis happened to have a house in Chelsea we could use for our trysts. It wasn't until several months later, when I decided to surprise him on a day we were not to meet, that I arrived to find the house…already occupied.'

She paused while he took in the meaning. 'Did you confront him?'

'Not then. I ran off, hoping, I suppose, to find some innocent explanation for what I'd discovered. There wasn't, of course. When he called on me later, we had a terrific row. I was hurt and angry, he defensive and rather insulting—something like George, when I refused him. He left after telling me that, as a widow nearly past her prime without any great beauty to recommend her, I ought to think again before breaking our engagement over so "trivial" a matter.'

'What a fine gentleman,' Giles said derisively.

'Hurt, confused, and bitterly disappointed, I had no intention of reconsidering, at first. Until I learned that… I was increasing.'

His eyes widened. 'Merciful heavens!'

'With that realisation began the most wretched month of my life. How could I marry Sir Francis—who, I'd discovered, didn't really love me after all, or at least not with the devotion I desired? But how could I bear a child out of wedlock, condemning him or her to the stain of bastardry, when all that was needed were a few words of contrition, and the child could be born within the confines of marriage? A miserable union for me, perhaps, but one representing safety for the child. Or if I were prepared to birth a bastard, how could I carry a child and give her up, be forced to deny her existence and never see her again?'

At that, he walked over to pull her into his arms. 'I'm so sorry. So, in the end, you did choose…'

'In the end, God had mercy, on me at least. I went back and apologised to Sir Francis—though I did not tell him about the child. Two weeks later and just before the wedding, I lost the babe. As soon as I recovered from my sudden "illness", I broke off the engagement for good. He was furious—I believe he incurred a number of debts, expecting that he would soon have my fortune at his disposal…to fund his gambling and his mistresses,' she finished bitterly. 'He never forgave me, and only his awareness of the damage Papa could do him if he maligned my name tempered the nastiness of the comments he made about me to society.'

'Did none of your family suspect?'

'Aunt Lilly may have, though she never asked me about it. I told Papa only that I'd discovered Sir Francis did not love me as Robbie had, and I wouldn't settle for less. Of course, all the world but me knew of Francis's little house in Chelsea, so Papa wasn't surprised. He even confided that he'd almost told me about it himself, to make sure I was aware what sort of husband Sir Francis was likely to be.'

She pulled away to take a turn about the room. 'After that, I was never tempted to respond to another suitor, since they were all of Sir Francis's stamp—Tories, who could use my wealth and connection to good advantage. How could I trust anything they said?'

'Surely you can't doubt how witty, intelligent, and captivating you are! Completely deserving of any discerning gentleman's love and devotion.'

His praise eased her bruised heart. 'It shook my confidence at first,' she admitted, 'but I recovered—left with only one deep regret.'

When he raised an eyebrow in enquiry, she continued, 'Glad as I was to have my dilemma resolved without having to marry Sir Francis, I still feel…guilty. Would I have carried the child to term, had I been thrilled, instead of filled with dread about it?'

'I don't think anyone knows how much influence one's feelings have over such a thing. I do think it beyond reasonable that you should blame yourself for it.'

'As I believe it beyond reasonable that you should feel in any way responsible for the fate of your mother?'

He smiled. 'You have me there, I suppose.'

'So you understand now why I can't continue? Of course, it goes without saying that I trust you will never reveal to anyone what I've just confessed.'

'Of course not,' he assured her, then halted. After a long pause, as if he were weighing his words, 'I'm only sorry you had to suffer so devastating an experience.'

She waited, perhaps in the very depths of her heart hoping he would say more, that though he understood why she must break it off, that he couldn't imagine not seeing her, that he cared too much to say goodbye.

Of course, he did not. While she mentally flayed herself as a fool, Giles said, 'You will let me know if there are any…untoward consequences from last night.'

'You agreed to an affair, nothing more,' she replied, the words as much to emphasise that truth to herself as to affirm it for him. 'That's all that was or is required of you. Besides, the timing is such that there is very little likelihood of any "untoward consequences".'

'But you would let me know if there were,' he repeated, gazing at her.

She shook her head. 'I was married once, to a man who loved me completely and wanted to spend the rest of his life with me. I won't settle for less than that.'

'You think I don't care for you enough.'

She gave him a sad little smile. 'Love comes to us,

unbidden. Like a wild fawn, it cannot be saddled and bridled and directed the way we want it to go. It simply happens…or it does not. I bear you no ill will because it did not happen for you, but I…I cannot be just your friend.'

'So you are saying…you don't want to see me at all,' he said slowly.

'Yes. I'm sorry, but that's exactly what I'm saying.'

'I see.'

He stared past her, as if he were having difficulty making sense of her words.

The little knives were sawing deeper, and Maggie didn't think she could bear much more. 'Then we've said all that needs to be said. Goodbye, Giles. God keep you safe.'

She curtsied, and looking shocked and disbelieving, he bowed. When he still did not move, she gestured towards the door, both frantic to end this and wanting to savour his presence until the last possible moment.

At length, he nodded and crossed the room, then paused on the threshold. Turning back to her, his expression troubled, he said, 'I still intend to discover who hired Godfrey to shoot at you. Shall I send you a note once I've uncovered the whole?'

'If you wish. And thank you,' she added belatedly. He would probably expect thanks for trying to figure out who had endangered her.

Somehow, that threat didn't frighten her nearly as much as the sight of Giles Hadley, about to walk out of her life for good.

Once the echo of his footsteps in the hallway faded, Maggie staggered back to the sofa, numb and stunned, like a boxer who'd just taken a powerful blow to the chest. She hadn't felt so bereft, so absolutely devastated and hopeless, since she lost Robbie.

The obvious implication finally occurred to her. It seemed so clear and simple now, she wondered why she'd not recognised it much sooner.

Of course she was bleeding inside. Of course the world without him seemed an agonising emptiness. Of course she'd wanted to belong to him completely, everywhere and as often as possible.

It was why she'd felt so strongly driven to intervene in his life and smooth his path. Why she was utterly content, just to listen to him speak about the politics that consumed him, though his opinions were so different from her own. Why, when she'd told him she meant to terminate the liaison, that still naïve child deep within had hoped he would refuse, proclaiming that he couldn't go on without her.

No point trying to deny the fact any longer: despite assuring herself she'd never let herself be vulnerable again, she'd fallen in love with Giles Hadley.

She didn't know when fascination had deepened into love, though if she were honest, she'd been tumbling deeper into enchantment from the moment they met.

Perhaps she'd secretly hoped, if she didn't call what she felt by its name, she might save herself some of the anguish now coursing through her.

She'd been wrong.

She allowed herself to retain only one tiny crumb of hope: if Giles cared as much for her as Robbie had, he would come back. If he did, then and only then would she confess that she loved him.

If he didn't, it was just as well for them to end it now. Continuing on would only entangle her heart and hopes more completely into his life and make the inevitable parting more difficult.

This was hard enough.

Aunt Lilly had been right to warn her, Maggie thought, struggling to get air in and out of her lungs. Hearts *could* break twice. And the second time was looking to be no easier than the first.

Chapter Twenty

Giles found himself back at his rooms at Albany without being able to recall precisely how he'd got there. He ached like the very devil, and he wasn't sure it was his hand that hurt the most.

He still couldn't believe that Maggie had ended their liaison. He'd been so focused on removing the threat to her so she could resume her—and their—normal routine, his chief worry the possibility that he'd have to shoulder the guilt of learning his brother was responsible for the attack, he'd never remotely considered it ending.

Not that he could be angry with her—not when her reasons were so undeniable and compelling. If he were honest, he had to admit that he had coaxed her into suppressing those very misgivings to win her agreement to begin the affair. She'd honoured him by trusting him enough to reveal the deeper reason behind those misgivings—a personal tragedy of which even her closest family wasn't aware.

His lip curled with derision when he thought of Sir Francis Mowbrey. How stupid and selfish the man must be to have remained ignorant of what a treasure he'd been offered! Concerned only with availing himself of her wealth, her connections and her body while giving her nothing but honeyed lies. Giles grieved for the innocent girl whose trust and self-confidence had been so callously shaken.

Small wonder she'd held herself at a distance from all subsequent suitors, too disillusioned to trust the love promises of prospective husbands who stood to gain so much by beguiling her into marriage.

Perhaps that was why she'd chosen him, Giles thought wryly. Her Tory connections were no help to him politically, and he wasn't on the catch for an heiress. As she'd said, he'd signed on only for a mutually pleasurable interlude with an interesting and attractive partner.

So why did he feel like he'd just been gutted?

He'd get over it, he told himself—just like the throbbing in this curst hand would end, eventually. Deciding some medicinal brandy might be good for all that ailed him, he hunted for the decanter and poured himself a glass.

His mind wandering, unable to focus on what he should do next, he automatically began to pick up the glass with his right—injured—hand. He dropped it at once, cursing at the excruciating pain.

Fury far beyond anything merited by that small miscalculation engulfed him. Seizing the glass with his good hand, he threw it into the fireplace, watching as the crystal shattered into pieces.

Like his world.

A week later, Giles was reading through some papers in the committee room when Ben entered with a stack of law books. His vision obscured, he bumped the table, knocking over an empty tankard that fell against Giles's injured hand.

After a stream of curses, he snapped. 'Watch where you're going, lunkhead!'

Ben set down the books with a thump. 'Here's all of Blackstone, as requested,' he told Davie, who sat at the table beside Giles. 'As for you, Giles, in future would you make sure you don't injure yourself while Parliament is in session? You've been like a bear with a thorn in its paw for the last week.'

Irritated and out of sorts, but knowing his friend was right, Giles was working up the will to apologise when a knock sounded, followed by the entrance of a runner, who handed Giles a message.

He read through it swiftly, then rose, going over to claim his hat and greatcoat. 'It's from Hines,' he told them. 'He has the information we've been seeking.'

'Shall I go with you?' Davie asked.

'No. One way or the other, I'll be fine. I'm just happy to end this at last.'

Ending it would mean he'd be able to write to Maggie, he thought as he hailed a hackney, giving the driver Hine's Bow Street address. He might even chance going to Cavendish Square to deliver the news in person.

His spirits rose at the idea of seeing her. Much as he hated to acknowledge it, missing her had been an ache as painful as his wound. Except, he expected, *that* pain would prove much more enduring.

A short time later, he climbed out of the carriage and hurried into Hines's office, eager to have the mystery cleared up at last. The investigator came straight to the point.

'Godfrey was hired by a Tom Brown—not his name, almost certainly. Brown hovers about the edges of society, along with the cent-per-centers and dealers in pawned merchandise, specialising in making discreet arrangements for gentlemen down on their luck who need to sell a family bauble that might not be theirs to sell, settle a bastard child obscurely in the country, or otherwise make inconvenient problems disappear. His reputation for doing so came to the attention of a gentleman who had such a problem, who contacted him to take care of it.'

'And that gentleman was?'

'As you suspected, your half-brother, George Hadley.'

Even though Giles had never been able to imagine anyone else being responsible, having the news confirmed still shocked him like a slap to the face.

'Shall I write and inform Lord Esterbrook?' Hines asked.

'Yes, he will want a full report. Thank you for your good work, Mr Hines. And for letting me come along for that dust-up we enjoyed the other night. Reminded me of my misspent youth on the Hampshire downs.'

Hines smiled. 'I imagine speechifying and law-making must sometimes seem a bit dull for an active man.'

He was about to participate in another dust-up—as soon as he ran down his half-brother. 'Total your bill and present it to my bank, and they will draft you the reimbursement.'

'Thank you, Mr Hadley. Right sorry about your half-brother.'

After exchanging bows, Giles quit Hines's office and raced down to the waiting hackney. Now to track down George at Abbotsweal House, and settle this for good and all.

But to his frustration, Giles arrived at the family town house to find the knocker off the door. Proceeding to the kitchen entrance, he roused a member of the skeleton staff, who informed him that Mr Hadley had been summoned home by his sire two weeks previous.

Thanking the man, Giles walked slowly out. Unfortunately, he'd not have today the reckoning he burned for. Even more unfortunately, he was going to have to make that long-delayed journey to Abbotsweal.

Three dusty June days of travelling later, Giles arrived at the village of Romesly and engaged a room at the local inn. Later, he would call on Mr Angleton and meet with the committee that had requested his presence. But first, he would visit Abbotsweal Hall and settle the business with his half-brother. And his father.

Following the directions of the innkeeper, Giles chose to ride to Abbotsweal, rather than take a carriage. Before anyone at the manor noticed a visitor approaching and gave the alert, he wanted to get a good look at the land that would eventually be his and the house he'd not seen since he was a small boy, and barely remembered.

To his surprise as he drew nearer to the house, bits and pieces of memories surfaced in his mind—a curve of road that seemed familiar, a sunny, open copse in the woodland where he must have played. Then the Georgian manor itself, vast as he remembered it.

The scent of roses brought back hazy images of a walled garden—which he spotted to the west of the main building. Then he was approaching the entrance, handing his horse over to a footman, being admitted by an elderly butler. 'Please inform Lord Telbridge that Viscount Lyndlington is here to see him.'

The old man drew in a breath. 'Master Giles? Is that really you?'

Giles looked over to find, to his surprise, an expression of gladness on the old man's face. 'I'm sorry, I don't—'

'I'm Wilson, sir, and of course you don't remember me! You were only a babe when you and…when you left us. I'm so glad you've come home, at last! Your father prefers to receive callers in the library—won't you follow me, sir? I'll let his lordship know you are here at once!'

'Is Master George here as well?'

'I believe he is out riding at present, but due back before dinner.'

Very well, Giles thought, following the old man into a large, long room whose walls were lined with cases filled with leather volumes. He'd deal first with Telbridge, then with his half-brother.

What a handsome room it was, he thought, idly picking up a book at random. It was disorienting to consider that, at some future date, this handsome library would be his, as well as this vast Georgian edifice and all the land he'd ridden through, including the village.

He was still trying to wrap his mind around that notion when the butler returned to announce Lord Telbridge.

Walking in behind him was the father Giles had not seen in over twenty years. For a long moment, they simply stared at each other.

Giles could see the resemblance to George: the same square jaw and hazel eyes, the silver hair that must once have been his half-brother's sandy-brown hue. Whereas he, with his blue-black hair and blue eyes, was entirely a reflection of his mother.

No wonder Telbridge had banished him with her.

'Telbridge,' he said, bowing. *They could at least begin with courtesy.*

The earl paused, apparently unsure what to call him.

'I'm Lyndlington,' he said pointedly, though he knew the butler would have passed on the visitor's name.

'Lyndlington,' his father repeated. 'I suppose we ought

to sit down.' Gesturing Giles to a wing chair, he took the chair behind the large desk.

A sudden memory surfaced—a young boy playing fortress in the wing chair, while a man looked on indulgently from behind that massive desk.

Pushing it away, Giles turned his attention back to the most important matter: the attack on Lady Margaret.

'I suppose you wonder why I've come here uninvited,' he began. 'It's not the obvious reason, although I will get to that in a moment. My primary purpose is to talk with George about an attack on Lady Margaret Dennison Roberts—a lady he courted, but who rejected him.'

'An attack on Lady Margaret?' Telbridge echoed. 'What do you mean? And what has that to do with George?'

'In brief, George had aspirations to the hand of the Marquess of Witlow's daughter, and when she refused his advances, he threatened her with retribution. I count myself fortunate to be a friend of that lady and her father. George previously warned me to stay away from her, and the knowledge that she persisted in befriending me after rejecting him certainly would have increased his anger and disappointment. However, no amount of outrage justified his hiring a man to take a shot at her while she was riding at Huntsford.'

'He hired someone to shoot at her? But that's madness! I know there is ill feeling between you. Surely that enmity has coloured your interpretation of the facts, for I cannot imagine—'

'Lord Telbridge, the *facts* are not in dispute. Lady Margaret's brother, Lord Esterbrook, had the incident thoroughly investigated by Bow Street. The perpetrator was tracked back to London, where he was apprehended and confessed. He had been hired and paid by an inter-

mediary, who had in turn been hired by George. I am
not speculating; if you doubt my word, you may apply
to Lord Esterbrook for a copy of the report Mr Hines of
Bow Street prepared for him.'

'But that is…fantastic!'

'Fantastic, indeed. Ill-judged, certainly, and prose-
cutable in a criminal court, definitely. Though I myself
would favour a trial and punishment, to spare the lady
and her family embarrassment, I imagine Lord Witlow
will prefer to proceed privately. But George must be dealt
with; the marquess will stand for nothing less.'

'I had some…prior knowledge of a problem between
them,' the earl admitted. 'I summoned George home after
receiving a note from Witlow informing me that George
had been harassing Lady Margaret; the marquess wrote
that he would consider preferring charges if I didn't bring
George home and exercise more control over his behaviour. But to endanger Lady Margaret…'

At that moment, the butler bowed himself back in.
'Master George just returned, my lord. Shall I have him
join you?'

'At once,' Telbridge said curtly.

There being nothing further he needed to say, Giles
remained silent as they waited for the earl's second son
to arrive. Davie would caution him to remain calm and
curb his temper—so he did not succumb to his strong
inclination to stalk over and floor George with a round-
house punch to the jaw the moment he entered the library.

'You wanted to see me?' George said as he walked in.
He stopped short, the smile on his face fading when he
saw Giles. 'You!' he spat out incredulously. 'What are
you doing here?'

'Surely you didn't think you could get away with this,'

Giles said, fixing his half-brother with a hard look. 'Don't pretend you don't know exactly what I'm talking about.'

Breaking eye contact with Giles, George looked over at his father. 'I don't know what sort of rubbishing story he's told you, but I assure you, it is false and exaggerated! What's he doing in our library anyway, as if he were a welcome guest? I would have expected you to show him the door!'

'That's quite enough, George,' Telbridge said. 'Take a seat. I'd meant to discuss this matter ever since you returned home, and now it can be put off no longer.' He nodded to Giles. 'Lyndlington, if you would explain?'

'George needs no explanation, being fully aware of the facts,' Giles replied. 'Which are, that at O'Malley's Gaming Emporium in one of the more…questionable areas of London, he sought out a Mr Tom Brown, who has a reputation for arranging matters of dubious legality for gentlemen who don't wish to dirty their hands doing them personally. George hired Mr Brown to find someone who would fire on Lady Margaret—or that's what the shooter, Mr Godfrey, insists. Unless you really intended to have her killed for refusing your suit?'

His expression stony, George remained silent, staring straight ahead.

'Well, George?' Telbridge demanded. 'Please tell me that Lyndlington is mistaken, and that you had nothing to do with this tawdry episode.'

When he still made no answer—trying to come up with an explanation for the unexplainable—Giles felt almost sorry for the man. But not quite.

'I require an answer,' Telbridge said, as if George's silence wasn't confession enough. Perhaps to accept that his beloved son could be responsible for such shocking events, he needed to have them confirmed by the man himself.

'Of course, I didn't intend for Lady Margaret to be harmed,' George said sulkily. 'Only to frighten her— maybe enough to realise that keeping company with *him* was dangerous—for such it proved, didn't it?' he added with a laugh. 'I thought she might come to her senses, and think again about my proposal. Although if the shooter's aim had been bad, and he struck *him* instead, I wouldn't have shed any tears.'

'If the shooter's aim had been bad, he might have struck *her*!' Giles retorted. 'He came shockingly close as it was! And if he did kill me, you'd have led a man into committing a hanging offence, just to soothe your injured dignity!'

George turned to Giles, frustration and fury in his gaze. 'If *you* had kept out of the matter, the proposal would have been accepted! Why shouldn't Lady Margaret marry me? I'm of impeccable lineage, belong to the correct party, and could maintain her in a position she prizes, as a leading political hostess! Whereas *you* only wanted to trifle with her. I tried to warn her!'

Giles sucked in a breath, needing all his willpower not to grab his half-brother and throttle him. Perhaps George's insidious words, added to the cautious scepticism she'd developed as a shield after her betrayal by Sir Francis Mowbrey, explained why Maggie had not seemed to believe how much he cared for her.

'So it's true, what Lyndlington told me,' Telbridge said, pinning George with his gaze.

'Well, yes, but there wasn't any harm—'

'No *harm*?' Giles cried, unable to restrain himself. 'You put Lady Margaret's life at risk, alarmed her family, and forced her into hiding! Not to mention, your hirelings could be brought up on offenses that could get them transported, if not hung. All so Lady Margaret might— *reconsider your suit*?'

'That's enough from you, too, Lyndlington,' the earl said. 'George, you will go to your chamber and wait for me to decide how I wish to proceed. It will require careful arranging to avoid having our family name tarnished by seeing you brought up on charges!'

'Very well, Father,' George said, bowing. 'I know you will figure a way out of this.'

While Giles shook his head in disbelief, with a great deal more nonchalance than a man in his position should be feeling, his half-brother walked out.

'You don't really think you can get him out of this,' he asked the earl once the door had closed.

'No,' Telbridge said quietly. 'I've…overlooked some questionable activities before, things I see now I should have put a stop to, but this appalling lack of judgement and consideration passes all limits. I fear I must implement the plan I'd been considering since I got the marquess's earlier missive. The family has mercantile interests in the Americas; I shall send George to our head office in the Bahamas to learn the business.'

'Lord help the office in the Bahamas,' Giles muttered.

'This time, he must act like a man and learn to make his own fortune. He's not an unintelligent lad. If he works hard and masters the details of the export business, he could earn a tidy income from it some day. As you will… eventually inherit here, he will need another source of income.'

Since you won't be here to siphon off funds from the estate for his benefit any longer, Giles thought. 'I had to come to Abbotsweal to find George anyway, but I did intend to also discuss the matter of the succession. After the election last month, a delegation from Romesly invited me to the village to meet the electors and the tenants hereabouts, wishing me to start becoming acquainted with them and their needs.'

'Doing for yourself what I had not done?'

Giles couldn't tell from his tone whether that was meant as comment or accusation. Refraining from answering, he continued, 'I never meant to tread on Abbotsweal land behind your back; I planned to call here first, and inform you of my intentions.'

'I'm glad you did call. I should have summoned—requested—you to return to Abbotsweal long since.' The earl smiled sadly. 'Inertia, I suppose. Plus, it is hard to admit one is wrong.'

Before Giles could recover from his surprise at that remark, the earl said, 'I admit, I've indulged George too much. And that, without any help from me, you've made an impressive name for yourself.'

'I'm glad you approve,' he replied, unable to keep an edge of sarcasm from his tone.

The earl laughed. 'I imagine you don't give a tinker's damn what I think—nor have I given you any reason to.' He paused, his gaze going to the far distance, as if his thoughts had wondered miles away. 'Did your mother ever give you an explanation for why I sent you away?'

Startled at the change of subject, Giles said, 'No. Until my aunt came to take me away to school, I had no idea we *had* been sent away. Aunt Charlotte explained it to me afterward, but…Mama died that same winter, before I could see her again and ask her anything.'

'Then it's time you heard the truth. All of it. Which will require some courage.'

The earl went to the sideboard and poured them each a brandy. Sitting back down, he took a long swallow and began. 'The cottage where you grew up was rented by an old friend, who used to go there for the shooting. My best friend, Richard Kensworthy, and I used it, too. A few years after your mother and I were married, I chanced upon the friend, and he asked me how I'd enjoyed the little taste of honeymoon before my wedding. I must have looked puzzled, for he reminded me that my wife had asked to borrow the cottage just before the wedding. I played along as if I recalled the incident, but I knew she hadn't gone to the cottage to meet *me*. It was Richard, of course.'

'I was in a rage when I returned and accused her. She made no attempt to deny it—it wasn't adultery, she said, because we were not yet married. And when I asked her if she could assure me that you were my son, she replied that she could not.'

'I *had* heard that part. And that because of it, you banished us both.'

The earl sighed. 'Actually, I didn't. It was Lydia who no longer wanted to continue our marriage. She said that she still loved Richard, she'd always loved Richard, that she'd only married me because of pressure from her family. I'd pledged to pay off her father's debts, you see. She said she'd tried to be a good wife, but if I was going to despise her for loving Richard and treat her son with contempt because he might not be *my* son, she would rather leave.'

'*She* wanted to leave?' Giles echoed, incredulous.

'Yes. Since you *might* be Richard's son, she said she wanted you all to herself. I see now that I should have waited, let us both have time to calm down and think rationally. But I was young, and stupid, and ferociously jealous. Because I did love her, you see. I always had, even though I knew she preferred Richard. I felt almost…

guilty, taking advantage of her situation to win her hand, knowing her family would never allow her to marry a penniless younger son. I thought I could make her love me, and when she confirmed I had not, I was furious. She told me she was going to take you and leave, and advised me to divorce her.' He smiled bitterly. 'So I might marry again and have a son I was sure was mine.'

'So you did,' Giles murmured.

'So I did.'

'Why did you allow society to believe you'd cast her out?'

'Pride. How could I admit to the world that my wife would rather live in a cottage on the downs than with me—' he gestured around them '—in this great old manse? The only concession I won from her was her agreement to live with you in that cottage. Where I could make sure you were both all right, with enough food and such few presents, like books and art supplies, that she would allow me to give her.'

As memories returned in a rush, Giles felt like George had punched *him*. Mama, receiving a wrapped package with a new book, or some watercolours. A merchant from the nearest village, arriving with a basket of vegetables, a side of beef, flour and supplies to make bread.

The truth dawned in a horrifying rush. '*You* own the cottage on the downs?'

The earl nodded. 'It's part of the estate. You will own it one day, which is why I was not willing to sell it to you when you made enquiries, some time ago.'

'Did your second wife know?'

'I think she suspected. She knew I never loved her, but there was no pretence of that union being anything more than a marriage of convenience. I wanted a son I knew was mine, and she wanted to marry an earl.'

'Why did you not come forward when my aunt sent me to school? I know my uncle paid my fees and expenses.'

'My second wife was still alive then. I knew I could always reimburse Lord Newville later, which I intend to do.'

'Does no one else know about your connection to the cottage?'

'The friend who used to rent it—but he was killed at Waterloo. And Richard, of course, but he died in India. I recognised almost immediately that remarriage had been a mistake, but by then it was too late. And by the time my second wife passed away, Lydia was already dead, too. I tried to transfer all my love and devotion to George.'

He shook his head, his expression full of grief. 'In the process, I ruined him and created a breach with you I didn't know how to heal. For so long after Lydia died, I didn't have the heart to try. So you see, the son I loved too well turned into selfish, shallow, reckless man concerned only with his own wishes; the son I spurned has become a man any father would be proud of. After this business with George, you have no reason to like or even respect me, but the estate will one day be yours. It's past time I began showing you how to run it. I'd like to begin again, if you'll let me.'

With everything he'd ever believed about the relationship between his mother and the earl turned on its head, Giles hardly knew what to think. Regardless of the maelstrom of conflicting emotions raging inside, the earl's offer was a reasonable one—the best resolution he could have wished for, for the good of the estate and himself.

'I'm not sure how to begin over either,' he admitted. He might never be able to conquer his anger and resentment for the man who'd allowed him to grow up fatherless all those years. 'I will try. And I will certainly accept your offer to acquaint me with the estate.'

The earl held out his hand. Giles shook it.

'Can you stay?' Telbridge asked. 'I'll have the house-keeper prepare rooms for you.'

'No, I must get back to London as soon as I've spoken with the delegates in Romesley. I've hardly held my weight the last few weeks on finishing the final preparations for reading the Reform Bill out of committee. If it's agreeable to you, once it's passed—it will pass—and Parliament adjourns, I'll return.

'Besides,' he added ruefully, 'you had better not trust me under the same roof with George. Perhaps by the time Parliament dissolves, you'll have dispatched him to those poor unwary souls in Bermuda.'

The earl held up a cautionary hand. 'As you've not given up on me, after all my poor decisions these many years, I'm not yet ready to give up on George. He may yet find the tiller that can right his ship.'

'I will pray he does,' Giles said. *Although that transformation would be a daunting task even for the Almighty.* 'Now, I need to return to Romesly. I sent Lord Witlow a note before I left London, promising to return as soon as possible and let him know what would be done about George.'

The earl nodded. 'I will write him as well, offering my sincere apologies and assuring him George will cause no more trouble. Also, to give him my thanks for choosing not to resolve this in a public manner that would cause embarrassment to us both. Will it be possible to obtain mercy for the two men George hired?'

'If the marquess chooses not to press charges, probably.'

'I will request it in my note. Perhaps they, too, can be…relocated.'

Giles stood, and the earl stood, too, offering his hand again. Giles shook it firmly.

'Goodbye, Lord Telbridge. I'll send you a note when I know when I can return.'

'Do that. Goodbye…my son.'

Chapter Twenty-One

Giles rode back to Romesly, almost dizzy from the velocity of the thoughts and questions whizzing around in his head about what the earl—his father—had just revealed.

His *mother* had wanted to end the marriage.

The earl had always loved her, had watched over and protected them all the years he was growing up.

The earl would have forgiven her and continued the marriage—but she had wanted to live apart. To treasure her son by herself.

He was not the cause of her ruin and banishment.

He'd always told himself he didn't believe George's taunt, but as he began to fully assimilate the truth of the relationship between the earl and his mother, his entire soul felt suddenly light, as if a terrible burden had been lifted. Perhaps, he thought wryly, he'd believed it more than he'd realised.

Mr Angleton and the voters of Romesly would be thrilled to learn he'd reconciled with the earl—removing any worry about possible retribution against them for ousting George from his Parliamentary seat.

He knew one other person who'd be thrilled to know

he would be taking up his proper role for the estate. His chest expanded with anticipation and delight at the thought of telling her.

But…Maggie had asked him not to call on her again. Because she believed, deep down, he was only 'trifling' with her, as George had warned? How *could* she believe that, after all they had been to each other?

He'd been so shocked and dismayed when she'd broken with him, he'd hardly made sense of her words. Suddenly, some of them recurred to him: *Love simply happens… or it does not. I bear you no ill will because it did not happen for you…*

For *you*. Was that to say love *had* happened, for her?

He had missed her as he'd never missed any other woman, longed for her as he'd not longed for any other woman. And he could not imagine wanting any other woman by his side when he took up the tasks that would be his destiny.

'I love you, Maggie mine,' he whispered with incredulous delight, and then laughed out loud for the joy of it. Perhaps it had taken learning the full truth about his mother's love and the earl's heartache, to free himself from the past and leave him open to recognising a love of his own.

Whatever the reason, he suddenly knew, with as much certainty as he knew his own name, that he loved Maggie Dennison Roberts.

Love comes to us, unbidden.

So it had, but given the earl's salutary example, he wasn't going to let his slip away from him.

And he was prepared to use every weapon at his command, including that explosive passion they both had so much difficulty resisting, to woo his shy fawn back to him.

* * *

A week later, Maggie sat in the little study at Cavendish Square, planning out the seating arrangement for Papa's dinner. It had been two weeks since she'd given Giles his *congé*, but she'd made little progress in banishing the aching sadness that afflicted her during every waking moment and haunted her sleep.

With the danger of further attack removed, she'd thrown herself back into her duties as hostess for her father and mistress of his household. She'd tried to fill up any odd spare moments shopping for new gowns, perusing the shelves at Hatchards, and making calls on acquaintances in town she normally never bothered with. All to keep herself from brooding about how much she missed him, and how dreary her life was, now that she'd banished him.

But new gowns only reminded her of how he'd unlaced her out of her bodice, and Hatchards of the books they'd discussed, and making calls of their secret rendezvous, she waiting with breathless anticipation for him to ride from the park and slip up the stairs at Upper Brook Street and join her.

Only by recalling the memory of Francis and the dire consequences of succumbing to passion, could she keep herself from summoning him back.

She'd fobbed off Papa, when he'd asked in concern what was ailing her, by saying she was still recovering from the shock of being shot at. The shock of loving and losing Giles was far greater, of course, but she *would* get through it, she kept telling herself. It *would* get better.

She pushed away the depressing thought that she'd never really got over losing Robbie. What made her think recovering from this second blow would be any easier?

Would Giles come, if she summoned him?

Exasperated, she squelched the useless speculation. She would not summon him. If he ever returned, it would be because he could not stay away. Because he'd belatedly realised he loved her, as she'd finally come to realise she loved him.

As she reached that conclusion, Rains walked in. 'Viscount Lyndlington to see you, Lady Margaret.'

So completely wrapped up in thinking about him had she been, at first she wasn't sure she hadn't just imagined hearing his name.

'W-who did you say?'

'Lord Lyndlington,' Rains repeated.

'Oh,' she said faintly, her heart commencing to beat so hard in her chest she had difficulty thinking. 'Show him into the Blue Salon.'

Rains peered at her with concern. 'Are you all right, my lady?'

'Quite all right,' she replied unsteadily, knowing it was a lie. 'Tell him I'll be right in.'

After the butler went out, Maggie rose from her desk, unsure what to do next. *Check your* coiffure, *make sure there are no ink smudges on your nose or fingers,* she told herself, having difficulty recalling what would normally be second nature.

Go to him.

She tried to ground the great, ravenous bird of hope that was flapping its wings in her chest, trying to take flight, making it hard for her to breathe.

He'd probably come to tell her the final results of the shooting incident. Though her father had already shown her Mr Hines's report.

Go in and see, looby.

She walked to the parlour on legs that seemed stiff and awkward. When she opened the door and saw him waiting for her, joy consumed her, and it took every bit of restraint she possessed not to run across the room and throw herself into his arms.

'Giles, what a pleasant surprise,' she said instead, making herself walk at a decorous pace. 'So, have you finished your quest?'

He came over and took her hand, those marvellous blue eyes scanning her face as he brought her fingers to his lips. She bit her lip against a whimper of delight.

'It's wonderful to see you, too, Maggie. Yes, the quest is complete. I'd thought to write you a note, but there was so much to say, I decided to come in person. I hope you don't mind.'

Oh, she minded! Torn between telling him to leave, before the ache of needing him grew any sharper, and begging him never to leave, she simply nodded and gestured towards the sofa.

Prudently seating herself on a chair, she got her unruly thoughts under control. 'What did you discover?'

'As your father might have told you, the investigation showed that George had indeed paid for Godfrey to fire at you. When I went to confront him, I discovered he'd returned to Abbotsweal, so I was obliged to follow him there.'

'So you met your father at last—and survived, I see. I assume you did not murder George?'

'No, though I certainly considered it. It turned out to be a...surprising meeting, in many ways.'

'Can you tell me about it, without violating any confidences?'

'I intend to.'

They paused then, Rains returning with wine. While

he poured, Maggie thought how wonderful it was to have Giles sitting in her parlour, confiding in her as they had so often when they lay in each other's arms at Upper Brook Street. How she ached for the precious hours she had not appreciated nearly enough when she had them!

After the butler walked out, Giles said, 'I'd feared Telbridge would support George, despite the evidence of his wrongdoing. The threat of possible prosecution by your father might have influenced him, but for whatever reason, of his own volition, he's decided to send George to the Bahamas to learn the management of the earl's export business there, with the possibility of running it himself one day, if he does well.'

'Perhaps he will, with a change of place and occupation. And a knowledge that he cannot count on the earl to support him for ever.'

'Yes. However, what I learned about my mother was even more surprising.'

He proceeded to tell her what the earl had revealed about his relationship with Giles's mother. 'It seems your belief was accurate,' he concluded. 'I was not responsible for my mother's divorce and banishment. The earl would have forgiven her lapse, and taken us back.'

'I knew you could not be responsible. I hope now, you believe it, too. So you reconciled with the earl?'

'Yes. I'll return to Abbotsweal after the session is over—at the earl's invitation. You'll be pleased to learn he has decided to do his duty, as you always insisted he should, and begin showing me around Abbotsweal himself.'

'That's excellent news!' she said, truly happy that the man who should bring Giles back into involvement with his birthright had finally accepted the responsibility. She smiled. 'How does it feel, knowing you're about to join the opposition?'

'Strange,' he conceded, smiling back. Oh, how charming his smile was, setting those compelling blue eyes aglow! 'But not all peers oppose the Reform Bill. I may have some company, when I finally enter the Lords. But that, please God, won't be for many years.'

'You may manage to get the institution disbanded before then,' she said with a twinkle.

'Perhaps I will,' he replied. 'More importantly, though, the startling news about the earl and my mother made me think more deeply about my own…relationships. About how much I missed you—and I missed you dreadfully. About what an amazing, intelligent, passionate woman you are. I realised it had been a mistake to let you send me away, and I wasn't going to follow the earl's example and let you go.'

The bird inside was flapping harder. 'You aren't?' she whispered.

'Several things you said in that final interview, that I only half-heard in the shock of the moment, gave me hope. That you'd been married to a man who loved you completely, and wouldn't settle for less. That you bore me no ill will because love hadn't happened *for me*. Which, can I believe, implies that love *did* happen for you? And that you would consider marrying me—if you believed I loved you enough in return?'

She hardly dared trust what she thought she was hearing. 'Are you trying to tell me that you *do* love me?'

'Absolutely, totally. Even if I was such a nodcock, it took me far too long to recognise it. Could you love me back, Maggie mine? Teach me to run an estate, stay by my side, in my parlour, in my bed, now and always?'

A happiness she'd never thought to experience again suffused her.

'Yes. I can teach you to be a good Tory, too.'

He laughed, the joyous sound an echo of her own joy. 'I won't go that far! Perhaps I'll teach you to be a good Radical.'

She chuckled, so delirious with gladness she wanted to run to the window and shout her happiness to everyone in the street. 'Sounds like we shall have to debate that.'

'That, perhaps, but never this: I love you, Lady Margaret Elizabeth Charlotte Dennison Roberts. I want you to be my wife and live with me all my days.'

With that, he dropped to one knee. 'Will you marry me, Maggie mine, and make me the happiest man in Christendom?'

She clasped his dear face between her hands, gazing down into the blue, blue eyes that had captivated her from their first glance. 'Yes, my darling Giles, I will.'

With a whoop, he jumped up, seized her hands, and danced her around the room. Stopping at last to kiss her soundly, he said, 'Shall we summon Rains? This calls for champagne!'

'I had a better celebration in mind. Why don't we repair to Upper Brook Street?'

His eyes blazed with excitement of another sort. 'In the middle of the afternoon? What about your elderly cousin?'

'Remember, I told you she's very deaf.'

Chuckling, he bent to kiss her nose. 'She's going to need to be. Shall I ask your father for your hand first?'

'He'll say "yes"; ask him later. I've already waited long enough to return to Upper Brook Street.'

He lifted her in another hug and whirled her around,

then set her back on her feet. 'Come with me now, then, Maggie mine. Come with me, and never leave me again.'

With that, he clasped her hand and led her from the room.

* * * * *

COMING NEXT MONTH FROM

HARLEQUIN®

ℌISTORICAL

Available April 19, 2016

PRINTER IN PETTICOATS (Western)
by Lynna Banning
Jessamine Lassiter is striving to keep Smoke River's newspaper afloat. So
sparks fly when Cole Sanders rides into town to start up a rival business!

IN BED WITH THE DUKE (Regency)
by Annie Burrows
When Gregory, Duke of Halstead, wakes naked in bed with no memory
of the night before, next to a beautiful stranger, he finds his life will never
be the same...

MORE THAN A LOVER (Regency)
Rakes in Disgrace • by Ann Lethbridge
Respectable Caroline Falkner buried her scandalous past long ago to
protect her son. But will Bladen Read unlace all of her secrets when his
touch proves too tempting to resist?

THE BLACKSMITH'S WIFE (Medieval)
by Elisabeth Hobbes
Joanna Sollers is determined never to love again. But when she's forced to marry
blacksmith Hal Danby, she discovers a burning desire for her new husband!

Available via Reader Service and online:

PLAYING THE DUKE'S MISTRESS (Victorian)
by Eliza Redgold
To prove to his cousin that all actresses are title-hunters, Darius Carlyle, the
Duke of Albury, *must* persuade leading lady Miss Calista Fairmont to accept
his marriage proposal...

THAT DESPICABLE ROGUE (Regency)
by Virginia Heath
Determined to expose Ross Jameson for the rogue he is, Lady Hannah Steers
dons a disguise and infiltrates his home as his new housekeeper!

**YOU CAN FIND MORE INFORMATION ON UPCOMING HARLEQUIN® TITLES,
FREE EXCERPTS AND MORE AT WWW.HARLEQUIN.COM.**

HHCNM0416

REQUEST YOUR FREE BOOKS!

♦HARLEQUIN®

ℌISTORICAL

Where love is timeless

2 FREE NOVELS PLUS 2 FREE GIFTS!

YES! Please send me 2 FREE Harlequin® Historical novels and my 2 FREE gifts (gifts are worth about $10). After receiving them, if I don't wish to receive any more books, I can return the shipping statement marked "cancel." If I don't cancel, I will receive 6 brand-new novels every month and be billed just $5.69 per book in the U.S. or $5.99 per book in Canada. That's a savings of at least 12% off the cover price! It's quite a bargain! Shipping and handling is just 50¢ per book in the U.S. and 75¢ per book in Canada.* I understand that accepting the 2 free books and gifts places me under no obligation to buy anything. I can always return a shipment and cancel at any time. Even if I never buy another book, the two free books and gifts are mine to keep forever.

246/349 HDN GH2Z

Name	(PLEASE PRINT)	
Address		Apt. #
City	State/Prov.	Zip/Postal Code

Signature (if under 18, a parent or guardian must sign)

Mail to the **Reader Service:**
IN U.S.A.: P.O. Box 1867, Buffalo, NY 14240-1867
IN CANADA: P.O. Box 609, Fort Erie, Ontario L2A 5X3

Want to try two free books from another line?
Call 1-800-873-8635 or visit www.ReaderService.com.

* Terms and prices subject to change without notice. Prices do not include applicable taxes. Sales tax applicable in N.Y. Canadian residents will be charged applicable taxes. Offer not valid in Quebec. This offer is limited to one order per household. Not valid for current subscribers to Harlequin Historical books. All orders subject to credit approval. Credit or debit balances in a customer's account(s) may be offset by any other outstanding balance owed by or to the customer. Please allow 4 to 6 weeks for delivery. Offer available while quantities last.

Your Privacy—The Reader Service is committed to protecting your privacy. Our Privacy Policy is available online at www.ReaderService.com or upon request from the Reader Service.

We make a portion of our mailing list available to reputable third parties that offer products we believe may interest you. If you prefer that we not exchange your name with third parties, or if you wish to clarify or modify your communication preferences, please visit us at www.ReaderService.com/consumerschoice or write to us at Reader Service Preference Service, P.O. Box 9062, Buffalo, NY 14240-9062. Include your complete name and address.

HH15

"Prudence," he said, turning to her, a tortured expression on
his face. "Perhaps I should have warned you, before we got
here, that—"

He broke off at the distinct sound of footsteps approaching
from the other side of the door.

"Too late," he said, shutting his mouth with a snap.
Never mind. Whatever it was, she could weather it. If she'd
managed to survive these past two nightmarish days, she
could weather anything.

But then, as the door swung open, something very strange
happened to Gregory. He sort of closed up. He deliberately
wiped all expression from his face, turning into a hard,
distant, cold man. He looked just like the man she'd first
seen in the Bull—the man from whom everyone kept their
distance. Even though she was still holding his hand, she got
the feeling he'd gone somewhere very far away, inside.

A soberly dressed man opened the door and goggled
at the sight of them. Which was hardly surprising. Not

many people looking as scruffy as they did would have the effrontery to knock on the front door of a house like this. But Gregory didn't bat an eyelid.

"Good morning, Perkins," he said. "Something amiss?"

"No, Your Grace," said the flabbergasted butler.

Your Grace? Why was the butler addressing Gregory as Your Grace?

"Of course not, Your Grace. It is just—" The butler pulled himself together, opened the door wider and stepped aside. "We were not expecting you for another day or so."

Gregory raised one eyebrow in a way that made the butler shrink in stature.

"Your rooms are in readiness, of course," he said.

"Why," she whispered as Gregory tugged her into the spacious hall, "is the butler calling you Your Grace?"

"Because, Miss Carstairs, I am a duke." He turned back to the butler. "This is Miss Carstairs, Perkins," Gregory— or whoever he was—said, handing him his valise. "My fiancée."

"Your—" The butler's face paled. His lips moved soundlessly, his jaw wagging up and down as though words failed him. Prudence knew how he felt, having just sustained as great a shock herself.

Which made her realize her own mouth had sagged open upon hearing Gregory claim to be a duke.

Don't miss
IN BED WITH THE DUKE
by Annie Burrows, available May 2016 wherever
Harlequin® Historical books and ebooks are sold.

www.Harlequin.com

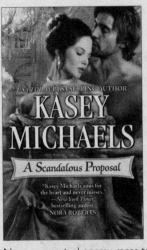

HARLEQUIN®

A *Romance* FOR EVERY MOOD™

JUST CAN'T GET ENOUGH?

Join our social communities
and talk to us online.

You will have access to the latest
news on upcoming titles and special
promotions, but most importantly,
you can talk to other fans about your
favorite Harlequin reads.

Harlequin.com/Community

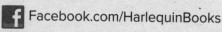 Facebook.com/HarlequinBooks

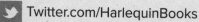 Twitter.com/HarlequinBooks

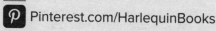 Pinterest.com/HarlequinBooks